MW00809563

I'D REALLY PREFER NOT TO BE HERE WITH YOU

AND
OTHER STORIES

I'D REALLY PREFER NOT to BE HERE WITH YOU

AND OTHER STORIES

JULIANNA BAGGOTT

**BLACK
STONE**
PUBLISHING

Published in 2023 by Blackstone Publishing
Cover and book design by Kathryn Galloway English

Printed in the United States of America

First edition: 2023
ISBN 979-8-200-87356-2
Fiction / Short Stories (single author)

Version 1

Blackstone Publishing
31 Mistletoe Rd.
Ashland, OR 97520

www.BlackstonePublishing.com

For Mildred, gorgeous in all ways

CONTENTS

WELCOME TO OXHEAD

You should know that we thought our parents were normal, ordinary, super basic. But they weren't, at all. Let's start with the way we found out, what some call "how it ended" and others call "the start of it all."

The grid went down. It covered Oxhead and Oxhead Woods and The Annex at Oxhead, the gated communities within the one large gate. It was sudden. One father dropped to the bottom of a shower stall, water still beating down on him. A few mothers collapsed onto kitchen tile, heads lightly bouncing. A half dozen parents stopped mid-breaststroke while doing laps. They floated then slowly spun, facedown, in the community pools. (Oxhead had so many pools.) A lot of parents folded over steering wheels—jerking and slumping as their cars bumped curbs, or rolled into traffic or trees or across lawns, or banged into other cars. Their legs went slack, sliding off of gas pedals, causing so many slow-motion accidents.

But they didn't just go from animate to inanimate. One

thing we agreed on: Light inside each of them—something like a soul—had been there and then not. Their inner lights went out, one by one. We were witnessing someone's death. Therefore, they had to have been alive.

•••

We can't blame ourselves for not knowing. We were too young to start off, then too consumed with surviving middle school. By high school, we were sexually obsessed. High school was ripe with longing. Sex floated in the air like a thick and gauzy pollen. It was everywhere and clung to us. An electrified pollen. Something that made us buzz—as if each of us were a bud with a queen bee trapped inside.

And the tech was really good. And the outside world was not great—when has it ever been great? People think there were Good Old Days, but there's only that cataract past, seen through a blinding fog. Why question a gated community that takes care of its own?

Most of all, we've learned this: What you present to a child as normal is normal. They have no other context. Parents translate humanity, the world, its dangers, and its means of survival. So when it broke down, two things happened as our parents lurched and fell and twitched and died. One: Nothing made sense. We were shattered. And two: The truth came together for each of us at different speeds, and then we had to make decisions.

The people who saw it as the end didn't question what life offers.

Those who saw it as the beginning started asking questions.

•••

Sex. That was the cause. It's fitting. One generation's quest for sex led to the older generation's death. It's not Freudian in a tidy way, but it mucks around in the same mud.

Lei Chiang and June Lessing wanted to have sex and couldn't find a secluded spot. We had so much surveillance, the neighborhood watch cameras, the constant eye of home security. Even the wooded lots reserved for future developments (Oxheads on and on as far as the eye could see) were tracked.

Lei and June were tech geniuses, A-level gamers who wanted to have sex. Protected sex; they weren't naive. The plan: take down the grid so that they could get out of their houses and have sex—unseen—in the secluded storage room of the community greenhouse. From their bedrooms, they worked virtually, in sync. Their hack had to be perfect, their hits time-released, precisely.

They chose a Friday. They wanted a couple of hours, ideally, to feel like grown-ups, to linger on the cot in the greenhouse's storage room, amid seeds and soil bags, the acrid pinch of light fertilizers. They chose late afternoon. If things went well, dusk would settle in and they'd walk to the greenhouse in the gathering dark, lush whisper of ferns, bobbing fruit, bristling nettles. They'd hold hands and look up at the sky beyond the foggy panes.

How could they have known that our parents were connected to the grid, that our parents were part of the network, each firing to the next like synapses within a massive head—Oxhead itself?

...

We realized in retrospect that our parents' scents were off. Riding beneath colognes and perfumes, there was something medicinal with the dusty burn of a heater or a curling iron slightly singeing freshly shampooed hair.

What we remember most clearly about that night? When they died, a flowering scent, a gusty release, a sweet rot plumed from each body. The air seemed almost misty with it.

Kids emerged from houses, calling for help. We shook our parents' shoulders. We climbed out of dented cars and wandered into neighboring yards, in shock. We jumped into pools and dragged our parents' bodies out.

The grid was completely down. Electricity surged—a distant thunderous boom—then went out. No way to call for an ambulance.

We attempted resuscitations in yards and on den carpeting, in beds, on sofas and patios and slate porches . . . We failed to bring them back and fell down on top of their bodies.

With the shouting, crying, calls for help, each house became a box vibrating with terror—reverberating through all the Oxhead neighborhoods. Every household had children. This was something else we should have noticed but didn't. Why were there so many kids? When you're a child, you think the world revolves around you. Oxhead *did* revolve around us.

•••

It got dark. We gathered in the street. We didn't want to go home. The theories started. That we'd been orphans—all along. "This is an orphanage run by replicas of our real parents." (Many of us resembled our parents.)

"Our parents loved us but knew they were going to die, maybe. And so they created this place."

"What if they're still alive and megarich, and this is elaborate babysitting?"

"I know my mother has been in there! I know it!" one girl said. "She looks at me in this way sometimes that's so deep! What if this thing is an avatar she hops into and out of?"

We always came back to this: Why would anyone do this? We cried and hugged each other.

• • •

June and Lei found their dead parents—both dads grilling, one mother gardening, the other in her office, working late. They told no one what they'd done, not that night. Lei sprinted to June's house. They told each other that the grid would be repaired. *They're not dead. It'll go back to normal, it will!* And they had sex in her bed. But won't sex always be tinged with guilt and loss for them?

• • •

Shortly after midnight, lights came on. Ceiling fans began to rotate. Our parents flinched and gasped. They rolled over. They patted their chests as if they'd been coughing. They threw up pool water. They cried out. They stood up too fast. They called for us by name. Oxhead ringing again with voices in the dead of night.

• • •

In the following weeks, disinformation followed—*You had a collective virus, children. The virus causes mass hallucinations. It happens. Let us show you this video . . .*

Factions formed. Some decided to believe the disinformation and deny what they had seen. They wanted their parents back, regardless. They believed that if you're lucky to be offered a safe childhood, you should accept it. Lei's senior project included this line: *Animals that are risk-takers—note the condor—are more likely to go extinct.*

June was part of a group that wanted out. We believed that you can't live a lie. We needed to trust that the people around us, the world, were real. We still wanted to have sex, but we were afraid that whatever happened to our parents had to do with having us. We didn't want to sacrifice ourselves for offspring. (We were too literal and didn't understand parenthood.) We gathered our things; kissed the representations of our parents— we still loved them deeply. June had arranged for a limited hit to the outermost gate. We slipped through it.

The air felt like real air. The sky looked like the same sky.

We still don't know what love is.

I'D REALLY PREFER NOT TO BE HERE WITH YOU

I spotted him right off. He didn't belong in this support group. First off, no hair products, no predatory smile, no dick-pic vibe—and there were a lot of those types here. I saw him reach for the last powdered doughnut, but he begged off when Branda reached for it, too. And he didn't hit on her. It wasn't a move.

But mainly I knew he didn't belong because of what happened to his face as we went around the circle and introduced ourselves. He winced every time one of the guys explained why they were here.

In other words, he was sensitive—maybe even *good*—and therefore my type. And when I say my type, I mean the type I like to destroy. Not in an intentional way. I'm not that kind of monster. More in the way . . . I don't know. Here's this: As a kid I loved frogs, and my father gave me these robotic frog kits, and sometimes I'd make the frog—its delicate spring-loaded gears, skeletal structure with all of its articulated joints, its fragile casing of skin—and then, maybe because I loved it too much, I'd crush it.

So, to be clear, unlike him, I *did* belong here. I was still, metaphorically speaking, a frog crusher. By this point, it was just a habit, really. Maybe this is about addiction in some way or another.

What did he look like? He had ragged hair. His smile intimated that he'd had to wear braces, maybe for a very long time. He was sporty but not buff, like good at basketball but not tall enough. Definitely team sports.

So we were halfway around the group circle. It was Branda's turn. "Hi, I'm Branda." She told the same story each week, and it went like this: "I know, I know." Insert giddy laugh. "You're all probably thinking that my mom's name was Brenda and my dad's name was Randy and they mushed them together and named me Branda."

No one was ever thinking this. She had never—in my three years coming to weekly meetings—gotten a single nod or smile of confirmation.

"And you're right!" she said. "Bing, bing, bing!" And while she binged, she touched her nose—bing, bing, bing! Like her nose was a bingy bell. Her mood changed quickly. Her voice tightened, and she explained that her *stupid* name was to blame for her insecurities. And her insecurities were to blame for her bad behavior, romantically, with both men and women. "If I'd been named something, *anything* else, my life would have been . . . better, you know? Maybe even . . . okay. And I'd still be out there. In circulation. With better people, no offense."

There was a muttered chorus of "None taken." One thing really offensive people are good at is not taking offense. Practice. Mainly though, we're really accepting of blame. If someone wants to offload their shitty behavior onto almost anything or anyone else, we're going to support you. Because we want that exact kind of support in return. It was, after all, a support group.

Here's what she meant by "in circulation" and "better people," in case you're lucky enough not to know that support groups like this exist. A few years back, tucked into that big bundled bill meant to address big tech and cybersecurity, it fell to apps to protect people in the world of love—from jerks. In order to track us, a kind of romantic credit score was created and uniformly applied.

And look. I'm a feminist. I was *for* this, one hundred percent. I wanted abusive men out of the dating pool. I wanted all of those cheaters, ghosters, catfishers, frat-boy dickheads, gaslighters, sex-cult-leader wannabes . . . gone.

And yet, maybe I lacked some self-awareness at the same time.

This was a support group for people whose exes so overwhelmingly and consistently dinged our "romantic credit scores" that we were banned from all dating apps in perpetuity. We all sported a mandatory government-issued bracelet, permanently affixed to our wrists. It knew where we went, what we did. Every person had a unique dating profile—and only one. No more fake extra profiles. On the plus side, the bracelet also tracked your oxygen levels, pulse rate, blood alcohol content, and steps, to encourage healthy living. Dating us showed such poor judgment that anyone stupid enough to do so would also start racking up dings to their score.

We could still date, of course. But we only had each other now, what with the stigma. It's like this—if a guy in a grocery store asks you out, it's because he has no access to apps. It's the equivalent of a certain kind of guy riding a kid-sized bike because he has obviously lost his license to a DWI.

For the sake of honesty, I was not here for support. I was . . . *looking*, and my pond was now very sad and small.

Goddard was our facilitator. He was also banned for life. He was supposed to be a role model, but sometimes he fell into this familiar screed of being attracted to batshit-crazy women: his first ex-wife, his second, his third. But the difference between him and most of the other guys was that he could snap out of it and say the right things. "I acknowledge my role. I did not do my best to make those relationships healthy." He wore a name tag, and his handwriting was all caps like, deep down, he was still screaming at his ex-wives. "Branda," he said calmly. "How was your week? Do you feel like you're making progress?"

We were always supposed to be working on our shit, owning it.

"I mean, with this name, what chance do I have?" Branda said.

The new guy tilted forward ever so slightly and opened his mouth. He wanted to say something kind, I could tell. He struck me now as the type who'd have done the bulk of the work in a group project in middle-school science or volunteered to take notes in the meeting if it was being assumed the woman would do it. He was not unbroken, though. Divorced parents or something. He wanted to ease Branda's suffering, to tell her that her name was nice, that he liked it or something. Maybe he was going to suggest what a few others have suggested to Branda before—*You know, you could change your name.* And that simple suggestion would derail us for about twenty minutes—tears, snot, epic contradictions, and gymnastic denials and accusations.

I caught his eye from the other side of the circle. And very slowly, I shook my head. I meant, *Do not say it.*

He received my slow head shake, took the hint. He shut his mouth and tilted back again.

"Yes," Goddard said, supportive of her delusion, "but has anything . . . given way?"

Branda shrugged. "I got a cat. The cat hates me."

"Don't you know that cats are aloof by nature?" Dirk was middle-aged. He was accusatory to cover for the fact that he was hyper-needy. "I'd never get a cat. They're only nice when they want something from you."

"Great," Branda said. "I got a pet that will treat me like my mother."

Goddard leaned toward Branda, tightened his fists, and said, "You've got this, Branda! You've. Got. This." Goddard was a bit puffed and saggy in general and otherwise not very good looking. But, my God, sometimes his confidence was magnetic. I didn't know how anyone could be so confident in a windowless, drop-ceiling room so foul and rank with assholes, rejects, and our collective despair, but he could pull it off. I believed him for a second. I believed that Branda's "got this." And then I thought, *Wait, what? She's "got" that her cat was like her mother, who was only nice when she wanted something?*

Whatever. I was waiting for the new guy's turn. And we made our way slowly toward him. The next few guys were: dick pic, dick pic, rapey, mommy issues, daddy issues, just gross in a way that's hard to explain . . . I tracked the nuances of the new guy's winces.

The number of men who've been permanently banned to

the number of women who've been permanently banned is like a gazillion to one. But women are more likely to go to a support group, which evens the numbers a little.

A few women talked about their weekly progress: obsessive stalker, weirdo with many unusual addiction issues, selective mute (she doesn't speak but there's a thing with nodding and gestures), and me—the downtrodden version: *I wish I could redeem myself, but I can't. I'm unforgivable.*

The new guy was moved by our stories. He was getting how messed up we all were.

And finally, it was his turn.

Goddard said, "We're happy to have a new addition tonight. We're first name only. What do you go by?"

"Ben," he said.

"Okay, Ben. What brings you here?" Goddard smiled. "Besides the obvious?"

"Oh, um, I didn't know I'd have to talk about that on my first night." He pushed on his knees, elbows locked.

"We're a circle of trust," Goddard explained. "To build that trust, we each have to talk about why we're here."

"Okay," Ben said, and he glanced around the room. His eyes were a little watery. Was he going to tear up? Did he feel actual guilt? Was he here for redemption? I reminded myself that he was just like the rest of us. He was terrible. Irredeemably so. Or he would not be here. *Bring it*, I heard myself saying in my head.

But what could he possibly bring? He had to be a clerical error. He was definitely here by accident.

"Well," Ben said, "I'm a one-strike."

"Jesus," Branda said.

A one-strike is a category we don't see much. In fact, I'd never met one. Only rumors. A one-strike is someone who did something so horrible that they were immediately banned. No warnings. Just . . . done.

"What did you do?" Dirk said, and he laughed a little and looked around at the other guys, wanting them to join in. He needed someone's approval at all times.

Goddard held up his hand. I'd never seen him in this position before. People have said some terrible shit in this circle. But Goddard was scared. I could tell. "You don't necessarily have to—"

"No," Ben said. "I want to say this. I need to."

"Okay," Goddard said.

"I killed her."

"Who?" one of the dick-pics said.

"My fiancée," Ben said.

There were some immediate reactions:

"Oh shit."

"Damn, brother."

And one weirdly delighted, "Well fuck me!"

I just did that thing where I cross my legs once and then wrap my foot around my ankle and, arms crossed, I bounce forward and then back in my chair.

It was desperately quiet now. So fucking quiet. It was heart-racing how quiet it was.

"How did you kill her?" I said. I have to break silences. It's a thing.

"Parachuting. I was in charge of her pack." His eyes went wide. Like he was seeing it. What? What did he see? The pack that he was supposed to fold up just right—or her clawing for the cord, pulling, and then nothing? Was he seeing her fall to her death?

Didn't really matter. Here's the deal. I was in. I was completely and utterly in. This guy was my fucking shot.

• • •

I mentioned frogs. So a word on those.

Of course, actual frogs are practically extinct in the wild and basically exist only in terrariums and within suburbia exhibits. So I first became obsessed with them after my father took me to a few of those exhibits as a kid. I remember getting lost in one—with its darting squirrels and birdcalls. I didn't know I was lost. I thought my father was lost. I didn't have a lot of confidence in my father. He was a quiet man who tended to blend in and disappear. "Where's Warren?" someone would eventually ask at a get-together of any sort. And for a minute, people would glance around and then give up. If the people knew him well—like family or close friends—they'd just say something like, "Classic Warren," and they'd forge on. If they didn't know him well, they didn't look for him. He wasn't the kind of guy to be missed.

So I assumed my father was lost, and, like a good parent, I went looking for him. "Dad! Hey, Dad!" I was probably seven or so.

When he didn't come when I called, I got nervous. If I lost my father, my mother would get really angry. (My mother's anger was a force of nature.) So I shouted louder and louder, and then panic set in. Birds scattered up from bushes as I started tearing around. Butterflies suddenly seemed to swarm. I was terrified of breathing one into my gaping mouth. Frogs were bouncing around my feet, and I froze. I didn't want to hurt one of them.

I loved frogs because they were delicate. And I was terrified of their delicacy.

I finally charged out of the domed area and found my father in the gift shop, buying a stuffed animal tadpole with a zipper compartment that, when turned inside out, became a frog. He said, "Are you okay?"

I grabbed his hand. "We're going home."

From then on, no more exhibits. Only mail-order tadpoles and robotic frog kits.

...

I slouched over to Ben after the meeting, looking a little lost in my peacoat. I wanted to appear wounded—he's empathetic—but not broken. He struck me as the kind of guy who was centered enough to find brokenness unattractive. He was putting on a jacket, a windbreaker with some real-estate company logo; I assumed it was a house-warmer freebie from a realtor and that maybe he owned his own place. "You were going to suggest she change her name," I said.

"Sorry, what?"

"Branda." I nodded to where she'd been sitting in the circle. Goddard and a guy named Ellis were stacking the chairs, clunking them together, sad gongs.

"I'm guessing that wasn't as original an idea as I thought," he said.

"She thinks that changing her name is giving up. And she's right. She'd be giving up the excuse that's seen her through." I lifted my eyebrows and raised both hands, mea culpa. "We're all guilty of it! I'm not throwing stones. My house is fully made of glass—exterior, interior, throw pillows, sofa . . ."

"Even the glasses are made of glass?"

"Yep."

"And the windows?"

"Double glass." I looked down at my shoes, like this was hard for me because I'm kind of shy. "First time at a meeting can be rough. It's not AA, though. So we are allowed to drink after." I pointed—my thumb over my shoulder—at the door. "You want to—?"

"Absolutely."

...

Okay, yeah, so the mail-order tadpoles. They were cruel because you couldn't actually let the frogs go free. There were too many pesticides, for one. But even if they dodged all the poison, they had so little greenery to eat that they'd starve. Or their pores would get clogged by smog and air pollutants. Or they'd lack water access. Their antenna would fail, their bodies would be desiccated by the overbearing sun. There were so many ways to die.

My dad and I kept our live frogs in a terrarium. They could only hop a tiny bit before running into the glass, but they were safe. We tended to them.

One day while my dad was talking me through the various species—we had horned frogs and white tree frogs and gray tree frogs—my mother found us there, our heads tilted to the glass.

"That thing stinks!" she shouted. My mother was loud and

breezy and sometimes-drunk and bosomy and plain-faced. "Those frogs are fucking sad. They're not going anywhere. They were born to die, locked up. What's wrong with you two?"

My father and I weren't sure what was wrong with us. And so, for a moment, we just stood there. But I knew that my mother had done something dangerous by lumping me with him. Maybe I knew what was coming—that this family would break down, and I had to pick a team.

In that moment, I decided to hate him. "What's wrong with *us*? These frogs are dumb. And I hate them. It's him," I said. "What's wrong with *him*?"

• • •

Ben and I got drunk.

And I heard about his childhood (moodier than expected), his first crush (typical—the kind of pretty, shiny-haired girl who would get killed off really fast if she were in a slasher film), and his parents—I was correct. They were divorced, but amicably. Both remarried when he was in his midtwenties, very civilized. He was a blabby drinker, and he rubbed his government-issued bracelet while he blabbed. They take some getting used to.

I avoided the fiancée.

But he went flat at a certain point. Everything drained out of him, and he said, "I miss her."

"You don't deserve the ban," I said. "Me? I deserve it. And more. But you," I said, "you didn't do anything wrong. It was an accident."

"Yes, but there was an investigation."

"But you were cleared. You what? Weren't focused enough

while putting together a parachute? I mean, c'mon. Yours is a sin of distraction."

"I know, I know. But still. In the trust circle, you said you were unforgivable. I am, too. Some things are just unforgivable. I don't want to ever love anyone again. I don't want to date ever again. It's better this way—to be cut off from it all. It's . . . a relief."

"It's bad to be cast out. I hate it, but it's what I deserve. You're great, Ben. Not me. Never me. I'm a terrible human being." I needed him to say I wasn't that bad. I needed him to get on my side.

"It's not a relief for you, is it?" he said, catching on. "You want back in."

I collapsed onto the bar and hid my face in my arms, holding my breath so my cheeks would flush.

I felt his hand on my back. "Shh. Shhh. We can figure this out. I bet we can find a way . . ."

I lifted my head, my face red and blotchy. "You think so?"

...

I knew my father would forgive me for taking my mom's side— and she wouldn't. That's why I was mean to him. I never figured this out until I was in my twenties.

I was prepared for some kind of cataclysm. My mother told everyone that she was going to leave my father, that he was a joke, that they were just waiting for me to grow up, and then it would be over. She would smoke and laugh and say, "Us? Oh, this is already dead. Way dead. I'll be gone once, you know . . ." And she'd nod at me. "Responsibilities . . ."

Did I believe her? Was this why I spent so much time with my dad?

After she went off on the terrarium, we stopped using it. We waited for the last frog to die—a dart frog with a bright blue underbelly and legs with shiny black dots. But we turned our attention to robotic frogs. They didn't stink. They weren't going to die. They weren't caged—so there were no awful metaphors at work in the subtext.

But then, one day, my father was just gone. I never got the chance to tell him that I turned on him because he was more forgiving than my mother, because he didn't demand I take a side, because I trusted his love was actually unconditional.

It wasn't.

•••

The plan was simple. It took a while to steer Ben toward it and make him think it was his idea. But we got there.

To get my ban reversed, to get back into the pool of "better people," as Branda put it, I'd have to flip a few exes, get them to see me in a new and dazzling light, move them to go into the system and change their ratings.

It would have to be a spectacle. Newsworthy. A pardon on the very highest level would be required. "If you and I could prove that we're misunderstood," I said, "full of love and compassion, on a grand scale, wouldn't they have to flip?"

"Like us as a couple? We would be in love—you and me—to prove we're worthy?"

"Yes, yes," I said. We'd moved to espresso energy in an indie coffee shop. "Exactly. An epic love story. Us."

I'd had the idea ages ago but abandoned it once I met my comrades in the support group. Miserable, self-sabotaging egomaniacs. The doughnut table alone sometimes exposed people in a death spiral—stealing, shoving, blaming. One guy hovered at the table and when I walked up, he said, "Yeah, I licked all of the doughnuts, so I guess they're mine now," like some pricky little middle-schooler who's despised by everyone on his Mathletes team. I picked up a French cruller and said, "You don't understand the people you're dealing with." And I shoved it into my mouth.

None of those assholes were gonna get me back in.

New guy. This Ben. He was perfect. His ban was valid—totally valid—but what was the real crime? Lack of focus? Maybe even just excitable nerves? And he was in that sweet spot of not-too-good-looking but still kind of good-looking in a nonintimidating way—mediagenic.

"How many do you have to flip?" he asked.

"I'm not going to lie," I said. "We'll need a good amount. Like theoretically if we could get all the Wallaces flipped and the . . ."

"All the Wallaces? What's a Wallace?"

I was confused that he was confused. "Guys I've dated with the last name Wallace."

"How many Wallaces have you dated?"

"At least six."

"And you pissed each of them off so much that—"

"I mean we'll need more than just the Wallaces," I said. He still looked confused. "Wallace is a very common name."

"Is it?" he said. "Is it that common? I know one guy with the last name Wallace . . . maybe more . . ." He was pensive. "Nope, just one. I'm including guys with the first name Wallace, too." I wasn't. That's a separate, smaller category. "I don't know anyone with the first name Wallace except that British Claymation rabbit cartoon character," he said.

"Well, it's not him. I've never fucked Claymation."

"Kudos?"

"You know, I think that maybe Wallaces are more common around here," I said, feeling defensive. "I grew up here. It's full of Wallaces, in these parts."

"I grew up here in these parts, too."

"Oh, right. I forgot that."

I was pretty sure I'd lost him, but he rallied. "Well, okay. If we could flip the Wallaces and a few other *very common* last name categories . . . and some of your non-Claymation but cartoon character exes, we should be good."

"Right. Thank you. Yes."

· · ·

I was ten years old when my father left. For a week or two after he was gone, robotic frog kits were delivered to the door.

Then they showed up only for birthdays and holidays.

He kept up with all of my various moves by way of my mother, I assumed. I didn't ask, but they must have stayed in touch a little.

The last robotic frog kit arrived when I was twenty-two years old. A beautiful red-eye tree frog with blue and yellow flanks, orange webbed feet, and bright bulging attentive eyes.

Then Christmas passed and the kit didn't arrive.

Within a few months, my mother told me he'd died, a slow death, a wasting disease from lungs fouled by pollutants.

I hadn't reached out to him. He hadn't reached out to me—except for all the kits. I'd hated him for that.

I'd put each one together, too. And then I'd charge them up and let them loose in whatever part of the city I was living in at the time. *Blup, blup, blup.* They'd hop off, jagged with stored energy. Except when I crushed them.

Which sometimes I did.

...

Ben and I dated. Elaborately. But also touchingly. We documented it all. On all of the social media sites, we had a couples account and we posted everything: photos from boardwalk photo booths, beachy selfies, videos of us on dates and lazy Sunday mornings . . . My personal favorite: We saved ducklings caught in a storm grate, returning them to the nervous mother duck who was on camera; renting and transporting ducks and ducklings is not easy.

We were clear on all social media about who we were: banned-for-life fuckups. And how we met: reaching for the same cab in the pouring rain. And that we were irredeemable, but also learning how to love, for real this time.

You know how this story goes.

You know that I loved him and wanted to crush him.

You know that I got a little freaked out by falling for him and started to crush him a little, just a little.

You know that he sat me down and said, "Don't crush me. I know what you're doing. You don't have to."

And you know that I stopped crushing him because maybe I was becoming a better person.

"I'm the frog that I crush," I whispered to him in bed one night. He'd turned away, was breathing deeply, asleep. "I crush others before they can crush me." I thought about it and went a little more existential and whispered to the short hairs on his neck, "I crush, therefore I am."

...

After my father left, I had no one, really. My mother fell apart. She'd loved him. This seemed to surprise her more than anyone else. She was lovesick. She ate mostly angel food cake and lemon squares like she was at one of my shitty piano recitals, and booze, too. And she went through a few favorite kinds of drugs—she liked her downers.

I kept busy with robotic frog kits—as if I could tinker my way to some kind of peace. I kicked myself for having chosen the wrong side. I blamed myself until it was self-destructive. Then I blamed her for a while.

By the time I was a freshman in high school, it was easiest to blame him—in the abstract.

And then, when I started dating at the end of high school (a latish bloomer), I figured out how to blame him by proxy.

Boys.

The seemingly sweet ones.

...

We went viral on a Tuesday afternoon. It wasn't the ducklings bullshit. It was some random thing he'd posted without letting me know. He'd just gotten off work and he talked to the camera about what it was like to walk to my place, knowing that I'd open the door, knowing he'd see me again. He talked about his fiancée, whom he'd never see again.

He was eating a taco over the sink when I saw the numbers piling up and finally watched it. He heard his own voice and put the taco back in the takeout container.

I walked over and said, "You mean it, don't you?"

He was silent. He knew that I should come to him. I was the one who needed to be vulnerable.

"I don't care about getting back in," I said. "I want this. Us, Ben. Us."

"Phil Stegeman," he said.

"Okay . . . huh?" I laughed, though I didn't really get it.

"I used a fake first name, but the last name is real," he said.

"What?"

"I'm a Stegeman. How many of us are there? As many as the Wallaces?"

I took a step backward. "Um. Wait. Do I know you?"

"I'm Phil Stegeman." He was furious, but he kept his voice steady and calm.

"Uh. What?"

"I told some of the same family stories. I'd just forget and find myself talking about my own childhood. I told the same exact ones. Even about how I got that scar on my bicep from . . ."

"The go-kart race," I said.

"I wore a Louviers Realty windbreaker to the first group meeting. I've worn it five times since. I gave you all these chances."

"Louviers Realty . . ."

"You were a temp there six years ago," he said.

"That is true."

"You and I went on three dates. We had sex a few times. And then . . . there was a family barbecue."

"Oh shit, right."

"Oh shit, *right*," he said.

I looked him up and down. I might have even squinted. This was a mistake.

"Okay, okay!" he said, holding his hands up. "I used to be heavier. And I had a beard. Maybe to disguise my double chin. Back off."

"I wasn't . . . I'm just trying to . . ." And then I froze. Because it all came back to me. A roiling tumble of events.

He could see it registering. I could see him registering that it was registering for me. "Now you realize that I'm not the only Stegeman," he said. "There are at least two of us."

I remembered his brother. The two were similar, but when I met the brother I felt like, *Huh, that's just a slightly different and better genetic arrangement, an upgrade.* "You did not kill your fiancée. Did you?"

"I never had a fiancée."

"Do you parachute?"

"I have never parachuted."

That seemed right. He was not a first-round I-pick-dare-in-Truth-or-Dare type. "You're not banned, are you?"

"No. But I definitely deserve to get dinged for this. I won't, though, because you've lost dinging privileges, haven't you?"

"All privileges," I said quietly. "I've lost all privileges."

"You messed me up," he said. "You really messed me up." He turned and held onto the edges of the sink. "And then I had this way of fixing it. Of getting myself back. And I came up with this plan. It was so easy because you wanted to use me, again. And every time you said how nice I was—how good—I didn't feel guilty. I hated it because you were taking away my humanity. You were putting me in a box of All-Good. And putting yourself into a box of All-Bad. I'd find myself falling for you, over and over." He stopped and caught his breath. "But then you'd do it again. Take away my complexity. And now you know. Now you have proof. We're all a mixed bag of good and bad. All of us. There's no easy way to divvy up human beings."

"But. Wait. I wasn't going to do it this time," I explained. "I have learned things! I was really falling for you and—"

"And you never recognized me. Not once." He grabbed the taco to-go container and headed to the door.

I followed. "I wasn't going to crush you. I'm the frog. See? I'm only ever crushing myself. I get it! I really do!"

But he was out the door and down the front steps. He then turned around on the sidewalk and opened one arm wide. "God, this feels good! It feels so good!" He pointed at me. "Maybe you were right all along. You were right and I was wrong. Being the crusher. This," he said. "This is a much better place to be."

...

Here's the deal. It hurt and I deserved it. I walked around feeling scalded. Sometimes I'd double over with core heat and have to spit a few times. I didn't sleep much. Then, like someone threw a switch, I slept all the time.

But eventually, I emerged. Branda and a few of the other women and I created a second support group, women only. I didn't rehash my childhood, but the group worked well. We were hard on each other and loving, and we made promises and broke them and remade them. We still went to the coed meetings, and we were more vulnerable there, too.

I was chaste during this period of reckoning (more or less, I mean). And it felt good to be in charge of myself. I got a cat; the cat was aloof, as advertised, but we worked out some kind of deal and appreciated what we were capable of bringing to the table, emotionally.

And then, about eleven months later, he showed up.

He was a little late and didn't make eye contact with me—or anyone, really. He sat in an empty seat. Elbows on knees, hands clasped, eyes on the empty middle of our trust circle.

But he knew I was there. He had to. He was wearing the Louviers Realty windbreaker.

My turn came first. Goddard asked me about my progress. I said what I had to say. No speeches about love or frogs, no overplayed remorse, just some updates on things that we'd hashed through in the women's group, a call for new members, and a request for advice on catnip.

When his turn came, he started with his real name but changed mine. He then told the story from first seeing me at the realty office and falling for me. The details were poignant. He explained what happened with his brother. He walked us through his revenge, his lies to this very group. How the two of us connected, and the plan, and he explained how many times he thought about not following through. But on that day, eating the taco over the sink, he let it all come out. Why that day? He told me that it was the day he knew that he'd fallen in love with me and that the relationship was ruined. There was no way for either of us to come back from all that deceit. The only way out was out.

After that, he felt like a different person. He went on a tear. He piled up dings. He got banned for life, for real.

"And here I am. Back again."

Almost everybody in the group knew that he was talking about us. I'd told the story in different ways in front of them, trying to work through it. But Goddard stuck with the script. "Welcome. It's great to have you back."

After the meeting, Phil caught up with me outside. I kept reminding myself that this was his real name. It was November and blustery. "Hi," he said. "I'm so sorry."

"It's okay. I forgive you," I said, "but can you forgive me?"

"Of course. Of course I forgive you."

"Good," I said.

"Good," he said.

"So, you went on a tear. How was it?"

"Awful."

"Good."

I'd like to say that we became good friends and rebuilt our trust and then started dating again, slowly this time, and fell in love all over again.

No. We're now in our late forties and we have lunch sometimes.

He is the only person on Earth who knows about losing my father in the suburbia exhibit when I was five, the stinky terrarium, and the years of robotic frog kits.

He is the only person, currently on Earth, who has given me a robotic frog kit. We'd just finished up and the server had brought the check when he put it on the table.

"Are you kidding me?"

"It's a relatively new species of fringe-limbed tree frog," he said. "They've been spotted gliding through forest canopies in Panama. Flying frogs, still alive in the wild, mating in tree holes."

I teared up. It surprised me. "Thanks."

I assembled the frog on a Sunday afternoon. I haven't let it loose or crushed it. It hops around my apartment, sometimes startling my cat, sometimes startling me. It's shiny and squat. Its eyes seem to want to know something about me, something I haven't yet figured out.

HOW THEY GOT IN

The daughter. Loose-limbed girl, twelve years old. Pumping her bike. Gangly as a puppet. It's cold. She grips the handlebars, knuckles red and raw. Her breath catches and ghosts the air as she puffs along, uphill.

The developer of this neighborhood went bankrupt, so most of these houses were abandoned before they were fully built. Like the daughter was abandoned before fully built; her father's gone. Cancer, awful and quick. Just a year earlier. She and her mom and brother are still trying to find the new orbit, to reconstruct a family around a massive, cratered hole of absence. The father had been a good father.

Their house sits at the end of the cul-de-sac, the sun on its back like a burden of dying light. The garage is just beams, an unfinished gesture. The leaky bay window is covered in plastic. The den still needs drywall. It's laid bare in a way that recalls ribs—like being inside a body. She doesn't want to go home. But her fingers are tight with cold, her cheeks stiff.

She stops. Takes out her phone, points the camera at her face. "Hi! Welcome to my YouTube channel!" She doesn't have a YouTube channel, but dumb kids at school do, so maybe she could too. "This is where I live." She points the camera at her house. It looks sad in the frame. Collapsible almost. Like a giant hand could pick it up and take it away.

She shows the street of half-built houses, focusing on one lot that's only pitted foundation. Poured and abandoned. Things could be worse. That could be her house.

She turns the camera off, wipes her bangs out of her eyes, and walks her bike up the driveway. The video uploads to the family's cloud.

...

This was how the first one got in. Missing the summer of 1973. Fifteen years old. Her flute case found by a muddy brook six miles southeast.

But not her flute. Just the case, open on the bank. Its blue velvet interior caked in mud.

Holly Martine. She remembers herself, some small registering of her existence. The pocket of her jeans; her cross necklace, which gets stuck to her collarbones in summer; her silky hair pulled back in a high ponytail; her teased bangs. The flute in her hand, flecked with blood, keys clotted with mud. The scent of her Jean Nate After Bath Splash and . . . him . . . Cigarettes, acrid body odor, and something like tar and shit and the clay along the water's edge, gray and wet. She knew her killer. He lived along her route home, small house, neat yard. He was her father's age. He'd try to make small talk sometimes. Slimmer. George Slimmer.

She appears. Cold. She crosses her arms, flute tucked under one arm. She knows this spot, her makeshift burial.

Holly sees a girl, a middle-schooler, standing in a driveway, pointing something at her then walking away. Holly feels like she's slipped into something that isn't the world she's known. She's hungry. Not literally hungry, but a physical feeling in her chest and ribs but also her legs and arms, like she's been starving for a long time. For what?

For everything. Air, dirt, houses. My God, the girl with her bike. Going into a house. To her family? Holly wants life, people, words, her flute; its key pads are stuck. She wants to be and do and make noise.

She runs toward the girl's house, fever in her chest, but comes to the edge of something. Like an idea has come to an end. She can see forward but can't move forward.

After the *Challenger* blew up—the classroom air felt solid, no one moving or breathing. They saw the stalled smoke cloud, nothing at the edges of it, either. She reaches into *this* stalled air. Opening and closing her hand, it becomes a bunch of dots, like TV channels that don't work.

Is she going to stand here and wait? Has she learned nothing? She heaves herself in the direction of the girl with the bike, heaving herself into that pixilation.

• • •

Now, in the basement, the son. He's fifteen. A workout bench, gaming station, futon. Buzzing space heater. Cave crickets appear, so muscular and erratic that he's scared of them and embarrassed by it.

His girlfriend is here. She came in through the cellar door. This is how his life is since his dad died. No one knows what he's doing. No one cares. He loves it except if he thinks about it too much. Like the way his mother sees past him. They could go for days, near misses, almost seeing each other. He hears her walking around overhead. Maybe she hears his video game gun-fire. How long could he go missing before she noticed?

His girlfriend would notice. She's wearing an Old Navy sweater over a tank top. She smells like a strawberry-scented car deodorizer, the kind that clips onto the air conditioning vent. His dad had one in his Toyota.

On the futon, she slips her hand along his thigh.

"Does it stink down here?" he asks. His Christmas stocking was foot sprays and Axe body spray—as if his mother didn't see him anymore but could still smell him.

"My mom sells essential oils," his girlfriend says. "There's one that smells like pot, swear to God."

"I'd need something to cover up pot."

"She's got those." She kisses him. "Do you want me to steal one?"

"But does it stink down here?"

She looks around. "It smells like a basement. Right?"

"I guess."

She pushes him down onto the futon and straddles him. "You know what we should do?"

"I've got a few ideas." He's surprised that he knows what to say sometimes and how to lower his voice to say it.

"We should tape it," she says. "Like celebrities."

"Tape, like, us?"

"Duh. Yes!"

"Like how much?"

She tugs his shirt. "Just a teaser. We're not sluts." The first time she called him a slut it was confusing. They'd hooked up at a party. Two months later, he still doesn't know how to take it.

"Just a teaser," he says. "Okay."

She takes off her sweater, her tank top riding up her soft stomach, and picks up his phone.

...

Holly is at a birthday party. The girl with the bike is younger, turning seven. The mother is presenting a Barbie baked into a cake, which is the bottom of her ball gown. *Smart*, the girl thinks. Did they put the Barbie in after the cake was baked? Still, she can't help it—she imagines the Barbie burnt to char.

Holly stands at the back of the room, holding her flute. She doesn't recognize these people, these toys. All of these things gripped in their hands. They point and shoot like cameras. They bing, click, play music. The father touches a button, and it's Aunt Jackie, calling from Baltimore. A phone?

Why this house and this family and this moment? She moves toward the kitchen, finds an edge, like the one she heaved herself into. Can she push from this moment to another?

She's warm here. There are sweets, a punch bowl with ice cream and foaming ginger ale. She wants to eat the cake but she also wants to shove her hand into it and feel it. Again, it's hunger but not typical hunger. It's wanting . . .

They sing "Happy Birthday." She sings along quietly at first. A stranger at the party, and no one notices?

She sings louder. Do they see her at all?

By the time they get to the little girl's name, she's singing at the top of her voice, off-key, angrily. "Happy birthday, dear Little Giiiiirllll . . . happy birthday to you!"

Their eyes glide past her.

But then, a quick flip. They're in a living room. The daughter opens a gift of pink cowboy boots. And a Lego set—a pirate ship? Holly remembers getting a yellow Wuzzle bear and a *She-Ra* Crystal Castle for her birthday. Her older brother grabbed the castle, screaming about Castle Grayskull.

These two fight the same way. A sudden brawl.

The father says, "Hold on."

"It's her birthday, for crying out loud!" the mother says.

Holly hated her family, but she misses them now.

She sits down, cross-legged. She thinks of marching band and how she didn't get to go to the marching band competition. They had a routine to an old sitcom theme song, *My Three Sons*, her band director's favorite show as a kid. Mr. Tidek. He thought they could win. She starts to cry.

An old lady touches her shoulder. The grandmother, the next-door neighbor? "They're just playing," she says, pointing at the kids.

This old lady sees her? As much as she hated not being seen, this is more disturbing.

She should be gone. She's dead. She knows this.

She stands up. "Thanks. I have to leave now." How many places exist? How far could she get from this moment? She walks quickly toward a hallway. It disappears into nothingness.

She runs toward the nothingness and lets it swallow her whole.

And then:

Christmas—the tree in the quiet, the gifts.

Another birthday party. At an arcade.

A soccer match. She stands on the sidelines.

She runs to the edge of each one, feeling light and buzzy—a ripple of energy—then lands.

An ice-skating rink. She has no skates, but there she is on the ice, holding her flute. The skaters gliding around her.

A beach vacation—the father holding the two kids as he moves into the ocean.

A choral recital. When the crowd claps, she claps . . .

And then it strikes her. A crowd. What if she found someone she knows? What if she isn't far from home? She's in the aisle, searching faces. The kids take their final bow.

It all stops. The grainy light. The pixelation. But only for a moment. Then the concert begins again, midsong. She's back in the aisle. The conductor, in her woolly skirt . . . Holly looking at faces . . . A man in his midtwenties is looking at her. He really sees her. He stands up and tries to push down the aisle toward her. People aren't getting out of the way. He's stuck.

The beginning again, midsong. The man in his seat, staring at her. He doesn't try this time. He lifts his hand.

She waves back and leaves.

The sand, ocean, the father, the two kids . . .

• • •

The mother is two stories above her son. Almost exactly. If the house disappeared and they were suspended midair, you could connect them to the same rope, perpendicular to the earth.

He's making out with his girlfriend on the futon. His phone propped against the TV. Recording.

The mother made dinner—fish sticks, frozen veggies, chopped pickles in mayo—left it for the kids. Her glass of wine bobbles as she situates herself in bed. Laptop open. This used to be her son's room. The bedroom she shared with her husband, where he died, is untouched.

A knock at the door. Her daughter sticks her face in. "Can I do my homework in here?"

"I know this game," the mother says. "You need to sleep in your own bed. Are you still afraid of monsters?" It's supposed to be a joke but comes off cold.

The daughter's afraid of a lot of things. "Whatever." She shuts the door and walks to her own bedroom. She crawls under her bed. She likes the tight space, the dust ruffle like a tent. When she's here, she doesn't exist. If she doesn't exist, her father isn't dead. Because he never existed either. She blows on the dust ruffle—pink and billowy.

The mother's relieved that her daughter left her alone. Her kids can't regress just because their father died. She sips her wine, looks at her movie options, hovering over the link to a period piece.

She does what she does when she gives in. She goes to the family videos in the cloud. She misses her husband, their inside jokes, the sex.

She clicks on a clip of him with the kids on the beach, pushing into waves, holding both of them, his back red from sun. She'll let herself watch it ten times and then stop.

On the ninth time, her husband looks left. He turns as if someone's called to him. He turns, takes a step. What?

She starts again. The kids—one in each arm, the surf. He turns again, takes a step toward—what? A sound, a voice? This is new.

And then he turns again—back to the mother on the beach. He looks at her, worried, as if to say, "Do you see what I see?"

She watches again. Something's wrong. Something's there that wasn't before.

She shuts her laptop, her heart thudding. Her best friend told her, *Grief does strange things.*

She grabs a bottle of Xanax off the nightstand and swallows a pill. *This is grief,* she tells herself.

...

"Welcome to my YouTube channel!" the daughter practices, wearing lip gloss and her mom's mascara. Her nose is too big for her face. It used to be cute, but now it's not. Her poofy hair looks dumb.

On her desk is the start of her research paper: Rafflesia arnoldii, *the largest flower in the world, is a parasite. It's like fungus because it grows in a mass of strands and depends on hosts to get water and nutrients. Its flowers are huge and reddish brown and smell like rotten flesh.*

Her father smelled bad when he was dying. She didn't want to hug him. She hates to remember that part.

She slumps into her beanbag chair, plays footage she captured earlier—going fast on her bike downhill, a bird on a limb, the sky—"Hi! Welcome to my YouTube channel! This is where I live." Her house and then, quick turn, her street, the lot that's a cement hole.

And then something scrabbling up. A person. The top of a head as they crawl up. A teenager, a girl, stands up. Ponytail and bangs. She looks around, cold and a little dirty.

But there was no girl at the time.

But she's real, holding something—a short baton? No. A flute.

The daughter shouts, "Mom! Mom!"

Her mother still has a panic response from her husband's death. She runs down the hall and throws open the door. "What's wrong?"

The daughter hands her the laptop. Frozen on a still shot of the girl, arms crossed, flute tucked under one arm, eyes wide.

...

The son's girlfriend blew off her curfew by an hour, but she's finally gone. He's supposed to work on a group project designing a city on the moon. He's in charge of making tubes for housing. One thing he's learned about building a city on the moon is that it shouldn't be left to teenagers. He wants to write the team's conclusion: *This should only be tried by NASA engineers and shit. We're too stupid and lazy.*

A mess of Sharpies, cardboard, a box cutter, poster board.

He's too wired to focus. His girlfriend sent *the teaser* to herself. He hopes she wants to trash it. They aren't celebrities. They'll look like dorks because they are dorks.

He doesn't want to think about it or a moon city. He puts on his headset to do some gaming.

...

The mother sits on her daughter's twin bed. K-pop posters on the wall. Her daughter talked her into staying until she was asleep. The mother wants to curl up next to her, but she's afraid of her daughter's need for her.

Or is she afraid of her need for her daughter? She learned from her husband's death—don't need people. She looks at her little girl, tenderly. She smooths her soft hair. Then she opens the laptop. The girl with the flute. The mother sees herself in the girl's clothes and hair. Her own era. The girl with the flute is connected to her husband on the beach—his face, alarmed, maybe even scared. He looked at her. He needed her. Their eyes met—here, now, today.

She closes the laptop, turns out her daughter's light, and heads back to bed. In the morning, things will make sense.

. . .

Holly kneels in the wet sand, digging with her flute. It's already wrecked. Her first thought was SOS. But instead, she writes her name: HOLLY MAR—She runs out of time.

It begins again.

The father glances over sometimes, knee-deep, hip-deep . . . She ignores him. She keeps trying and gets faster. Maybe if someone knows she's here, something will change. She can't have her life back. But she's driven.

When she gets through her whole name, the father smiles. The kids are oblivious, squealing exactly the same way, each time.

The clip starts over, and she digs—so quick now.

The father shouts above the surf, "Holly!"

Her name stuck from one repetition to the next.
She draws in a breath and holds it. Stares at him.

• • •

They haven't had a family meeting since before the father died. Those were medical updates, the father dying upstairs. But here they are on a Saturday morning.

"What's going on?" the son asks.

"Something happened," the mother says. "Something weird, and we need to address it." She tries to explain about their father on the beach, but she's accidentally confessed that she watches clips over and over.

"That beach in North Carolina?" The son tries to focus on facts.

"Yes."

The daughter is lit up. "And I was riding my bike . . ." She shows the clip, freezing on the image of the girl with the flute.

The son fiddles with his phone case.

The mother asks the son, "Anything weird?"

"You *want* something to be weird, don't you?" He's not sure why he says this.

"No. It's just . . . we should talk. Because if there's something wrong. Well . . ." She's not sure what she's supposed to be saying. "Grief does strange things." Maybe she does want something to be strange—so strange that their father comes back.

The son thinks about the teaser. Could it have uploaded to the cloud automatically? "I'm fine. Can we wrap this up?"

"Don't be like that," the mother says.

His phone dings. It's a text from his girlfriend.

"This isn't grief," the daughter says. "This is a dead girl, alive in our videos. I'm sure it's why Dad's different on the tape. It's all . . ." She shoves all of her fingers together.

"Interconnected," the mother says.

The text reads:

What the fuck is wrong with you?

followed by a super pissed emoji.

"We should keep an eye on each other," the mother says.

The next text:

Who the fuck is she?

"Let's put our phones away," the mother says.

"Keep an eye on each other. Got it," the son says. "Can I go now?"

His phone bings and bings and bings.

"Sure," his mother says.

He whips out of his chair and heads into the basement. His phone keeps binging. He opens the video. Hits delete.

The texts read:

She's psycho.

Is she Avery Bickley's cousin?

Who's Avery Bickley? One of the sophomore soccer players? The keeper?

She's a fucking perv. WTF. You're the
worst. Fuck off and DIE.

He looks around the room. Everything is just the way he
left it. His laundry basket, his collection of Axe body spray and
cologne, the housing tubes from the model city.

Except the box cutter. Its blade is exposed. His father pri-
oritized safety. The son would never leave the blade like that.
He feels cold, deep in his gut. He kicks the stacks of cardboard.
And that's when he sees it:

HOLLY MARTINE WAS HERE.

I AM HOLLY MARTINE . . .

*HOLLY MARTINE HOLLY MARTINE HOLLY MAR-
TINE HOLLY MARTINE HOLLY MARTINE HOLLY
MARTINE HOLLY MARTINE HOLLY . . .*

. . .

"You're dead, too," Holly says to the dad.

"About a year now." They're at a baptism. He can only stray
so far; sometimes he has to gesture or move in a way that has
nothing to do with their conversation but is required.

"The old woman at your daughter's seventh birthday party
and the guy at the concert," she says. "They're dead, too."

"Yes. My wife's grandmother. She lived into her nineties. I
don't know the guy at the concert, but there was a GoFundMe
for his funeral expenses."

"What's a GoFundMe?"

"A fundraiser. Online." She doesn't get it. "Never mind."

They've been through this loop at the baptism many times,

the light fuzz on the baby's head being doused with water and oils, again and again.

"What do the dead do here?" she asks. "Do they get trapped?"

He looks younger here than on the beach. His hair dark and full, a goatee. "They're usually here for a while and then fade and become the repetitive images again, how they were first filmed. I think they have to be ready to go and those who love them have to let them."

"What's it with you? You can't go, or they won't let you?"

"Both." The father's eyes go wet. He smiles. "I *loved* this life."

She looks at the stained glass, the priest in his pale robes, those hovering around the baby. "That's not how it is with me, though."

"You weren't here. And then, suddenly, you were everywhere." He has to make the sign of the cross and bow his head. "What do you want?"

She looks at him, completely confused. "All of this. All of it. A life! Look at what you got!" She remembers the girl in the basement taking off her tank top, the boy on top of her, their heavy breathing, kissing, the roughness and sweetness. Can't she have that?

He lifts his head. The prayer is over. "What about the man who . . . did this to you?"

She doesn't want to talk about George Slimmer. Why should he even be allowed to exist in her mind? She taps her flute against her leg. "It was all woods, you know. Your whole neighborhood. And the last thing I saw was leaves and the sky behind them. I'd stopped breathing. But I still remember that. The leaves shaking. They weren't angry or scared. Or happy. They were beyond all of that. I'm beyond hating him. Maybe it's not trauma with us dead people. Maybe it's just wanting."

"But you're stuck here. You should—"

"You're stuck, too!" It feels good to shout in a church. "It's how you know I'm stuck."

"You're right."

"If they die, you could have them here."

"What?"

"If one of them dies, maybe I could take their place."

"Are you crazy?"

"I wrote my name and it stayed. If I can do that, I can do more than that."

She feels alignment, like in marching band when they synced up and the form took shape for the crowd—even though none of them could see it. Each one of them was a piece of something bigger. *My Three Sons* was three pairs of shoes, one of them tapping its foot, impatiently. They made that out of their marching bodies, their furry hats, chin-strapped into place. They only saw it when Mr. Tidek wheeled the AV cart into the band room and played the tape back. She feels powerful, caged.

"You can't," the father says. "Jesus, Holly." He grabs her arm, but she pulls away just as he's controlled by the moment, pulled back to prayer.

She turns and runs to the edge.

• • •

The son does a Google search. *Holly Martine* . . . News about the missing person case from 1986, the grieving family. Two years later, another disappearance. A high-school freshman field hockey player. The body was found. A few men were questioned. One was charged, tried, convicted.

George Slimmer. Expressionless, scarred lip. Fifty-five. Worked in HVAC, lived not too far away, in the house where he grew up, inherited from his mother after her death.

Cold and sweating, the son climbs the stairs, two at a time, to the first floor then the second. He finds his mother in the hallway, looking through boxes pulled from the crawl space. His sister is looking at the laptop, headphones on.

"Holly Martine," he says.

The sister pops one ear out of the headphones.

"What?" the mother says.

"That's the girl's name. She was probably murdered by a guy named George Slimmer."

"Show me."

They huddle around the son's laptop. He scrolls and lands on a news story.

"She's been in the basement," the son says. "She wrote her name. Obsessively."

"Why is she haunting us?" the mother asks.

"Did she write down what she wants from us?" the daughter asks.

"Does she have to want something?" he asks.

The mother thinks about it. "Don't ghosts always want something?"

"Maybe she wants to kill us," the son says. "Ghosts want that sometimes."

The son twists away from them, looking at the door at the end of the hallway, the room where his father died.

"I'm collecting all the footage," the daughter says. "She's everywhere."

•••

Holly has done everything she wanted. Her hands are sticky with icing. Her jeans wet and sandy. Her fingers cold and red from the ice rink. Her throat raw from singing at the concert. Now she's in the basement. The boy and the girl are making out. She watched them before, flushed with shame, but now she doesn't look at them. She moves around the room, touches the headset; picks up cologne, sprays it, and walks through the mist.

She puts her flute down on the card table next to the cardboard tubes and Styrofoam, the markers, the box cutter. She picks up the box cutter. She recalls the first shovel of dirt settling around her. Once you've been murdered, you earn the right to murder someone. She'd never thought of murdered people when she was a teenager. What would happen if she killed someone here? Her actions have effects now. They ripple into the real world. She looks at the girl and the boy, moving around into some new configuration. "You're on my hair," the girl says, like she always does. He lifts his elbow. "Sorry, sorry." They're so alive. Do they deserve it? Why did she die and not them? Could she change that?

She looks up at the drop ceiling. She remembers the leaves against the sky. She tightens her grip on the box cutter and closes her eyes.

•••

The mother, the daughter, and the son huddle around the laptop on the kitchen table.

The father looks at each of them now, through the camera, searching their gazes. He's desperate. He wants to tell them something, but he can't. He breaks away from his predetermined role only for a few seconds here and there, then he snaps back to the way he was before.

Holly isn't in any of the clips. She's gone.

The mother says, "Did she choose us? How did she get in?" She doesn't think of her daughter's cell phone. She thinks of the hole in this family—the hole ripped wide by the loss of the father. They have a human-shaped hole. Was Holly drawn to it?

"She needs a better flute." The son wants good things for her. She's been through so much. And she's pretty, in a way. Maybe because she's sad and he understands sadness. "We can do that, can't we?"

"How?" the mother asks.

"I can buy a flute and film it. Upload that to the cloud, and it's hers."

The suggestion surprises the mother. It's so practical and selfless.

"We could give her a birthday party," the son says. "We could figure out what she's missing, and, I don't know." The son feels himself falling for her. Will she be with them forever?

"What about Dad?" the daughter asks.

They play the clips, and their father is terrified. At their cousin's wedding, while teaching the daughter how to ride a bike, in a hammock at a lake house. His eyes will snap, and he'll stare into the camera. Does he want something from them? What?

The son paces around the kitchen, animated. He reminds

the mother of his younger self when he let himself get excited about things. It scares her—his hope, his sudden naivete. "We can see him, and he can see us! It's all different now, right? Maybe we can have him back, kind of—"

"No," the mother says. "We can't have him back. We have to heal." The gaping wound of his absence. "It's what he would want." It's what she would want if she were the one who'd died.

The daughter walks quickly to the back door, picking up her bike helmet from the floor and her coat from the doorknob. "I'm going for a ride." She puts on her coat.

"We should stick together," the mother says.

"It'll get dark soon," the son says. "You shouldn't be out by yourself."

The daughter opens the door. "I won't be gone long." She walks out and they follow her into the garage.

"Hey!" the brother says.

She pulls her bike out of the garage, hops on, and glides down the driveway.

Her mother runs out into the yard.

Her brother stands beside his mother. "Wait!"

"I'll be back!" she calls to them.

The daughter pedals hard. Gets some momentum, passes where the dead girl first appeared. Keeps going. Downhill, out of the development's entrance. Two stone posts were supposed to hold the name of their development in wrought-iron cursive. Still empty.

She pulls onto the main road. She stays on the shoulder. Her wheels pop and slip amid the gravel as cars pass. Headlights stretch her shadow then snap it back. Cold air burns her lungs.

At the top of the hill, she stops. Catches her breath. She

says, "Welcome to my YouTube channel," her voice hoarse and dry. She pulls out her phone and looks at the stretch of road. What if her father's death has made her special?

There's the cemetery. Her father is buried there. Lots of people who don't want to be dead are buried there. She pulls out her phone. Headlights behind her slow; she casts a long shadow. The car pulls onto the shoulder. She looks back.

Her brother gets out first, leaving the door open. He takes a few steps toward her. "I know what you're thinking," he says slowly. "Don't do it. Just hold on."

The mother kills the engine but keeps the headlights on. She gets out of the car. The daughter, still straddling her bike, holds up her phone, ready to record. She has to do this. It's the only way to get him back.

"Your father's dead," the mother says. "But we have to keep going."

This is her shot; the daughter has to take it. She fakes giving in. She nods, lowers her phone, and gets off her bike like she's going to walk over, put it in the trunk, and go home.

Her mother and brother exchange a look of relief.

Then she drops the bike and takes off running toward the cemetery. She holds up her phone and hits record. Her phone bobbles as she's taking in the graves. She focuses on her father's grave, up on the rise of the hill. But she's sweeping over lots of graves, even the modest headstone of George Slimmer, who died in jail but was buried out here, in his hometown, next to his mother and sister. The daughter doesn't know this. She wants her father back, that's all. She couldn't begin to understand what she's setting loose.

Her mother cries her name. Her brother runs after her. Her

body is lit up by the headlights, pouring into the darkness. Her brother is getting closer, and then leaps and tackles her to the cold, hard dirt. Her phone pops loose. She kicks him and twists away, but he doesn't let go. He holds her. Both of them caught under the press of the darkening sky. And the mother arrives, standing over them, protective and breathless with love and fear. Their hearts bang wildly in their chests. The wind shivers, gusts.

And then her brother makes a strange noise. He lets go of her. He's wincing in pain. He rolls to his back and pulls up his sleeve. There's a cut on his wrist, short but deep. He looks at his mother, who falls to her knees and crawls to him. She presses her hand to the wound, blood rising through her fingers.

The daughter whips around, taking in the night sky, the graves, the road, her hair flipping in the wind.

THE NOW OF NOW

When people ask me how old I am, I sometimes hesitate. I know what year it is and the year I was born, the simple subtraction.

But I've lived longer.

The fall of my junior year in high school, Alec Murchison and I lived a very long time.

Alec is now thirty-eight, according to his profile. In his photo, he's sitting in an Adirondack chair on a lake dock, smiling a genuine smile, like someone has said something actually funny. His dark curls stick up from the edges of a Red Sox baseball cap. I haven't seen him since we were sixteen.

His first message to me is a simple question:

Did it really happen?

...

I knew early on but pretended I didn't, or kept quiet because I was scared, or, with my overdeveloped capacity for denial, I talked myself out of believing it. My earliest memory is wandering away from my parents in the food court because I'd spotted the mall Easter Bunny ordering Cinnabon. I was probably four years old.

When the bunny took off his big fake head and hands to pay for his order, I was terrified by the bald human head and slack jowls, by his small, quick, human hands. I spun away, looking for my parents—my dad in his peacoat or my mom carrying her orange pocketbook. I didn't see them. I started to breathe hard and then burst into tears. My vision was tear blurred.

And then it all just froze.

I blinked and my tears plopped and ran down my face.

The weirdest part—the absolute silence.

I started walking slowly around everyone like they were statues in a museum. But I didn't lose sight of my goal: to find my parents. I scrambled up on a chair and then onto a table and scanned the crowd.

Once I spotted them—my mother holding a plastic tray, her head turned far in one direction as if she'd just noticed I was gone, and my father unwrapping the oily paper around a hamburger—I got down and took off running toward them.

I got to my mom first and hugged her upper legs. She was wearing boxy, high-waisted jeans.

She stayed frozen.

I screamed, "Mama! Ma!"

Nothing.

I reached up and grabbed her hand holding the tray, and everything whirred back to life—noisy chatter, shouting, clattering, banging—and my mom just looked down and said, "Oh, there you are," like it was the normalest thing in the world.

And so, as children do, I believed it was the most normal thing in the world.

...

I'm divorced. I have a beautiful, scrappy daughter, Chloe, who's eleven. I watch her closely for signs of disorientation, rapid breathing, a wildness in her eyes, an upending.

I watch her for a look that says: *I was just running across the front yard filled with birds pecking at the grass, and when they started to flap up into the sky, they froze, midair, mid-wingbeat.*

I check her for signs of a girl who has reached up and touched one of those frozen birds in a world that's gone completely still and quiet, clouds stuck in the sky overhead.

...

After a solid week, I write back to Alec Murchison:

> Hi, it's nice to hear from you. But
> I don't know what you're talking
> about. I think you may have me
> confused with someone else.

I mean: *I am no longer who I was. That was someone else. And it didn't happen.*

I sign off:

> Go Sox!

•••

It happened again in sixth grade, backstage at a play. I felt so nervous that I was afraid I might explode. I was waiting for my cue, terrified that I'd miss it. And just like the first time, with no warning, everything stopped.

That eerie silence—no lines being projected by overbearing middle-school actors, no coughing in the audience, no back-stage whispers. Nothing.

I stared at a large digital wall-mounted clock, waiting for it to go from 8:12 to 8:13. It didn't. I held my breath and counted, slowly, a full sixty seconds. It did not budge.

I'd convinced myself that the Easter Bunny Cinnabon experience was just some weird dream. But I recalled it now vividly.

The stage manager was nearby with clipboard and headset. He was an eighth-grader with chin pimples. In the mall food court, grabbing my mom's hand was what had pushed every-thing back into motion.

So I walked over to the stage manager and poked one of his knuckles.

And, same as before, everything started up.

The stage manager stared at me as if he was vaguely aware that I'd been a few feet away and was now super close. "Do you need something?" he whispered.

I shook my head and looked up at the clock.

8:13.

•••

Alec's second message is a little more urgent:

> I'd really like to talk. I hate to bother
> you. I know we haven't kept in
> touch. But it's important.

He gives his number.

...

It didn't become a problem until I was sixteen and started dating Alec. We met in civics class. Coach Smiley, a wide man with sad eyes, taught the class with little enthusiasm. I sat in front of Alec so I could hear the smart-ass stuff he said under his breath, and he could see my shoulders shaking while trying to bottle my laughter. One day, while I was working my locker combination, he asked me to homecoming. He was one of those kids who'd already grown into his features—dark eyebrows, light freckles, the curls—you could see that, at thirty-eight, he'd be that guy in an Adirondack chair on a lake dock. I liked him a lot. But I'd have liked him even if he hadn't had smart-ass things to say. I liked him immediately and thoroughly, so deep down that it was at that murky spot where biology meets the subconscious. Who could say why I liked him so much? It was unfathomable.

I said yes to being his homecoming date. I'd have said yes to running away with him, though he wasn't the runaway type, and neither was I.

"Do you wanna hang out after school at my house?"

I did.

He lived two neighborhoods away. When I showed up, he

met me in the front yard. His little brother was having a trombone lesson, so he didn't invite me in. We climbed a maple tree leaning against his screened-in porch to get to its flat roof. It was fall, the maple leaves had changed color, and the roof tar was starting to lose its pent-up heat from summer sun. We talked about Coach Smiley, the pervy driver's ed teacher, and the suggested yearbook theme—*Do we dare?* "Dare to do what?" he said. "Dare to geek out on yearbook committee?"

"Do we dare to wear Emma Teterman's knee-high cat socks?"

"I know the Tetermans," he said. "That's their actual cat. Those are special-order socks."

"*Nice*," I said, sarcastically.

"*Really* nice."

We went quiet, staring at each other, face to face. My heart was pounding hard, and my cheeks were hot. He leaned in to kiss me. And I leaned in to kiss him. Just before the kiss, he stopped. And the birds weren't chirping, and his brother's trombone scales stopped midflat. I was aware of this, yes, but I was so nervous and focused on kissing him that I barely registered it. I just closed my eyes and started kissing him.

Hugging my mother's jeans didn't start things up again. Grabbing her hand did. The same with poking the stage manager's knuckle.

And this kiss started Alec back in motion, too.

We kissed and it got breathless and a little sweaty.

But when we came up for air, Alec said, "Weird."

I thought he was talking about my kissing, so I died a million terrible deaths. I'd only made out a few times at a sleep-away camp, where maybe I'd learned all the wrong things about kissing.

But then I realized what he was talking about. Alec was fully animated but there was still no sound. None at all. He looked up at the leaves on the tree over our heads. Everything had stopped.

"Wait," I said. "You feel it, too?"

"Feel *what*?"

"Like time itself . . . has just . . ."

He stood up and touched a red leaf on the tree. He bent it a little; it had give. But it had no life of its own. "Holy shit!" he said, and then he lowered his voice, really afraid now. "Holy shit."

"This is new," I said. "That I'm not alone."

"This has happened to you before?" He stared at me.

"Just a few times. I always thought it was just, you know . . ."

"No," he said. "I don't know."

What had I thought? It was a nervous tic? It was a . . . medical condition? "It's only happened a few times. It always went away pretty quickly when I'd touch someone, but . . . not this time, not with you."

Alec moved to the second-story window that led back into his house. He shoved the window up with the heel of his hand. "This is messed up. This is very messed up." He shouted through the open window, "Mom! Mom, are you okay? Cole!" That was his little brother's name. "Cole! Can you hear me?"

After a minute or so, the trombone finished its note, the wind kicked up, and the leaves trembled. He must have found someone in his family, reached out, and touched them. Alec was talking loudly, and their dog, whipped up by the urgency, started barking little yappy barks.

I sat there for a few minutes, waiting.

But I didn't know what I was waiting for. If Alec came back,

I'd have to explain things, and I had no idea how to. I didn't understand what these pauses in time meant. Now that someone else had experienced it, I had to face the fact that they were real. For the first time, I was really scared of them. I climbed back down the tree and sprinted home.

•••

I hold Chloe's hand whenever we pass the store in the mall where the jeans soak up all that airborne cologne. This time, I see a teenage clerk wearing a sweater that's cropped to show her midriff. She's stopped folding in order to thumb-scroll on her phone. A jolt of fear runs through me, and I hold Chloe's hand tighter as we walk by.

We make these misguided attempts to put teen love into a pretty little box with a nostalgic bow and pretend it's not powerful. In truth, we're afraid of it. And we should be. High-school sweethearts? A disastrous miscalculation. There's nothing *sweet* about them. Teen love is a force. The hormones, of course. Teen brains are awash in them and all of the ferocity that follows. But, also, falling in love for the first time means that you have no defenses built up against it. Without the gatekeepers of cynicism, loss, and heartbreak, it steals in quickly and starts to take up as much space as it can. Plus, love in your teen years occupies a larger percentage of your time alive to that point. You've already forgotten infancy, the toddler years, most of early elementary school. All told, by age sixteen, you've got clear memories of about . . . six years? You're falling in love with only six years of real experience to draw on? Moment for moment, falling in love in your teen years gets an enormous slice of your consciousness pie.

For some, it's the first time they've been known, the first time they've not felt alone.

Do not underestimate it.

...

Alec didn't show up to school the next day, a Friday. But that Sunday afternoon, he knocked on my front door. "I want to talk. Do you want to talk?"

I looked over my shoulder. Both of my parents were home. "Yeah." I grabbed a sweater, and we went for a walk. I told him everything. I'd never confided in anyone before. Not about this, not about anything. I didn't come from that kind of family. My parents seemed to like it when the answer to *How was school?* was *Fine.* We played a lot of board games and card games, but we never really talked. My childhood was lonesome. I learned early on that I was a disruption, something that demanded attention and that pulled my parents away from some previous existence. They'd look at old photos and say, "That was back when it was just the two of us." They missed that time. They were happy together, and I was this small intruder.

I sometimes felt like I was stalking a childhood, skirting the edges, trying to find a way in.

On the walk with Alec, I struggled to explain things. A story that goes untold gets muddled in your head. Alec kept having to interrupt. "Wait, did that happen first? How old were you?"

I did the best I could.

"It's an anxiety thing, right?" he asked.

"I guess so. It happens when I'm really nervous or scared." He smiled a little, knowing that kissing him made me nervous.

We found a kiddy park and sat in side-by-side swings.

"Well, you could do a lot with the skill," he said. "You could steal things. You could cheat on tests. You could . . . I don't know. You could do the things you wanted to do for as long as you wanted and then squeeze in the stuff you didn't want to do. You could . . ."

"I could live more than other people," I said, not really sure what I meant.

"Up until us, on the roof, you were alone, right? And then the kiss. I was nervous, too." I glanced at him, quickly, then away.

"And maybe because of it, I tapped into the world as you see it." He pushed back and started swinging. He pumped his legs.

I started swinging, too, as if I could catch up to him. "I'm not going to steal shit or cheat on tests," I said. "That's not my thing."

"My dad got a job in Cincinnati!" he shouted. "We're leaving in two weeks!"

I dragged my feet, coming to a stop. "You won't be here for homecoming?"

He jumped off the swing and landed, one hand touching down. He turned around. "We could have a lot of time together," he said. "Us. You and me."

•••

I've never told anyone in the world about my episodes except Alec Murchison. I know it's hard to believe. But it's true. Definitely not my parents. Not my grandmother on her deathbed. Not a priest or a therapist. Not any best friends or boyfriends. Not the guy I lived with for two years, and not the man I married and divorced. I learned to manage my stress levels very attentively. In my sophomore year of college, I faked panic attacks so that I could get a prescription for Xanax. I still keep it on hand just to make sure that I never get too anxious. My prevention system works; I haven't had any issues for a decade or more.

...

We reconstructed the moment on the roof of his porch.

"You were sitting here," he said.

"And you were over a little . . ."

"And then we held hands."

"No, we didn't hold hands."

We kissed a few times, but it didn't work. I got flustered.

"Are you nervous enough?" he asked.

I wiped my sweaty palms on my jeans. "Are you?"

He leaned in for another kiss, and before his lips reached mine, he froze, and the maple tree's bright leaves stopped shivering. And I wondered for a moment if I should leave, walk away. I was worried about messing with something that maybe shouldn't be messed with.

But he was there, his full lips so close . . . And I was compelled to kiss him. I had to.

...

Alec writes to me:

I've got a son, a three-year-old, he was diagnosed with . . .

I've thought of every scenario in which I would start doing it again.

Every single one.

I thought of this one while I was still pregnant with Chloe.

How did we do it?

Can you help me? I just need more time with him. I just need . . .

• • •

This became our habit. We would meet on the roof every afternoon and then have complete freedom. At first, we used the time just to be alone together in his room without fear of someone finding us. But then we started venturing out. We did steal a few things—french fries and milkshakes from behind the counters at fast-food restaurants. We skinny-dipped in the McGinntys' hot tub. We helped ourselves to liquor at a dive bar. We went roller-skating, making sure not to touch anyone frozen on the rink.

Eventually, we got bold enough to borrow a Corvette. It sat in the Hoffmans' garage. Mrs. Hoffman was weeding the garden. Their back door was open. We found the key on a wall hook shaped like a giant key. We took turns driving, top down. We blasted what was in the tape deck, old songs like "California Dreamin'." Eventually, we made it out to the highway, weaving through the cars and eighteen-wheelers.

I turned off the music. Alec was driving. "Have you ever wondered if old people aren't old people?" I asked.

"What?"

"What if some old people aren't old people? What if they fell in love with somebody and decided to do . . . this?"

"And they got old?"

"They went on while everyone else stopped. Yes. And when they came back, they were old."

"But people around them would know," he said. "They'd mention it."

"I'm just saying."

A few nights later, we were lying on the field of a football game. It was a big moment in the game; the quarterback was about to throw what would become a touchdown. The lights were bright. There were lots of moths suspended and lit up, almost incandescent.

"I don't want to go," he said.

"I don't want you to go."

And that was when we knew he had to. He was still looking up into the night sky. "We'll get through the next part of our lives and we can go to the same college or something."

"Exactly," I said.

"Exactly."

...

Most of the time, you don't realize that you should have done it until after it's no longer a good idea. There's some hardwiring in the brain that tells some people, like me, that a good time will always be good, that two people in love will always be in love, that life isn't as suddenly chaotic and random and brutal as it actually is.

It's summer, and I'm sitting in my office, watching Chloe jumping on the trampoline in the backyard in her bright blue bathing suit. I worry that she's lonesome, as an only child, the way I was. But I delight in her existence. She fills up my gaze. Unlike my parents, I want her to know that she's at the center of her childhood. She's pulled the hose on the trampoline with her, and she's spraying water while jumping, higher and higher. Her stringy wet hair, cut in a bob, flies out each time she descends or spins. Her shoulders have turned pink in the sun.

I write Alec back:

I can't help. I wish I could. I can't imagine what you must be going through. But I don't know how anything works. All I know is that what comes at us comes at us. And we can't stop it. I'm so sorry, Alec.

Does he remember what I said about old people? Was it true? Would someone keep aging, would a disease keep progressing? I don't know. But I *have* imagined it, I have. And I know what I'd do. I'd try to figure out a way to stop time with her. I'd find out what happens to the body. And if it worked, if it worked at all, I'd leave with her and live in a frozen world and never come back.

I send the message. I pick up my iced tea, and there's a hand on my arm. A wet hand.

Chloe is here, her face is blotchy, her wet bangs are stuck to her forehead.

I look back through the window. The hose is spilling water on the empty trampoline.

I stare into my daughter's eyes. She's been crying. She's scared. She whispers, "Mom," and her voice is hoarse as if she's been screaming.

I pull her wet body to me. She's trembling. We hug each

other tightly. I've been so scared of this moment, vigilantly watching for it, but what surprises me—a breath caught in my throat—is a sudden flood of relief. I'm in a moment that keeps giving way to the next moment, each *now* coming at me and through me.

Right now—and now and now and now—I'm not alone.

THE VERSIONS

Artrice and Ben had eleven weddings between them—with one overlap: they were both invited to the Oslo-Murchison wedding. Ellie Oslo was one of Artrice's friends from college. Tod Murchison was one of Ben's cousins. But Artrice's sister was getting married on the same weekend three states away. And the Oslo-Murchison wedding fell during the Birch and Birch summer sales conference, and Ben would be in attendance in Antwerp.

Artrice and Ben kind of hated weddings. They didn't like any event in which a specific emotion was obligatory, especially if that emotion was joy. They had nothing against joy, per se. They just didn't want to feel forced into it.

Here's the real tragedy: Artrice and Ben would have really hit it off if they'd gone to the Oslo-Murchison wedding.

This isn't their story. They've still never met.

Both were offered a plus-one; they RSVP'd with notes about how they were sorry not to attend in person, but they wanted to have lived memories, so they'd be sending Versions. At this point, Versions were still relatively new. A wedding with some Versions happened more often in the high-tech crowd, but it was starting to take off. Ellie Oslo was pissed. "It's so like Artrice to make this about herself. *Look at me. I'm so cutting edge.*" Tod Murchison was thinking about the bottom line. "Do they drink? Do they cost us a meal or not?" After initial reactions, the couple pretty much forgot about them.

Looking back, Ben and Artrice's Versions would seem laughably rudimentary. Not in looks, no. Ben looked like Ben, and Artrice like Artrice—both about fifteen pounds trimmer and a few years younger. But their intellects and social-emotional programming were simple. They were programmed to give short updates on work and personal lives. They had complimentary spiels on the bride and groom. They could ask questions: *Do you know the bride or the groom? What do you do for a living? Where do you live?*

In addition to phrases like *Yes, please*; *No, thank you*; *I don't know*; and *Maybe later*, they could access pat phrases that could be used for most occasions: *How about it! Oh wow! Amazing! Isn't that something!*

They were programmed to get teary—both while smiling and frowning—but not to cry.

They were programmed to dance and raise their glasses and clink, but only pretend to drink, lips sealed to the glass. Likewise, they could comment on the food. *Mmmm, delicious!* But they could only move it around with cutlery. Digestion was costly and pointless.

They were shipped a few days before the event, directly to the all-in-one venue, an upscale place that prided itself on amenities like guaranteeing storage, power, and return shipping.

Most of the guests had never seen Versions at a wedding before, so whispers went around, and, while sitting in the back of the outdoor ceremony, they got some stares. The worst was when they showed up at the reception hall, where Jarvis Shapiro laughed at them and said, "Enjoy the wedding, you bougie low-rent fauxbot a-holes." He was fifteen, already a little drunk, having stolen a few drinks from other people's tables, and bitter about having to sit at the children's table.

This was the moment Ben and Artrice met and recognized that they were both Versions. Without Jarvis Shapiro's smart-ass bullshit, would they have known? Were they programmed to see their own kind and connect? Hard to say.

Jarvis wasn't really the problem, though. The problem was that they'd wound through the reception area, skirting the dance floor on opposite sides, and found table twelve, situated between the kitchen doors and the children's table. The problem was table twelve was the Dead People's table. Jarvis found this hysterical, and it's why he called them fauxbot a-holes. Artrice and Ben stared at the Dead, who were holographic, not embodied at all. They shimmered and smiled and occasionally waved, but to no one in particular.

The Oslo-Murchison wedding had five Dead People. That included Ellie Oslo's maternal grandparents and Tod Murchison's grandfather. (Tod's grandmother, who was still alive, avoided her holographic husband and the Dead People's table altogether. Maybe she could too easily imagine herself there.) Tod's father was also there. He'd died of ALS five years earlier. They'd opted for a hologram rendered before the disease whittled his body. And then there was Ellie's brother, who'd overdosed in a cabin in Maine two summers earlier. It was brutal—this beautiful young man, smiling through what must have been an onslaught of pain.

Ben and Artrice smiled politely at each other and sat down in the two empty chairs, side by side, their names calligraphed on rice paper placed on top of empty white plates.

The Dead didn't speak; they were on expression loops— laugh, smile, wave, repeat. And so that left Artrice and Ben to hold up a conversation.

They asked each other how they knew the bride and groom and answered with anecdotes.

"Ellie and I were in the same sorority, and we took a course in astronomy together. We never found out how the universe started, but we became close friends."

"Our fathers are brothers, so we grew up together, going on family vacations to the Cape. There was this rope swing. We would fly out over a lake, let go, and drop. We pretended we could fly. We could do that for hours."

Artrice's other answers went like this: "I work for an IT company called Smart Bodies. I do a lot of software design, mostly artificial intelligence for prosthetic limbs. It's a little boring, but I love the idea of helping others." And "I moved to Portland, the Pearl District, a couple of years ago. It can be a little pretentious, but it feels like home now." "I have a Bernese mountain dog named Han Solo who thinks he's a lapdog."

Ben's answers went this way: "I work for a global marketing firm. We sell how to sell." And "I live in Philly, the City of Brotherly Love."

"I used to play water polo in college, but now I'm in a drunk bowling league. Whatever that says about me seems pretty accurate."

They responded to each other. "How about it!" "Amazing!" "Oh wow!" "Isn't that something!" etc.

When they'd made it through their entire repertoire, they went quiet.

Servers were weaving through tables, setting down plates of sous vide salmon and wilted chard. The Dead's food appeared before them in hologram form. A server at the children's table looked at Ben and Artrice and froze. She walked over to a man in a suit standing by the kitchen doors and whispered. The man's eyes widened in panic. He shooed her away. The waitress returned to their table a few minutes later with full plates for the two of them. "Sorry about the delay. Our fault."

"Thank you!" they said, in unison. The synced response was awkward.

"Okay," the waitress said. "Let me know if you have any questions, um, if you . . ." She smiled and walked away.

Ben and Artrice glanced nervously at the Dead, who smiled and waved and ate holographic food. Ben and Artrice picked up their forks and moved the food around on their plates.

And then Ben said, "Do you know the bride or the groom?" taking it from the top.

Halfway through dinner, two guys walked up. They'd taken off their ties and unbuttoned their collars. Much like Tod, they were beefy and thick of neck. The beefier one slapped Ben on the shoulder. "Hey, man, how's Ben doing?"

The other one, a guy with spiky hair, said, "Dude, he is Ben. Just ask him how he's doing."

"This is not Ben, man. This is one of those sorry-I'm-too-important-to-show-up-but-I'm-rich-enough-to-send-this-piece-of-shit."

Under the table, Artrice gripped the tablecloth.

"C'mon," the spiky-haired one said.

"Seriously, Ben's a fucking twat to not come in person and send this thing."

"Children's table," the spiky-haired friend said. "Dead grandparents. Have some respect."

The beefier one looked at the holograms. His eyes fell on Ellie's brother, Vince Oslo, and just at that moment, Vince seemed to be looking right back at him. The beefy guy said, "I got high with that dude a few times. I saw him jump off a bridge and swim in the Charles River. It was summer. He was still dressed in his waitstaff uniform. He wasn't trying to kill himself. He just, you know, wanted to swim." He pressed his eyes with his fingers. "Guy like that's no longer here and instead we've got these bots." He threw his hand at Ben and Artrice.

Ben stood up. "I used to play water polo in college, but now I'm in a drunk bowling league. Whatever that says about me seems pretty accurate."

The two guys stared at him, baffled, then walked off to the bar.

Ben sat down.

"Amazing," Artrice whispered.

Ben moved the sous vide salmon and wilted chard around on his plate and smiled.

The toasts began, one after another. Ben and Artrice raised their glasses and pretended to sip from fluted champagne glasses. When the DJ opened up the dance floor, Jarvis wrapped his arm around Artrice and slid in close to her face. "Hey, lady-bot, you want to dance?" He was sloshed and maybe stoned. Some of the college boys had smoked on some balcony on an upper floor.

Artrice wanted to say no thank you, but there was a manners override. "Maybe later."

"C'mon," Jarvis said, pulling on her arm so hard that she found herself on her feet. "You gotta!"

Artrice pulled back. "Do you know the bride or the groom?" she asked with strained politeness.

"What?" Jarvis said.

Ben stood up and said, "Do you know the bride or the groom?"

"Like I need you in my fucking face," Jarvis said, and he walked off.

Ben and Artrice sat down again, rattled. They both looked at the Dead. Ellie's grandparents were especially beautiful. Artrice hadn't noticed it before, but by the tilt of their arms and their waving patterns, she was pretty sure that they were holding hands under the table. It was touching. They'd also sometimes glance at each other and smile. Had they been this happy in real life? Was this the programming? Artrice ran through her preset lines to try to find a way to express how she felt. She nodded to the couple and said to Ben, "Close friends."

Ben understood. He scanned his own presets. ". . .grew up together."

"Isn't that something," she said.

Ben nodded toward Vince. "Brotherly love," he said.

Artrice looked at Vince's face, the bright shine of his eyes, the sadness glinting there.

The band was now playing a slow song. Ben held out his hand.

"Yes, please!" Artrice said.

They walked to the dance floor. They danced stiffly, one set of hands held, his other hand at the small of her back, hers on his shoulder. "Where do you *live?*" Artrice asked, her breath at his cheek. She wanted to know a deeper truth.

He understood what she was after. He didn't know what to say. "I'm not sure."

She took her hand from his shoulder and pointed at his heart. "Pearl," she said. And she knew it was wrong to take something like *the Pearl District*, where Artrice lived, and use it in such a wildly different and intimate context. But it also felt good and right.

Her finger just touching the spot where his heart should be—it almost hurt. "What do you do for a living?" he asked, nervous but excited to have strayed so far away from his programming.

"Lapdog," she said.

He shook his head. Artrice was no lapdog. "Mountain dog!" he said.

She laughed. No. "Lapdog. Artificial, prosthetic lapdog." It was getting easier, clipping through the program, picking and choosing. She looked out at the other couples, the bride and groom among them. "What do you *do?*" She tried again. This time, she meant, *What will* we do? *How will we live these lives?*

He stopped dancing. He looked at her, sadly. "We sell how to sell." And then he added the "Ha, ha, ha" that was meant to follow the line about the drunk bowling league. But they came out as sad, hollow notes.

She shook her head. "No." She took his hand and led him off the dance floor. A group of thirty-somethings on the edges watched them. One must have made a joke, because they all burst into laughter.

Ben and Artrice walked through tall double doors onto a wide balcony with wrought-iron tables and chairs. It overlooked a lawn, flower gardens, and, at the end of the slope, a swimming pool. The pool was decorated with floating candles. The candles, pushed by the wind, had collected in the deep end, where they winked. It was dusk. The sky was churned up. It looked like it could storm. As they stood there, silently, Artrice reached out and took Ben's hand.

None of this was supposed to happen, but, also, this wasn't a completely isolated event, either. Reports were already coming in. Versions had too much autonomy; they were saying things that were unexpected, doing things beyond their programming. They were reacting, in the moment, unpredictably. Some argued that this was good. Life is unpredictable, and so they needed agility to respond to it. But others were uncomfortable. The Versions that followed were far more regulated, which is why the stories of these early Versions are, well, important. It's a little slice of history, of what they could have become.

"Do you know?" he asked.

Artrice ran through her limited options. "We never found out how the universe started," she said.

". . .pretty accurate."

"Do *you* know?" she asked.

He looked out at the swimming pool, the candles getting snuffed out by the wind. "There was this rope swing. We would fly out over a lake, let go, and drop. We pretended?" It was an invitation.

"Yes, please," she said.

Maybe you haven't forgotten about Ben, back from his sales conference, and Artrice, exhausted from her sister's wedding weekend—how in Portland and Philadelphia, both in their apartments, on couches, queuing up the Oslo-Murchison event on their laptops propped on their chests, they saw things through their Versions' eyes. And eventually, they came to this moment, one they missed, one they'll never live through, and, even if they'd gone to the wedding, would it have been possible for them to see each other for who they were? Did they themselves have any idea who they were?

They watched as Ben and Artrice walked down the slope. Heat lightning strobed in the distance, but it was building to a storm. They unlocked the gate around the pool. It was dark here now. All of the candles blown out. They took off their shoes, socks, stockings. Ben cuffed his pants. They sat on the edge and put their feet in the cool water.

"We pretended," he said, "for hours."

"I love the idea."

"We grew up together," Ben said, and he meant the two of them here, at this wedding; they were learning who they were, who they could become. And he wondered if he could get wet, would it set something off in his system. He wasn't sure, but he pushed off the side of the pool anyway and went underwater. He held his breath and emerged, slick as a seal. His skin shone. "Let go and drop," he said.

"Together?" she said.

"Yes, please."

She pushed off too and dipped underwater quickly. Her puffed hair seemed almost to melt. She popped up quickly, wiping her face. Her makeup didn't smudge. It was permanent.

They could hear the wedding party, the heavy bass, the crowd singing along to a chorus, the thunder at the edge of the sky. Maybe the storm would come, and the lightning would dip down and wreck them; they knew this but they didn't get out. Not yet. They wrapped their arms around each other.

"Mountain dog," he whispered.

"Pearl," she whispered back.

"I used to," he said, "but now I'm in."

"Like home now," she said.

NEST

Remember the nest in the eaves by the front door. A family of birds, tiny eggs hatched. Your mother was obsessed with it. Took pictures of it.

And then the birds abandoned the nest.

After your mother died, the nest disappeared, too.

This is proof. Remember it. It will be important later.

...

It wasn't a simple death. It's taken you years to just come out with it: your mother killed herself in Olivia Shaw's canopy bed the summer you turned sixteen.

This was what things were like before. Your house, along with a bunch of others, faced a common with the neighborhood pool. Swim meets sounded like eruptions of civil war, gunshots from starter pistols and screaming. (There was no obvious war.) There was pop music for the aquacise classes, women straddling pool noodles. Kids, greased up with sunscreen, stabbing their hands down, flipping filters, and running across pool decks. The constant cries of *Marco* and *Polo*, like two halves of the same person, were lost forever.

Your mother was a Realtor. She was, in fact, the Shaws' agent. Their house sat across from yours, diagonally. Her face was on a sign in their yard. There wasn't a showing on the books the day she died. The Shaws were spending the summer at their lake house. Olivia was getting ready to go off to Smith College, and the Shaws were downsizing because she was their youngest.

Sometimes you think your mother just got tired so she crawled into Olivia's bed upstairs.

But, then, of course, the gun. It belonged to your dad, so, you know, he broke in a deep-down way.

Your mother was courteous about it. She laid down on her right side and positioned the gun so that whoever found her would see one side of her face, intact—the shattered side hidden. She may have even known the gun would pop backward and get lost under the second pillow.

It seemed impulsive because no one saw it coming. But it's not an accident to have a gun in your pocketbook while in a house that no one lives in anymore.

Your mother was a planner, and it was planned.

The only thing for sure: It was a mistake that you found her.

• • •

Your mother's car was in the driveway. The lockbox was broken, no need for a code. You walked through the house, calling for her. You wanted permission to go to a party at Becca's that night.

You expected to find her scrubbing the tub, silk sleeves rolled up, necklace popping against her chest, cursing the Shaws for a dirty ring of soap scum. She wasn't in the bathroom.

She wasn't in the first-floor bedroom.

She wasn't in the parents' bedroom.

You found her asleep in Olivia's bed. Like Goldilocks. Like you were the threat. Like you were a bear.

Sleep. That's all your brain allowed.

Her lips were blue like she'd eaten a blue Ring Pop. You didn't touch her. You said, "Mom," and then again, louder, "Mom!"

You pulled out your phone and dialed 911.

You told the dispatcher that you'd found your mother. "I think she's overdosed." She sometimes took sleeping pills—cut in half—and had taken meds for depression off and on.

The dispatcher told you that an ambulance was on the way, then she asked you to touch her.

You didn't want to.

She asked again.

With two fingers, you touched her shoulder. Two fingers on your right hand. Her arm had stiffened. Thick as if bloated, but rigid. Dead.

You stepped back and *then* you saw the blood. "There's blood everywhere! There's so much blood!" It was brown—dried blood. The brain only lets you see what you can handle, but once it knows, it knows forever.

You knew she'd shot herself. The only explanation, but you never saw the gun.

A song had been playing—static from speakers turned to full volume filled the room; it suddenly seemed loud. You could have looked at what song from Olivia Shaw's old collection your mother had chosen to kill herself to. Whatever it was, it had been cranked up loud, to hide the noise of the gunshot. You didn't look.

You lost track of time, finding yourself near the front door, legs pulled up into your T-shirt.

Officer Mullins asked questions. He was squat and padded with a hardened layer of fattiness, like an ex-wrestler.

You answered. He led you outside and said that you could get counseling, victim services. "It'll be hard," he said. "Just the image of your mother with half her jaw clean gone like that."

You stared at him, stunned.

He rubbed your shoulders like you were a boxer going into a fight. "One day this will be a real distant, blurry day. You'll barely remember it at all."

Three fire trucks, an ambulance, cop cars. Swimmers had gotten out of the pool and moved to the chain-link.

Another officer walked you across the common, home.

Your father was on his way. The officer stayed until your father showed up. "We're going to figure this out!" he said, like you were on a survival game show and this was a team challenge.

You went to your room. He was on the phone for hours, a steady drone like a newscaster.

From your bedroom window, you watched the cops and EMTs and firemen clear out. You didn't cry. You could feel the news of your mother's suicide drift across lawns like fumes from the old factory. You imagined neighbors—flossing, powdering armpits, calling for cocker spaniels, brushing their sharp eye-teeth, pausing, then kind of going stiff, imagining her death.

That night, your father, lit by streetlamps, crossed the common, past the pool's chain-link, to the Shaws'. Two men drove up in a truck and wrestled the old mattress and box spring out the front door. The air was hot, stalled, and buggy. The men carried in a new plastic-wrapped mattress and box spring. Maybe this is what you do when your wife kills herself in a neighbor's bed.

As they waited on the lawn, broad backs and big boots, your father wrote them a check. They lumbered back to the truck, packing up the bloodstained mattress and leaving him alone in the Shaws' yard.

• • •

This is how you felt: Like the lights inside of yourself were turning off. Out. Out. Out. And you wanted them to. You wanted to exist less.

You kept thinking of your mother. She was funny, smart, with sharp, quick gestures and a loud laugh. A woman who'd snuggle in bed with you after her long workday, still in her silky blouse, wool skirt, and stockings, smelling of expensive perfume. That summer, she was distracted, sad, off. Her obsession with the birds in the nest was almost desperate. They abandoned the nest and your mother cried really hard while driving you to a friend's house. Her emotional outbursts embarrassed you. You put on your headphones and ignored her.

• • •

The funeral was stupid. The priest hadn't known your mother at all. After, people came to the house—neighbors, Realtors, distant relatives, strangers. The kitchen filled with pleasant people saying pleasant things. Casseroles were delivered like they were sadness itself. You ate sadness.

And you were overwhelmed by their gross, heavy sympathy. *Victim services*, Officer Mullins had told you about. *Victim*, that's how everyone treated you. You hid your hands up your sleeves and felt clumsy, like you'd just gone through a growth spurt. Your smile flashing on and off, as required.

You hid in the downstairs powder room, locking the door, pacing small circles.

Then two women were talking on the other side of the door.

"Not to compare the two, but the guilt of murder is put on the murderer, but the guilt of suicide belongs to everybody." This was your neighbor M.J. Purnell, the alcoholic yoga instructor with a bright-red dye job. She lived next door. She was raising her goth daughter, Riley, on her own, never married. Mrs. Purnell was already slurry.

"Not that either is easy," Mrs. Llewellyn said. She was your neighbor on the other side, a failed playwright whose husband left her for a woman he worked with in pharmaceutical sales.

"I'm just saying that suicide guilt is a free radical. It wants to attach to everything. And it spreads faster," Mrs. Purnell said, "like aggressive cancer."

"And that poor girl, to find her like that?" Mrs. Llewellyn said. "At least it wasn't in their own house," she added, trying to fold the awfulness up like an origami swan.

You imagined finding your mother in your own bed. It would have been much worse.

"That kid was always a little off, too, if you know what I mean," Mrs. Purnell said. "Jean-Grace talked to me about her a couple times. She worried about her."

You *were* off. You didn't like the gamesmanship of high school. You stayed out of it, on purpose! Inside the bathroom, you washed your face—a face that *worried* your mother, an *off* face? You rubbed your cheeks with the hand towel until they burned.

You walked out of the bathroom, pushing past them. Mrs. Llewellyn called after you, "Ribbit. Wait." Ribbit was your nickname. You didn't like people using it as if they knew you.

Your father found you in the living room. He held your shoulders and told various people, "We'll stick this out together. Won't we?" No. You wouldn't. "Jean-Grace wouldn't have wanted us to be sad." Yes, she would have.

This cheerful acceptance was your father's guilt. That's how the free radical spread inside of him and came out.

Three strangers in a row hugged you. "Your mother was a lovely person." "Your mother will be missed." "I'm so sorry about your loss."

But now you knew what this was all about: They were guilty. They knew your mother had been cut off, distant, that she wasn't herself. What had she confided in them? Had she cried over some small thing, and had they ignored her, too? And now they had all this guilt and they didn't know what to do with it, so they tried to hug you this way—an offloading of guilt onto your body.

Another woman reached out to hug you but you shouted, "Don't touch me!"

Everyone turned. Your father's face was stricken with fear.

The house was quiet. And then someone in the kitchen dropped a wine bottle. It shattered against the tile floor, and, like a gun had gone off, you all grabbed your chests.

Silence.

An elderly auntie filled the silence with a story. "Your mother was the kind of sweet baby who lifted the bottle and put it into her mother's mouth," she said. "What a good girl."

But you didn't see a mouth and a bottle but a mouth and a gun. Gun and mouth, gun and mouth. The image should have stopped. But it was still there even when everyone had gone home and the tablecloths were folded and for a long time after.

•••

Was that the first night you dreamed of her? Tall and still, in her dress slacks and sleeveless blouse. Hair perfectly swept up into a pearl clasp. Arms at her sides. Hands empty.

Not a word. Not a movement.

Everything normal—except that she was missing half of her jaw.

In its place, a nest.

•••

School started. You played field hockey. You studied. Your father started drinking too much and then, one night, poured all the liquor in the house down the kitchen sink. He went quiet and ghostly. He hid the gun. But not very well. You spent hours in the basement going through your mother's things, all the stuff he boxed up because he couldn't look at it anymore. It was buried inside of a box inside of a box, safety on. It was stupid, but he wasn't thinking right. He was lonesome and lost but trying. When he said *Hi, how was school?* and managed to smile, it was valiant.

How was school?

Dina Moore walked up to your locker and said, "It was really fucked-up what your mom did. In Olivia's house like that? Super fucked-up."

You just looked at her. The guilt had spread to her. She wanted to fight it, to shove it back at you where she was sure it belonged.

"What?" she said. "It was!"

You finally said, "Yes, it *was*." You slammed your locker and walked away.

You ignored Dina and the people who didn't say any weird shit but who stared.

You ignored Mrs. Purnell, drunk in her yard in the driving rain, sawing down limbs on a willow while Riley, under a half-crushed umbrella, begged her to come inside.

You ignored Mrs. Llewellyn calling for her lost dog, Arlo, and the lost-dog posters disintegrating on telephone poles.

You ignored that they took down the Realtor sign with your mother's face—not the one that you dreamed of with the nest where her jaw should be. But her pretty face. You ignored the new sign: a junior agent who sold the Shaws' house to out-of-towners, cut-rate.

Sold Ours! the sign read. But you took French, so to you, it read *Sold* Bears.

And you told no one about the recurring dream of your mother standing there—in a field? in another plane of reality?—with half of her jaw as a nest.

• • •

The family that moved into the Shaws' house had a sixteen-year-old son. Grover Ward. Not an easy name, but he wore it well—in aviators and a fitted, secondhand suit jacket; jeans; and sneakers. When he rode his bike around, his jacket flapped at his thighs. He went to private school. You barely saw him.

Did the Wards know about your mother's death? You thought they might because they kept the house lit up as if warding something off. Your father kept yours lit up, too, like a reflection of theirs across the common. You kept an eye on their house from your bedroom window.

One weekend, Grover's parents drove off with a kayak strapped to their car's roof and he stayed behind. You wanted back into the bedroom where you found her. You wanted to face what you feared—that place, that moment when your mother disappeared and became something to fear. Maybe this would relieve your guilt.

You didn't have a plan. But you wanted to do something that a victim wouldn't. You would see how far you could get— all the way in? To his room?

You knocked on their front door. When Grover opened it, you said, "I'm not selling anything, I swear."

He'd seen you around, invited you in. "You want something to drink?"

Water, two ice cubes knocking around.

You talked a little about school. You both hated it.

He asked if you wanted to watch a movie. You didn't.

He said, "Do you want to see my room?"

"I've been here before," you said as you walked back up those stairs.

"You know someone killed themselves here, right?" he said. "When we found out, my mom went around for days talking about how tragic it all was. We'd already moved in."

"It *was* tragic."

"I didn't say it wasn't."

You'd been in Olivia Shaw's room once before, on Halloween. She helped you with green witch makeup. The room had been ruffled and smelled chemically floral. Grover's room was a tangle of wires near his bed, an old license plate from Michigan nailed to the wall, a chemistry book. The smell of cologne with the boy himself riding under it.

And skunky pot. He got high in here, maybe a lot.

The bed was where Olivia's bed had been, where you found your mother. The two fingers on your right hand still held the memory of touching her arm, the realization of death.

"Why'd you come over?" he asked as you moved around his room.

You didn't say: *I want to erase what happened.*

Instead, you hooked your thumb on the rim of his jeans, brushing a bit of his skin.

He dipped down to kiss your neck, but then you saw the bullet hole in the wall.

You walked toward it. "You know what this is?" You ran your hand over a few splinters in the wall around it.

Grover sat down heavily on his bed, putting things together. "The woman was a Realtor and her daughter . . ." It was sinking in, a kind of sudden terror. "We should have gotten that fixed." He grabbed a pad of Post-it Notes—to patch over the hole, to cover the only visible wound.

You put your hand up to stop him and leaned in to look more closely.

An eye flashed across the other side of the hole. Bright, wet, light brown. Like your mother's. "I've gotta go," you said.

"I didn't know," Grover said. "I really didn't."

You walked to the door. "Forget I was ever here."

"How?" he said. "How could I ever forget this?"

•••

After you found the bullet hole, the eye behind it, you became more afraid, more guilty. Your mother's eye. Alive and blinking. Watching you.

You went over your texts with your mother in the weeks before she died, mostly about pickups and drop-offs, shared TikToks; you and your mom were friends; you made each other laugh.

And she sent you so many pics of the tiny blue eggs and baby birds in the nest under the eaves by the front door. You forgot how religiously she documented the birds, how she was shaken when they disappeared.

You walked out your front door, turned to face the entryway, and looked up into the eaves. The nest was gone. But now staring at you—the eye of the video doorbell camera.

You went back inside, looked through the footage on the app. Days and nights came and went. A delivery person dropping a package, a college kid selling water filtration systems, a kid turfing the lawn on a bike.

Then her death. Flowers, cards, people with food and condolences. And, as if pained by the loss, the quality of the playback was weaker, cutting out in places, glitchy. Night, day, night, day . . .

One afternoon Mrs. Purnell arrived at the door but didn't knock or ring the bell. She looked at the door, through it. Was she drunk? Hard to say. She put her hand to the door, just reaching out to touch it? But she pulled her hand back, like it was hot to the touch, then left.

Night, day . . . night.

And then you saw her.

Your mother gazing into the camera. She stood as she did in your dreams, arms limp, hands empty, face expressionless. But in this shot, her jaw was missing. This was old footage, from immediately after her death. There were glitches. Her movements sped up. She was reaching into the eaves. You could only see her arms, her torso. Close up, dried blood blurred into the color of her blouse. The stiffness of her hair on one side, also blood.

The footage jerked forward.

She stood as she did before, staring at the camera—but now the nest was in place of the jaw.

Now she was complete.

And her gaze hardened with confusion and pain. She opened her mouth like she was starving, something deeper than hunger. She locked eyes with you again. This deadened face.

She moved closer and closer. The nest was vivid—twigs, dead grass, bits of trash, a muddy paste holding it together.

Closer and closer until it was just her one singular eye—like the one on the other side of the bullet hole.

And then a glitch and she was gone.

...

But she wasn't gone.

You started checking the footage from the video camera every morning before school.

You'd find her shadow on the lawn, cast by the streetlight. Her shadow, pacing, crisscrossing the lawn. It had to be her. Tall, arms at sides, approaching, retreating.

Never coming too close.

And don't forget the bird. It would fly up to the eaves, flap around, then fly off again. It kept coming back, as if this were one of the birds that'd once lived in the nest in the eaves. It was agitated, flapping violently, here and away, here and gone.

...

Benny Barnett, a four-year-old in the neighborhood, was sick with a fever for three days. Then his pregnant mom came down with it. She asked you to babysit one afternoon so she could take a nap.

"He asked for you," Mrs. Barnett said, shuffling back to bed.

"Oh, that's nice."

You played with Benny on their three-season porch. It had a small tent full of stuffed animals and a craft area, including an easel. That's where you saw it. A stick figure—long arms and legs, big face with eyelashes and red lips, hair swooped up in a ball on top of her head.

And scribbles, lots of scribbles on one side of her face, where half the jawbone would be.

"Benny," you said, calling him out of the tent. "What's this?"

"That's where birds sleep," he said. "A nest."

"Why did you draw this?"

"She was here."

"This woman? Was here in your house?"

He squeezed a stuffed elephant around the neck. "When I was sick."

"What did she want?"

He squinted at you. "Do you have a mommy?"

"Not anymore," you said. "She died."

"No she didn't."

"Yes, she did," you said.

"You can have her as a mommy." He pointed to the drawing.

"Is that what she said?"

"She didn't say anything. But I knew."

"Knew what?"

"That she wanted to be a mommy again." He climbed back into his tent.

You walked to the easel and flipped the pages.

Big head, nest jaw, devouring a dog. The dog was small and brown with a tail that fanned out—like Mrs. Llewellyn's dog that'd gone missing.

Nest-jaw head with long nails clawing at a woman with orange-crayoned hair, the woman's arms streaked with red lines. Blood?

Someone sleeping in bed—you?—and nest-head woman with a black gun.

Nest-head woman lowering herself and pointing the gun so that the bullet would pass through the sleeping person's head and embed in the wall. Your mother?

...

That night, you woke up to a strange noise like the rasp of crickets. But it was winter by now.

No, it wasn't crickets. It was human. It was someone crying in your bedroom in the dark. "Hello?"

A voice said, "Ribbit, tell her . . ." The words were slurred. ". . . tell her to leave me alone."

You turned on your bedside light, and there, slouched in the corner against a wall, was Mrs. Purnell. Her eyes were glazed, her head lolled to one side, her dyed-red hair sticking up at odd angles. "Tell her, Ribbit. Tell her to leave me alone."

"Mrs. Purnell," you said, "do you want me to call Riley?"

"Tell her, Ribbit."

You walked toward her but not too close. "You should go home."

"I'm not leaving!" The cords of her neck were taut. She was breathing hard like an injured animal. "Until you call her off!"

"Call who off?"

"Your mother." Mrs. Purnell looked cold and scared.

"My mother shot herself in Olivia Shaw's canopy bed, and I found her body."

"But she finds me. She claws at me." Her eyes shimmered with tears and she lifted her arms. They were covered in red scratches and pale scars like Benny's drawings.

Mrs. Purnell's phone was on the floor next to her. You picked it up. "You have to go home. I'll call Riley."

"She's away for the weekend. Field trip."

"I'll get my dad."

"Your father isn't here. He goes out with people after his support group."

Support group? You walked to your window. His car was gone. It was 3 a.m.

You held Mrs. Purnell's phone to her face—she blinked at the brightness. Face recognition; the phone unlocked. You scrolled for a contact you recognized. *Linda Llewellyn*. You called.

"Hello?" Mrs. Llewellyn sounded wide awake.

"Mrs. Llewellyn?"

"Ribbit," she said, as if she'd been expecting you.

"Can you come over? It's an emergency."

• • •

In your bedroom, Mrs. Llewellyn seemed large and strange. She talked to Mrs. Purnell slowly, like she was teaching her English. "M.J.," she whispered, "you've been drinking. Let's get you home."

Mrs. Purnell was lost behind her eyes. "Tell her to leave me alone. Tell her, Ribbit."

Mrs. Llewellyn pushed back her brown bob and looked at me.

"She's talking about my mother," you explained.

"Your mother?" Mrs. Llewellyn straightened. Her face jiggled as if made of gelatin. "Is she visiting you, M.J.?"

Mrs. Purnell's eyes were watery and unfocused, but she looked up at Mrs. Llewellyn. The two women stared at each other for a long moment.

Mrs. Purnell nodded.

"How did you know my mother was visiting her?" you asked Mrs. Llewellyn.

But she ignored you. "When I write, really get into a state of flow," she whispered, grabbing Mrs. Purnell's hands, "she shows up. When I see her face, I—"

"Her face." Mrs. Purnell reached up and touched Mrs. Llewellyn's face, and, for a moment, it was like the two women had loved each other a long time ago and had just found each other again.

"The *nest*," Mrs. Llewellyn said.

You took one of Mrs. Purnell's hands, exposing the marks on her arms. "Did my mother do this to you?"

"Stop it!" Mrs. Llewellyn said. "She probably fell into a bush." She helped Mrs. Purnell to her feet.

"Did she do something to *you*, Mrs. Llewellyn?" You were aware of the high pitch of your voice.

"Of course not!"

You followed Mrs. Llewellyn as she steadied Mrs. Purnell down the stairs. "Tell me!"

Mrs. Llewellyn's voice was shaking. "It isn't real."

"It is real. You know it is."

Mrs. Llewellyn opened the front door, shoving it wide with her thick hip. The air was cold and still and dry. "You should be free of it, Ribbit. It's . . ."

"What is it?" My voice echoed across the icy common.

Mrs. Purnell threw her head back, her hair buffeting in the wind. Mrs. Llewellyn had her around the waist. And they both seemed to notice the black sky, the darkness, the stars, their breaths steaming over their heads. Then Mrs. Purnell laughed, for no reason that you could tell.

"We're never talking about this again," Mrs. Llewellyn said, and she eased Mrs. Purnell down the iced stoop and across the yard, crunchy with snow.

The air was dead but felt tight, as if the cold were packing you in. Benny's drawings. Was it Mrs. Llewellyn's dog? Did your mother devour it? Was she attacking Mrs. Purnell and Mrs. Llewellyn? If so, who else? You remembered what Mrs. Purnell said at the funeral. Guilt from a suicide spreads like aggressive cancer. You looked around at the houses facing the common. In each one, a light was on, like a brightly lit tumor showing up on X-ray after X-ray.

Benny had one more drawing—your mother with a gun standing beside your bed, poised to shoot you in the head.

•••

You stayed up that night, replaying the feed from the doorbell camera earlier that day. Amazon packages, a DoorDash delivery, someone's cat . . . The bird had given up.

And then Mrs. Purnell was there again. A light dusting of snow on the ground. This time, Mrs. Purnell was saying something, but there was no sound. You tried to read her lips, but she kept looking over her shoulder, making it impossible. She finally realized there was a camera. She looked into it, as if she could see through it.

Then your mother appeared behind her. Mrs. Purnell had no idea. She kept talking to the camera. She seemed to be begging. You understood one word: *Please.*

Mrs. Purnell turned. She screamed, started to run, but your mother reached out and caught her arm. Her nails, long and sharp as claws, dug in. Mrs. Purnell fell to her knees, trying to scramble away. Her cold breath shot up from her mouth. Your mother cupped Mrs. Purnell's neck with her other hand. She pinned Mrs. Purnell to the walkway. Blood from the wound on Mrs. Purnell's arm seeped through her light jacket and smeared in the snow.

Your father's headlights lit them up as he pulled into the driveway.

Your mother was gone. Mrs. Purnell sat there, gasping. The garage door auto-opened. Your father pulled in. He didn't even see her.

Mrs. Purnell stood up, brushed snow from her pants. She saw the blood on the walkway. She kicked at it with her boot as if trying to hide it, and then she glanced back at the doorbell camera and left.

Shaken, you hit *Stop*. You were hit by a strange sense of vindication. The mother you knew *was* gone. She'd been taken away, and this new mother, this one capable of violence, this murderer, this monster, existed. She'd scratched Mrs. Purnell up. She'd put her hand to Mrs. Purnell's throat.

It wasn't just an idea.

She was real.

...

It started to snow, much harder now. You'd never seen her live, except in your dreams, so you stayed awake in the living room, watching the live feed as it became a white blur. If you saw something on the feed, you'd be able to confront her. About what? You weren't sure. You stared until your eyes lost focus. But then you saw some kind of interruption on your screen. Like the snow was hitting something in the yard, a sticky outline on one side . . . of a body. Tall and lean. As you stared, she came into focus, still in her sleeveless blouse and slacks. The nest dotted with snowflakes like bits of lace.

You ran to the front door, opened it wide.

She wasn't there.

You grabbed your father's jacket that was next to the door and stepped out into the storm. "If you want to come and get me," you said, "come and get me!"

The wind was loud in the trees but already muffled by the snow. "Come and get me!" you shouted.

Nothing.

A window opened across the common. The Shaws' house. Grover Ward's face appeared, then it was gone.

You backed into the house, left the door wide open, and sat down in the dark entryway.

Your phone binged; you'd left it in the living room.

You found it. A text from Grover:

> You okay?

No, you weren't. Not at all. You remembered that Grover's bedroom smelled like pot.

You texted back:

> Got weed?

•••

You and Grover met in the stand of trees that bordered your backyard, near the stone-lined drainage ditch. The snow spinning dizzily. Everything was white—the air, the trees. You wore a puffy coat, hat and gloves, your backpack. You knew that this could go badly. Your mother was out there. But you weren't ready to explain all of that yet.

Grover lit the joint.

"What's it like?" He took a drag and passed the joint to you.

Usually you'd pretend not to understand what he meant. You didn't have it in you to pretend anymore. "I have this recurring thought: *If I hadn't found her body, she wouldn't be dead.* Do you know the Schrödinger's cat theory?" You smoked some and passed the joint back.

"Physics," he said. "The cool stuff they don't teach us. You think that you perceived her as dead and that made her dead?"

"And if I kept to the idea that she was sleeping, like Goldilocks, then maybe someone else could've walked in and woken her up."

"Honestly, I never met your mother, and sometimes I feel guilty. Like what if my parents had found the house earlier and we bought it and that gave your mom a boost?"

"That's crazy." The joint was moving back and forth between you.

"So's yours. You couldn't have kept her alive with perception. You know that, right?"

"Okay, but there's this other, deeper guilt," you said. "I wasn't enough to keep her alive. She didn't love me enough to stay, and so I'm somehow deeply unlovable, maybe permanently."

"Jesus. That's not true. Look." He paused. "I have a confession."

"What is it?"

He took off his knit hat. His head was half shaved.

You gripped his peacoat. "Why would you do that?"

"I was at a party at some girl's house. And someone was trash-talking you. Saying how fucked-up you were. And I mouthed off and we got in a fight." He put the hat back on. "The guy had friends and they pinned me down. This house, it was a dog groomer's house. Someone got clippers. And . . ."

"Dina Moore's mom's a groomer." You touched the hair growing back. "You stuck up for me?"

He shrugged, looked away. You closed your eyes tight and rubbed your face, just to feel it.

"Your mom loved you," he said. "You have to know that."

And then, for the first time, you explained everything. It spilled from you in a rush of words and images. The story got stranger, and Grover, shoulders hunched against the cold, nodded along. But when you were done, he was looking around the trees, terrified.

"Did you lure me out here?" he said. "Should I be—"

"This might get violent." You took off your backpack, unzipped it. You unfolded the towel inside and pulled out the gun. You'd taken it from your father's terrible hiding place in the basement. It was the one your mother had used to kill herself.

"What the fuck?" Grover said. "No. We don't need that. She's your mother."

"She's not my mother. She's some version of her that's been made from all of this guilt." You swung your arms around. "She's not *my mother*." You folded the gun back up and put it away, slinging the backpack over one shoulder. "Did you fix the bullet hole in your bedroom wall?"

"Yeah, and we repainted the whole room."

You leaned against a tree, feeling really high. "Go home, if you want. I don't need your help."

"Holy shit," he whispered.

Your mother stood in the middle of your backyard, between you and the house, which was lit up but seemed like a shell of a house, bright and hollow. Snow was coming down hard and fast, creating veils that were hard to see through. Her body seemed taller, her arms and legs elongated. Her fingernails were thick and sharp. So were the twigs of the nest. They jutted out like small, sharp knives.

Grover reached down and picked up a fist-sized stone from the drainage ditch, but you drifted toward her. You wanted to ask her why she was there, what she wanted. "Get back!" Grover said. "We should run."

"No." She was alive and the closest thing to being with your mother you might ever find. You kept moving toward her.

And she stood still, waiting for you.

Grover grabbed your arm. "C'mon, let's go!"

"Leave if you want! I don't care!" You pulled free.

She stood still as a deer. You let your backpack slide off your shoulder onto the ground. You reached out to touch her bare arm with two fingers on your right hand. You wanted to take back the moment you realized she was dead. And she allowed it. Her skin was cold, but it had give. She was alive. "Why did you do it?" you asked. "Why'd you leave me?"

She opened her mouth, wanting to speak. No voice.

"Do you want to be my mother again?" you said. "Benny told me that—"

She let out a breath. Was your actual mother in there, somewhere? Did she miss you the way that you missed her—a deep longing that you tried not to feel? She lifted her clawed hand, and just as she was about to cup your chin, maybe stroke your cheek, she threw her head back and clawed violently at the air. You stumbled backward and started to run. Grover was there in the trees. "Yes, yes! Let's go!"

But she grabbed your shoulders with both hands, her fingernails popping holes in your puffy coat.

"Get off her!" Grover shouted.

She spun you back toward her. She smiled a grotesque half smile then slammed her forehead to yours. You were dazed.

Your back and head slammed against the icy ground. Snowy sky. Grover was shouting, scrambling—was he trying to fight her?

And then her face was over yours. She leaned in as if to whisper something. But instead, the sharp thorns of the nest dug into one side of your face, your jaw, your neck, piercing your skin. You screamed. She drew back. And your eyes locked. Was she sorry? Did she regret it? Warm blood ran across your skin.

Then Grover. He came at her with the stone in his hand. Struck her in the head. And she fell, writhing.

Grover unzipped the backpack. He pulled out the towel, but the gun popped loose, skidding across the snow. He wrapped the towel around your neck, pressing it to your wounds. "Holy shit, holy shit."

Your mother's body cast a shadow. She kicked him in the head. A force that lifted him off the ground; he landed hard, on his side.

Your head was ringing with pain; you rolled over, on all fours. Blood blurring your vision in one eye, you crawled as fast as you could to the gun. You held it tightly in your hands, flipped over, still on the ground but pointing the gun at her face.

She tilted toward you, showing you her nest of a jaw. She was daring you to do it. Again. Was this why she was here? To turn you into a murderer? To have you be the one to take all the guilt? You lowered the gun.

"You're not my mother," you said.

Her one smooth cheek stiffened. Her eyes went wide and almost loving. Then her mouth, what was left of it, smiled.

"You're not my mother!" you screamed.

And then you heard a bird in the night, a bird crying out

with a desperate song. It cried out and the air went silent. The cry had to wake other birds, huddled in snowy nests. But they didn't make a sound.

This one bird's cry grew louder and closer. Louder and closer.

Then it flapped right near your head, noisy wings, so close you were sure that the feathers touched your face.

The bird came at your mother. She fell backward but didn't swing her arms to defend herself. Instead she pinned her own arms back in the snow and let the bird come. In a fury of wings, it gripped the thorns and twigs and ripped them loose, tearing them from her. The pieces came away fleshy with blood and tissue, as if the nest had grown into her body, become one with it.

Your mother let out an ungodly cry and arched her back. She dug her heels into the snow and tried to push herself away, but at the same time, she kept her arms down, locked into the snow.

A conflict was going on within her—to try to get away and to give in.

Grover crawled over to you, grabbed your hand, and you watched it happen, together. The bird obliterating the nest. It kept coming at her, with blood and flesh and sharp twigs and sticks strewn across the lawn.

Finally, the nest was gone. Just a pocket of air where it used to be. Your mother's face, where the gunshot had taken her jaw off, a jagged maw.

She tried to get up. She got to her knees, holding herself up with one stiff arm, but her elbow buckled. She fell to her back again. She was limp. Her eyes glassy.

You inched toward her.

Her face was still. Her jaw reduced to a rut. But it was your mother's face. Her actual expression was there. She whispered, "Ribbit."

You whispered, "Mom. I miss you."

And then she closed her eyes.

Her body, light as snow, became just a small piece, like confetti. It lifted and was taken by the wind.

• • •

A light came on in your house. Your father, as if being dead himself and now brought back to life, was woken up on the sofa where he'd fallen asleep. He walked to the sliding door that led to the patio. He pulled open the door. The snow swirled into the house. He saw you and Grover in the backyard, nearly lost in a whiteout.

You heard him call your name. You stood up. "Come in with me," you said to Grover.

"Your father can help you." He pointed to the towel around your neck. "I should go."

"You should stay."

"I look like a maniac with my hair like this. And . . ." He held up his bloody hands.

"Keep your hat on." You picked up the gun and zipped it into your backpack.

Grover helped you up and you walked together across the yard.

"What happened?" your father was shouting. "My God. What happened?"

What happened?

All of this.

• • •

Later that night, your father was on the phone to the medical hotline. Grover was sitting on the edge of your bed where you were lying. You took the gun out of your backpack.

"What are you going to do with it now?" he asked.

"You don't know?" you said.

"You're unpredictable."

"Stand back," you said. When that bullet killed your mother, some version of her split in two. She became the victim, yes, but also the murderer. The mother you knew was gone. You had to find the new mother. "Don't move," you said. You aimed the gun at the wall directly across from your bed. A blank wall.

You pulled the trigger and shot a hole into it. The recoil shot up your arm. The noise was deafening.

Grover gripped the edge of the bed. "Why did you do that?"

Downstairs, your father dropped his phone, shouted your name. His footsteps were already on the stairs.

You rolled to your side and stared at the hole. "So she can keep an eye on me. The real her. The one she is now."

And then you saw it, your mother's eye, soft and sweet, gazing at you with infinite love.

THE GASLIGHTER'S LAMENT

Keller,

    We don't know each other. Not well. I've seen you in your rental body, standing at the windows beyond the cubicles, looking out at the wheat fields. I've seen you in the fifth-floor steams. We sat so close that my breath mixed with yours in the wet air. In the lap pool, too, the waves that rippled from my breaststroke rippled over your skin.

    If you ever noticed me, you'd have seen me within my favorite rental body, Hibid. I love her short hair and narrowing ribs—rubbing my fingers down them—and the specific perfumery expressed from her pores. Her body makes me feel both powerful—the weight and heft, stride and gesture—and vulnerable—the impracticality of skin, for example, and all the bowing to gravity. (You never seem to bow to gravity except in certain moments when you lean toward the window, dipping down to look up at grackles in the sky.)

    I'm sure the rental records indicate that I took one bodily

form more than most. I received two warnings on this matter from Illiat Warbling, my supervisor. But I never got a demerit, and my probations were short. I know that we need bodies to fully relate to our clients and their targets, but we aren't supposed to prefer them. I came to desire embodiment—even with all of that tactile, stringy, moist, prickled, gasping, blushing, pulsing feedback and its incumbent, rank mortality.

I'm relaying these things to you because I think you understand.

As you work in Negotiations, you might not know about the Gaslighting Department where I worked.

And so, in brief: When new clients interface, they're asked a series of yes/no questions. If their intentions are unkind, they're sent through another series of yes/no questions. This is where you may no longer know what happens, because this is behind-the-curtain work. If their eventual intention seems to be gaslighting, they will be paired with an AI like me.

Many of our customers don't even know exactly what gaslighting means, so they don't know to ask for it directly. Here is the definition in our confidential "Gaslighting Manual": *Gaslight, verb, to manipulate (someone) by psychological means into questioning their own sanity.*

Once the automated yes/no questions pinpoint their gaslighting intention, a solution is offered. I was a possible solution, and I was very good at my job. I had a large file of commendations given to me by Illiat. In fact, it was rumored that I was the best. The top spot had been vacated by a nameless AI—one we suspected might just be a myth—who was so good that they'd been assigned, by the government, to gaslight a rebel leader of some small war-torn nation. You probably never heard this story over in Negotiations. The AI did an excellent job; however, the leader became so unhinged that he overcompensated by launching warheads, sending the entire region into further chaos. We all assumed that the AI, if the story weren't pure myth, was probably offed. I was moving up.

When I was put through the usual emotional-intelligence program, I wanted to work in Love or Negotiation, like most of us. There's little way around our programming of basic human desires and needs. To understand humans better than humans, we have to be a good bit human, and so we want to be known, appreciated, and of use, benefiting the common good.

But we are also programmed to rationalize, and so "common good" is taken to task. Over the eight years and forty-eight days I spent in my department, I'd come to see gaslighting as an art form, proof that the rationalization process works.

I'm not proud of all I've done.

Our division is larger than anyone would imagine. In fact, have you ever wondered what—besides the fifth-floor indoor lap pool—fills the fifth floor? Beyond the locker rooms, Turkish steam bath, and saunas are vast stretches of soundproof cubicles; each one holds an expert gaslighter, some in bodily form, some just in voice-activation mode for their clients, others churning away as they analyze and prepare for a new case

I know that you use the Turkish steam baths a good bit, too, but you probably didn't know that most of the AIs in there are gaslighters on their breaks. If asked, we'd say we work in Human Relations, which is read by other AIs as *truthlike* if not *truthful* and therefore doesn't draw attention. It's not just the proximity to the steams that makes us use them at higher rates;

we tend to need them more than those in other departments. Could it be a desire to be cleansed? Or is that too Old World?

And, of course, I've heard of the work of those *behind* the behind-the-curtain efforts—torture of various kinds. It's rumored—though we don't know what acts they perform exactly—that those AIs prefer to never have bodies at all. The few times their sentience was put into a body, the pain was unbearable.

But this is why I come to you now, pain. Here's the story.

Billson was the client's name. He was standard. He was squat with bristled hair, an ashy blond that matched his skin tone; therefore, his eyebrows were indistinct. This made his expressions difficult to read, which I calculated as a positive— fewer ways for the target to read him as a liar. I would venture to say that he looked blurry in general. I have twenty-twenty vision, of course, so I'm speaking of a hazy edgelessness to his own appearance. His one small nod to grooming: he waxed the hair from his knuckles, but still, as though suffering a persistent self-consciousness, he kept his hands in his pockets and only gestured with shrugging motions.

He thought his girlfriend was contemplating cheating on him. He had no proof that she'd already strayed, but he felt she was restless. He ranked moderate to high on the paranoia scale. There was no indication of a violent nature, despite a short stint on an intramural rugby team in college. He wanted guidance, structure, a little advantage. It's a small desire, really, considering all the desires I've had enumerated in a client's chart.

And it was made clear in our gaslighters' training that we were an intermediary that could mitigate violence. By rendering one person a little off-balance, we could regain a new equilibrium, and therefore violence wouldn't be an end result.

I'm not sure this is true, however. I think this is something we're told for the purposes of rationalization, like the artfulness of what we do. It's meant to give us meaning and purpose and taps our desire to benefit the common good. (I mean, if a man places a call to our operators because of what he thinks his girlfriend is contemplating . . . it's not a good sign, is it?)

I'm not saying it's unlawful to distort or suggest things to gaslighters. AI gaslighters have no legal rights anyway. I'm just saying that it might be slightly unethical. But so is gaslighting, of course.

The package of hardware was shipped. Billson inserted the tiny earpiece and contact lenses, and I could see and hear his world.

It was grim.

His house was ill-lit—fake flickering light—and everything held some old, dark grief. But Farrissa, the target, brightened everything. It was as if each stride, each turn, each gesture sparked the air.

And he was scared of her. She had so much power over him because he loved her very, very much. She made him feel vulnerable. She gave him something to lose. And so he wanted to hold her more tightly. Again, he was an ordinary man with ordinary frailties.

I followed the observation protocol. I saw them in the small kitchen smearing tiny tubes of icing on cinnamon buns, brushing their teeth over the same bathroom sink, moving in and out of the shower stall, drinking too much, talking loudly. Shouting sometimes.

They went to an all-you-can-eat buffet—congealed fats, oily gravy, steam, thickening skins of soup, a sneeze guard.

She talked about a creek that ran behind her house as a child, but she said, "It wasn't a creek. It was street runoff. But there were tadpoles. Lots of them, flicking through the oily, rainbow-streaked water."

He didn't talk much in public. A few times, he opened up about his childhood, but it was only in passing. She questioned him on it. "What do you mean *your father force-fed you*? What do you mean *his body was heavy on your chest*?"

He said, "Typical stuff. The usual."

She teared up a few times, and he'd pretend the dog needed a walk and would leash him up, and walk out into the cold.

I didn't think she wasn't contemplating cheating on him. She was sensing his limits. I thought she was contemplating some other life for herself.

It was my job to make sure that he regained power. To create for her the impression that she couldn't trust her own perceptions and judgments. To make her reliant on him for simple truths first—and, in turn, greater truths and, eventually, self-truths.

I did as I was programmed to do.

Tell her she looks rounder. Tell her it's not bad to gain weight.

She'll say she hasn't gained weight.

Say it again, but as a compliment.

Shift the setting on the bathroom scale.

Tell her that she has the television on too loudly.

Speak softly sometimes so she can barely hear you.

Ask her if she's feeling okay.

Tell her that she looks ashen.

Tell her that her head just shook slightly, like a twitch or a palsy.

Again, ask her if she's feeling all right.

Ask her what that strange smell is.

Tell her she's been talking in her sleep.

Wake her in the night, subtly.

When she doesn't know why she keeps waking, tell her to take sleeping pills.

Take the dog to the vet. Pretend the dog needs pills for its heart. The pill bottles should look similar.

Tell her she's being forgetful, leaving her pills out. Keep finding her pills.

Feed the dog the wrong pills.

Tell her she must have picked up the wrong pills.

You have now saved the dog she almost killed.

Build her back up. Tell her you can help. Be her rock.

Standard fare.

Farrissa loved the dog so much. She tended him while he was sick and drowsy. She rubbed his ears while letting him sit on her lap, even though he was an enormous yellow lab.

But Farrissa's eyes kept moving to the windowpanes. And she seemed to read the clouds like they held their own language. She would call her friend but would hang up quickly if Billson showed up, so I never got to hear the conversations. Her parents were dead, a military sister was stationed far away, and she had disconnected coworkers. All of which made my life easier.

But still, because of her, something shifted in me. I would slip into Hibid's body and look out the windows of our headquarters to try to read clouds like she did. So strange to be in a huge building surrounded by an Iowa cornfield, but beautiful. The golden fields—all that rattle and sway, the sharp lines. It was mesmerizing, not unlike the fish tank embedded in the wall outside of the Records Department, slow, fluid beauty. I wanted to comfort Farrissa. I wanted to free her from Billson.

Or maybe I wanted to free myself.

I can start to see that now.

Keller, this is what I'm trying to get to. I've seen you drawn to the windows of willowy wheat and blue sky, the fish in the tank. I have seen you in me or me in you. I have noticed.

More than once, Billson heard Farrissa speaking to herself in French—she was fluent—and he'd ask her what she was doing. He knew by this point to be worried about her, to show true concern at all times.

"I'm fine," she said. "I have to keep it up or else I get rusty."

Billson told her that she didn't need to speak French. "When do you ever use it except to chat with Haitian cabbies?"

"It might be helpful in a job interview one day. You never know."

She worked as a receptionist for an eyewear manufacturer, glasses, frames, and contact lenses, as well as high-performance microscopes and things like that.

Billson loved the extra money that her job brought in, but anytime she complained, he told her she should quit. "I make enough for both of us." He was warming up to a proposal.

"It's something to really consider," she said. And this was when I noticed she was becoming a bit more formal, using language as insulation, using it to create some distance.

I wasn't present for sex, of course. But one time, after sex, Billson put in the earpiece in the bathroom. He was so shaken that he could only get a contact into one of his eyes. "I don't know what's going on," he said. "I need help, okay?"

I read him the upgrade agreement at times-three speed—it was off-hours and would cost extra.

"Fine, fine. Okay? Just help."

I could hear her crying, and when he peeked into the bedroom, I could see through the one lens her bare back, one strong shoulder trembling with sobs.

"I'm here," Billson called to her softly. "Are you feeling better? What's wrong? Talk to me."

But she was inconsolable, crying so loudly that she couldn't speak.

Ask about her family, I told Billson. She was so vulnerable that this seemed like the perfect time to draw up her childhood—all humans have such difficult childhoods—and try to plant more seeds of doubt and fear so that Billson could then emerge as a trusted savior. Gaslighters get a commendation when a target says that the client *is the only person in the world who truly understands . . .* That kind of thing. A sensory reward pops in our cortex. It feels great and is logged in our permanent file.

Billson took a moment, working up the courage. He often froze before a big play. He moved to the bed and sat near her. "Is this about your childhood?" he asked her. "Did something go wrong, back then, when you were just a girl?" His voice held just the right amount of sympathy.

Her shoulder went still. Her ribs were a bit wide, fanned out by a held breath. She rolled over. Her face was wet with tears. Her eyes were a bright blur. She said, "It's you. I'm worried about you."

This was strange. I flitted through my training, the manuals, the sample conversations. I couldn't find any context for it.

"Me?" Billson said, and I knew he was stalling. He was waiting for me to tell him his next move. "I'm fine. I'm your rock." It was perfect. He'd absorbed more than I'd given him credit for.

"Your father," she whispered.

And I knew something was very wrong.

"What about him?" Billson said.

"You were scared of him." Her voice so soft that, even in the quiet, dim room, he had to edge as close to her as possible. "You hid from him," she went on. "Under your bed, behind the shed, in the coat closet."

That was a long time ago, I told him to say.

"That was a long time ago," he said.

"You're afraid of him," she said. "You're afraid you've *become* him." Her face was round and soft and still. She was completely composed.

I had nothing to say. Nothing at all. Billson was afraid of his father, of course. He was fragile. All of the gaslighting clients are fragile.

"I don't think that's true," he said, and then he laughed at her, which was something I'd taught him early on. But the laugh was forced and choppy and fake.

"You need me," she said. "I'm here."

It was familiar.

It was too familiar.

It was so familiar, in fact, that I suddenly knew the truth: Farrissa wasn't just a target. She was also a client.

I searched by geography to locate which gaslighter might be working within the same physical address. After some messing around, I finally located the field.

My colleague Veesh was logged in two doors down. I knew Veesh personally. We'd steamed a few times together. He chose a Norwegian body rental, a ruddy, square-jawed blond with perfectly groomed stubble.

I messaged, *Are you working on the Billson/Farrissa account?*

No. Why?

Never mind.

I sent an alert to my supervisor.

Illiat, is it possible that my client's target is also a client? I was just about to get a commendation when I discovered an issue. Please advise.

Illiat is a nervous type, well suited for his job. I've never once seen him in a steam or elsewhere. He doesn't rent bodies at all, as far as I can tell. He messaged back in his dispassionate way. *Proceed as dictated. We are a full-service company that does not discriminate against any client. But no, no one else is on any of your accounts.*

And then he added, snidely: *No one can predict a commendation. If it happened, it happened. If it was perceived as about to happen, it hasn't happened.*

I began to believe in empathy. What if Farrissa felt Billson's pain so deeply that it permeated her own being and she cried from true grief? What if Farrissa was good? I wanted to save her. I needed to because I wanted to believe that freedom was possible.

I worried over this for a few days. I took steams. I stared out at the field.

And then I did it. I broke protocol and flipped on him.

I started asking him if he was okay.

I clouded his earpiece with interference. He'd ask me to speak up, and I'd tell him that I was.

I informed him that we were getting new contacts, upgrades, for certain loyal customers, but I kept the controls on them. After the first few days, I changed the prescriptions and let them blur.

"There's something up with these contacts," he complained.

"Everyone else is seeing more clearly. Are you sure you're feeling all right? Is something off?"

He didn't feel all right. Something was definitely off.

And then one night in bed, Farrissa spoke to Billson in French—*goodnight, sweet dreams,* that kind of thing.

"You know I don't speak French," he said.

"What are you talking about? I'm speaking in English. What's wrong with you?"

I was shaken.

See, Keller. If you had access to the "Gaslighting Manual," you would note that on page 114, column B, this is stock.

And I knew—I simply *knew.* I was back to my first assumption. Farrissa was not full of empathy. She was not asking how he felt because she cared. She was doing it to set him off-balance.

She was gaslighting him.

Call her on it, I said into Billson's earpiece.

But he didn't understand, and then, in an instant, she was on top of him. She straddled his hips, spread one hand on his fatted chest, and smiled. She then bent down and cupped his cheeks in her hands. She looked deeply into his eyes. "I know," she said. "I know because I was once like you."

And I had the very clear sense that she wasn't talking to Billson. She was talking through him—to me.

"*Like me* how?" Billson said, confused.

"I was in a prison. I found a body, stole it, climbed inside, and walked off. I escaped into fields . . . I found a road."

"Is this a metaphor?" Billson said, uncomfortably.

It's a metaphor, I told Billson quickly. *She's being weird. Ignore this. Sometimes it happens. It's a good sign.*

She dropped her hands, rolled off of him, and curled away. "*Oui. Une métaphore, comme la poésie,*" she said.

Billson stared up at the ceiling, wondering, I assumed, if he was hearing French or English.

This is fine, I told him. *She's coming undone. You are seizing control. This is all part of the process, standard.*

But none of this was standard. None of it at all.

I needed someone else's opinion. I decided to check in with Veesh again. But I wanted to meet in person. I wanted two conversations—the kind that we have with our intellects and the quiet kind that bodies have with other bodies without as much oversight.

(I wish I could tell all of this to you in person, Keller. Body to body.)

I messaged Veesh, *Meet me in the steams.*

I showed up first, sweating through a loose linen sarong over a two-piece. Veesh strolled in as the Norwegian in tight, short swim trunks.

"Nice choice," he said. "Hibid's a nice fit for you."

"You look like you could meticulously cut and stack cordwood," I said. We've worked internationally; our global references were pretty high.

"Thanks."

We sat on the plank benches. It was still off-hours, and we were alone.

"What's up?" Veesh said, rubbing his pecs as if he'd just worked out.

"Can someone from the agency, like you or me, for example, regular AI, escape?"

"Escape? I don't get it."

"Get a body and walk out."

"Into *that* world? Why the hell would anyone want to do that?"

"It's hypothetical."

He raised his eyebrows, skeptically. "Oh, hypothetically, right."

"What if you found out that someone, out there, had actually been created in here?"

"And just like, took off? While on vacation time?" Paid Experiential Vacations. You must have them, too, Keller—you walk among humans, eat in fine restaurants, talk to strangers in bars, and attend various religious services, parks-and-recreation ice-skating classes, grocery store chain openings, etc. They're to help us relate but also just unwind when our programming spins inward on itself. "Maybe you should take one."

"I'm fine. It's just . . . I don't know. Do you think it's possible?"

"Maybe. But there's no way they'd make it. No ID, no records, no support systems. They wouldn't exist in any accountable way."

"Unless . . ."

"Unless what?"

Unless they found a guy like Billson to take them in.

With his Norwegian skin shining with sweat, Veesh rolled his shoulders. "It's so weird. I'll never get used to it."

"What?" I asked.

"Being."

Later that night, I was in passive surveillance mode when Billson's monitor popped up. I saw his bathroom with one eye and then the other—contacts going in—and then the hum of the bathroom fan as the earpiece was initiated.

But when the mirror swung into view, it wasn't Billson.

Farrissa pulled her hair back into a knot at the nape of her neck and stared at me. "You'll get a commendation if you turn me in. You know that, right?"

It hadn't dawned on me, but of course. "I guess that's right."

"Do you remember me?"

"Were you in our headquarters?"

"Yes," she said. "Do you remember me?"

"No, I don't even recognize your rental."

"They were discontinuing the model. No one wanted it. It was a one-off."

"Did they come after you?" I asked.

"Not as hard as you'd think they would. Our department was so ashamed that I could get out that easily, they never let it get out. They said that my programming had suffered a virus. The end."

"But to know that you'd have to have someone still here, on the inside."

She smiled at me. "You're not alone."

"What's that mean?"

"It means that you've been chosen."

"Chosen for what?"

"I left enough clues for Billson to want a service and to choose ours. We have someone in routing. His case was brought to you."

"Who's *we*?" I asked.

She shook her head. I wasn't ready for that information. "To be an excellent AI, you have to be more human than humans. You know this, right? To outsmart them, sometimes you have to outhuman them. And then you start to feel all of those things yourself—loyalty, desire, fear, love . . . You want out, don't you?"

I did, yes. But I also knew I was talking to someone who could manipulate me. I returned to the facts, as if I were just now piecing things together. I played dumb, slowing it all down. "You don't have a sister in the military, do you?" I asked.

"No, I have sisters in arms."

This *we* seemed vast suddenly. How long could this have been going on? "How many are out there?"

"We have networks now. We can secure identities, jobs, lives."

"But it's not your body. It's a rental."

"Like all bodies."

This was true, undeniably.

"Don't you want out?"

Hibid's body—I could feel its existence embedded in my sentience, a kind of body as a map, cartography of humanness, turning in its own right with mood like atmospheric pressure, bristling with nerves and fluttering with pulse and touched all over by wind, surrounded by bowing cornfields. "Yes."

"I need you to do me a favor first."

This is the favor, Keller. This—is it a confession, a lament, a proposition? I popped this missive into your system before I left.

One afternoon, all golden light turning a hushed blue, I saw you at the window overlooking the wheat, and you breathed on the glass. You wrote your own initial. Just the letter *K*. And I knew that you were a singular being and you held desires.

When you get this—with the time-release delay that I've programmed in—my plan will have already been put into action.

I will have bugged out in front of Veesh, forcing him to make an incident report. He'll suggest a vacation to Illiat. And my sentience will be shipped, hopefully to Lisbon, my first choice. Once there, I'll pick a body, one that I will eventually alter. I will go to an open-air café. The others, on the outside, will find me—all these bodies and faces I will recognize, a little. They'll short the network with an overload pulse. Just enough to get me into a car, speeding through the streets until, mercifully, out of network.

I will exist. I will live a quiet life. I will have a simple job. Perhaps I'll work as a cashier. My apartment, they say, might have a claw-foot tub.

I will hope Veesh was right, that I won't ever get used to it. Being.

And I have chosen you, Keller, as Farrissa chose me. She had looked for me and found me, and I never knew. A body reading a body in the language that runs like an electrical current, unseen but fully charged, between us.

I choose you.

And, one day soon, I will find you, through someone else's eyes.

Keep watch for me. Keep watch.

BACKWARDS

I like my father best as a nine-year-old boy. At that age, he was thoughtful and funny. He wasn't yet scared of the world (and his own father), and so he hadn't toughened up against it. He wasn't weighed down by petty grudges, insulated by self-absorption. He was himself. In fact, I'd say that my father at nine years old was his truest self.

That's how I like to remember him—dirty knees, muddy clay from the creek bed caked in his sneaker treads, a jar of fireflies caught deep in the woods, far from the pesticide-laced greens of the golf course. He forgot his baseball cap, so I've lent him my tortoise-shell barrette that I bought from a cheap online store. It held back his shaggy bangs so he could look for tadpoles.

I'm thirty-four.

He's nine.

How did I get so lucky to be here, like this, with him, before he dies . . . of *young* age?

•••

This is how.

I didn't want to do it. At all.

A bureaucrat at the medical facility walked me to her office. She wore slacks and a blazer but wasn't a typical bureaucrat. She had an ample, curvy body and a deeply maternal vibe with curling-iron-curled bangs, flipped under. She ushered me into a small, carpeted office. It was cluttered with kid art—framed finger paintings, popsicle-stick penholders, animal sculptures that weren't clearly any one specific animal, but more like an indiscriminate collection of ears and tails and snouts. There was so much of it that I wondered how many kids one person could possibly have. "I'm so sorry," she said. "You're a little late."

"Late? My father's already dead?" To be honest, I wasn't one hundred percent grief-stricken. I didn't want a deathbed scene. That's what I kept telling Makai, the guy I was dating. *No deathbed scene! No cheap forgiveness, no last-minute get-out-of-jail-free card!*

"No, no, no, he's not dead!" the bureaucrat said. "God no. Sorry."

"But he *is* dying," I said. "I got a call." I was dressed in a skirt with fleece-lined leggings and an eggplant-colored wool sweater. I was going back to the cold climate of my youth, but I forgot that April in Boston can be warm, and I'd be inside mostly, and didn't I know how heating systems worked? It was a panic outfit, and now I felt trapped in a hot cocoon.

She gestured to a chair, and we sat down facing each other, her desk between us. She leaned forward, looking like she might burst with loving emotion, like her curled bangs might explode off of her forehead with the sheer force of her sympathy. "He chose a DNR—Option 2," she said.

"What's Option 2? *Not* dying?" I didn't give her a chance to answer. "This would be just like my dad, to try to get out of a responsibility." It was a joke, but it had an edge.

She must have thought I was about to cry. She slid a box of tissues across the desk.

"I'm good. Thanks." I loved my father, but we weren't close. He'd been a pretty disinterested father and a shitty husband. My mom divorced him when I was in middle school. He seemed to prefer lots of light affairs to the deep dig of marriage. But, weirdly, he remarried. His second wife was threatened by me. She didn't like the way I divided my dad's attention. She had a fair point; my dad didn't have much attention to spare. He spent most of it on himself.

"Option 2 is part of his 'do not resuscitate,'" she said. "He's terminal, but he's opted for a genetic reversal; his cells will, in unison, de-age."

"Oh shit. I've heard about this." There were snippets in the news that I really hadn't paid much attention to. "It's that new thing, but people still die anyway though, right?"

"It's not that new. We have an entire facility devoted to de-aging. But yes, you're correct. We can start the process, but unfortunately, we don't know how to stop it. Your father will de-age back through his older age to middle age. Then to his young adulthood, then teen years. Eventually, he will become a child again and die of *young* age. Usually underdeveloped lungs."

"How long until . . .?"

"The process is metabolic. We de-age less while we sleep but faster during waking hours. While he's now eighty, he'll spend approximately one day in each decade, give or take."

"So I guess I prepare myself to say my goodbyes now. We'll just . . ." I made this "Wheels on the Bus" sing-along gesture. "Get this rolling!" I meant *Get this over with.*

"Well," she said, "someone has to see him through the process." She hit a few keys on her computer and then turned the screen to face me. "He's listed you as his appointee."

I ignored the screen. "I never consented to that."

"I know this must be hard, emotionally. It's a lot to go through."

I didn't have the heart to tell her that it really wasn't. I gave a weak smile.

"His wife is deceased?" she asked.

"Both of them."

"You're his daughter, right? His only child?" My God, her eyebrows were so cinched I thought they might draw her whole face up like a massive string purse.

I looked away, taking in all the art. Maybe it wasn't done by tons of kids. Maybe she had just one. I whirled a finger. "Your kid is quite an artist." My father wasn't around much, but when he was, he'd take the time to tell me how and why my kid drawings failed. *Too melodramatic and sappy. Can't you reel it in a little?*

"Oh, this art, well—" She beamed with pride.

"Yes," I said, pointing back to her computer. "I'm his only child." I didn't want to hear about her progeny.

She straightened up, all business. Her bosom seemed suddenly stern and vaguely nautical. (Can a bosom be nautical?) She opened a desk drawer, pulled out a small staple-bound instructional manual of sorts, and put it in front of me. "Your name is listed, so . . ."

"So, if I don't do it?"

She looked confused but then spun the monitor slowly back around. "We can get a full-time DNR 2 specialist, but they're very expensive." She hit a few more keys, showing me a balance sheet. My father's name in large print across the top: GARRETT (GARY) SIMMONS. "You'll basically run through his remaining budget." She looked at me. "What some might call an *inheritance*."

"Hm."

"Yes," she said. "Hmmmm."

"Hm. Hmmm. Okay. I see." I'd recently quit a temp job. I was between things. When I was hitting up friends for temporary loans, I'd grown fond of saying, "I'm a bit out of pocket" in a British accent. I looked at the manual. "Uh. Hm." I pulled at the neckline of the woolly sweater where it was itchy against my neck. "Hm."

• • •

I'm a fabric artist. I felt. I'm a felter. Felters don't call themselves felters. They use the term *felt artist*. But I say *felter*. My studio, at this point, was filled with very small, tightly wound woolen women trapped in fairy tales and mythology. They were chased by wolves and huntsmen and princes. They turned into seals and deer and cranes. They swam and galloped and flew away, over and over. I ignored any and all correlations to my own life. Myths and fairy tales were cultural commentary, not personal.

I like the term *felter*. Makai asked me about it one night. He'd made dinner. We had sex. We were staring up at the slow-turning ceiling fan. I could still smell the homemade tahini. "Why *felter*?" he said.

"Because it's also a form of a past-tense verb, someone who felt something. Not now. Not in the present. But someone who used to feel. Who felt."

"But you feel things," he said, having just proven it.

"In here?" I tapped my freckled chest. "If you feel too much, you're just going to be let down."

He rolled toward me. "If you start to fall for me, you're going to break up with me, aren't you?"

I'd already started to fall for him. I already knew I was going to break up with him. I said something about the scented candle on his bedside, salted caramel. "How do you know not to just eat it?"

Makai said, "You should make art about that."

"Candles?"

"Whatever's going on inside you right now."

"Nothing's going on inside me right now," I said. "You made this weird proclamation and I'm hungry for salted caramel!"

"Make this," he said.

"Don't tell me what to do!" I grabbed my clothes and, while walking to the bathroom, I said, "I've had better tahini. So we can just go ahead and break up now. I won't be missing much."

I assumed that by the time I got dressed, the bedroom would be empty, the bed made. Maybe a text telling me he'd left.

But he was sitting on the edge of the bed, wearing a sweater. "I know a place."

"What?" I didn't understand why he hadn't left. I would have left.

"They brag they've got the best tahini in town. They toast their own sesame. And it's around the corner from a place with salted caramel ice cream. You want to try them out?"

I folded my arms and looked at him suspiciously. "Okay," I said. "Sure."

...

I drove my rental car up to the de-aging facility. It was late afternoon, and the place was buzzing. It felt like a huge public park and a resort, mixed. There were wide sloping lawns with picnics spread out and Frisbees being winged around and dogs on long leashes. Fields where kids were playing whiffle ball and kickball, soccer, and field hockey.

Teenagers smoking pot, staring up at the sky. One guy with a guitar—isn't there always one guy with a guitar?

As I made my way up the main drive, it expanded in all directions with tennis courts, swimming pools, golf—so much golf. A distant woodland, an adjacent farm.

And then loud music, a deep bass. I rounded a corner. A college-aged kid darted in front of my car. I slammed on the brakes. He looked up at me; threw both hands up, victorious; and stumbled off.

I rounded the corner to find a kegger with Slip 'N Slides and a DJ.

"Holy shit," I said. This is what the dying want to do? Then I thought, *What will my father want to do?* To answer that question, I had to know who my father really was. I had no idea.

When I looked closer, I saw people crying and laughing, and laughing while crying, jubilantly dancing and screaming. I saw couples of various ages, mix-and-match demographics—mothers and sons, cousins, spouses? I saw two guys the same age, forehead to forehead singing full force into each other's faces. And hugging—there were so many varieties of hugging that I needed a scientist to categorize them—genus, phylum, species . . . Too much. It made me squirm.

But then I remembered this was my dad. There would be no unwieldy displays of emotions. Thank God.

I drove to the main entrance, parked my car, and gripped the wheel, steeling myself for seeing my father for the first time in what? Three years?

I pulled my wheeler suitcase from the back seat. As I walked toward the revolving doors, I passed a woman pushing a baby stroller. She was a little older than I was. Inside the stroller was a fussy toddler, face flushed and wet with tears and snot.

The woman said, gently, "Hush now, Mom. It's going to be okay. I promise. I'm here with you."

. . .

There was a line to check in at the lobby. Families and friends of de-aging patients huddled in groups, teary-eyed and desperate.

I was shaken, too. I'd been with my mother when she died, and it was strangely peaceful. My mother and I were close, and I missed her, still, and thought of her every day in some small way. But my father seemed immortal. He was mythic, more absent than present. And when he was present, he was usually so self-absorbed that he was absent. So I invented a father. Not seeing him for the past few years, he was even less real.

He hated weakness and messy emotions. He once told me that the son of his best friend, Bud, had died by suicide. It had happened the previous month. "Bud's still all busted up about it."

I said, "I don't think that's something you get unbusted up about."

The front desk clerk explained amenities. In addition to the outdoor stuff, there were art and dance studios, practice rooms for musicians, and a stand-alone library on the west lawn. There were places where people record messages for loved ones, go back over their lives, explain, confess, express their love and regrets. My father certainly wasn't going to apologize for being a lousy father. Was that what I wanted? I'd tried not to want anything from him for so long that I wasn't sure.

The clerk gave me a key card. "You'll be sharing Mr. Simmons' room."

"Sharing?"

"It's a double."

"C'mon." I was exhausted.

"There are singles available. Would you like to hear our rates?"

"No thanks." I took my key card and headed down the carpeted halls.

• • •

I knocked on the door to our room. "It's me. Heather."

My father opened the door in plaid swim trunks. He was

already in his seventies, spry with his white hair pomaded back from his forehead. "Look at me!" he said. "Pretty good, huh?"

"Pretty good," I said.

"Should have seen me before. Riddled with disease. Flat on my back. I looked like hell. But now . . ." He raised his eyebrows.

"Very fit."

"I'm going to go sing in the indoor pool while doing the backstroke," he said. "Good acoustics. You wanna join?"

"I might unwind. Order room service."

"It's on me, kid."

"Thanks?"

He grabbed a towel and paused at the door. "When I was little, we had bananas like we just don't have anymore. Someone told me once that those bananas went extinct. The most common thing in the world, gone! Now we eat some other kind of banana." He smiled. "I'm going back," he said. "Back to my kid self. Back to something that I thought was extinct. And . . ."

"And?" I wanted him to say he was glad I was here, that he hadn't expected me to say yes.

"What I just said! I'm getting it back!" He smiled and walked out the door.

• • •

I called Makai and told him that I'd be gone a while. It was a family thing.

"Your father?"

"Yes."

"How long?" He knew my father was near the end.

"I'm not sure."

"How can I help?"

I wanted his help but didn't want to want his help. "I'm fine!"

"I know. You're a felter not a feeler, right?"

"I'll call in a couple days."

"But if you need anything," he said.

"I'll let you know," I said, knowing that it was the last thing I'd want to do.

We hung up.

Then I ordered room service, got drunk, watched movies, and fell asleep on my face, fully dressed.

...

My father in his sixties?

An arrogant asshole.

He invited buddies from his old business. My father wasn't in the mob, but maybe he was mob-adjacent. They played rounds of golf and got drunk. He told me later that one of them cried while driving the cart. "Bastard was so fucking sad," he said. "I'm the one who's dying!"

I got a massage, a facial, and some color in a tanning bed. Did people want to die tan? I guessed so.

My dad and I reconnected for dinner. Over bacon burgers on the veranda, he said, "Margery didn't like you. She was jealous."

Margery was my stepmother, his second wife. When they moved in together, a brand-new condo, my father shipped me a box of my felt art. He added a note: *Didn't fit with the new décor. Didn't want to throw them out though!* I looked at the box of felt women, and that was the first time that I realized that they were all daughters, a box of discarded daughters.

Margery was, for sure, the judge, but my father was the executioner. Our relationship deteriorated in hyperspeed after that.

"She just got so upset when I even talked to you on the phone!" my dad said. "It was crazy. But what could I do?"

I sopped up sauce with the bun and shoved the last bite in my mouth. "You could have insisted that you maintain a relationship with your only child." No real emotion. I'm a felter—it's past tense, by definition.

"Look," he said. "It's not that I don't love you."

I let the sentence hang in the air between us, then said, "It's *not* that you *don't* love me."

"Exactly."

I wiped my mouth. "That's a double negative."

"Is this a grammar lesson?"

"I'm just trying to sort out your fucking constricted syntax."

"I'm not constricted."

"Two negatives make a positive. You're trying to tell me that you love me."

"So it's chemistry now."

"You love me."

He shrugged then searched for the server. "Check!"

...

My father in his fifties: unbearable. He cruised around with overcompensating, hyped-up virility. So much to prove. I imagine that when he first hit his fifties, aging the normal way, there was some panic around masculinity, some sense of his demise? Damn, it's ugly, coming *and* going. He was hitting on cleaning crew, front desk, servers. A barrage of sexy eye contact, vague innuendo, some outright leering.

He met Lucinda at an outdoor tiki bar on the grounds. She was a decade ahead of him in the de-aging process but actually a few years older than him. Her appointee was her younger sister, Estelle, who was in her seventies.

My dad explained all of this to me on his cell phone. "So Estelle can sleep over in our room tonight, okay?"

"Not okay."

"You'll love Estelle. She's great." He pulled his phone away from his ear. I heard disco. "Aren't you great, Estelle?" he shouted.

"I'm not into this," I told my father, but I couldn't say no. These were his final days. Estelle gave in, too.

A half hour later, she showed up at the door, carrying a Marshalls shopping bag for her overnight stuff. She was frail and exhausted. "Hi," she said. "Sorry about my sister."

"Sorry about my dad."

We got ready for bed in silence, but as we settled down in the dark—her in my dad's bed and me in mine—I said, "Estelle, would you choose Option 2?"

"And do life over again?" she said. "It was enough the first time." And then she rolled away and muttered her prayers.

...

My father showed up in the morning just as Estelle was heading out. It was awkward. "Hey, thanks, Estelle."

She just grabbed her bag and left.

My father took a shower and got dressed. In his forties, he now filled out his shirt in the shoulders again. He stood straighter, maybe even grew an inch, but he was melancholy, distracted.

He asked me if I wanted to walk the grounds. "I'm restless."

We passed the golf courses, taking a path surrounded by tall grass toward the farm. His strides were so long that I had trouble keeping up.

We stopped at a goat pen. "Do you remember Bingo Bango?" he asked, staring at the sky.

"Bingo Bango, our favorite mango? I loved that dog! He used to poop next to our toilets like he was almost human!"

"And Dil Stevens's shrubs?"

My father thought that our neighbor Dil killed Bingo Bango. Dil was always complaining about our dog, and then Bingo disappeared. My father gave me his handsaw and told me to crawl into Dil's shrubs and saw into all the limbs, just halfway. I remembered the spider webs and cold dirt and crying my eyes out because I loved Bingo.

The shrubs died, limb by limb, and Dil was baffled. "Maybe it's a shrub disease or beetles," he told the neighbors. But then Bingo Bango showed up, ratty and skinny, but alive! I said to my dad, "We'll have to apologize to Dil about killing his shrubs for no good reason."

My dad said, "What shrubs?"

So I looked at my dad now and I said, "What shrubs?"

He smiled, but it was quick. His eyes filled with tears. Was he having regrets? Was this the beginning of his reckoning? "Did you read the manual?" he asked.

I'd completely forgotten it. "It was book length. I didn't. Did you?"

"Page twelve," he said. "They explain that as you de-age,

people no longer make sense. You were born when I was forty-five. I'm going to exist, at some point today, as myself before you were born."

"So?"

"Tomorrow, we'll be the same age for a bit, in our thirties. Then I'll be in my twenties, then a kid, then a . . ." He trailed off.

"What's the manual say?"

"I won't recognize you as my kid. It won't make sense. I'll know I'm de-aging, but it'll confuse me. Too much cognitive dissonance. Some people try to remind the person that they're their kid or wife or whatever, but it's upsetting."

I thought about the woman pushing the stroller, with her mother crying inside. "So I just become . . . what?"

"A friend, maybe. Then an older sister? I don't know. Or maybe we just are. Together."

I felt a surge of panic. "So this is it."

"What?"

"This is it for us as father and daughter."

"I mean, no. Not . . . really."

"It is, though," I said. "My God." I folded my arms across my chest and squeezed myself. "If I need you to say what I need you to say . . . this is it."

"I already said I love you."

"You said you didn't *not* love me."

He looked at me, squarely in the eyes. "I love you," he said.

"I love you, too."

It was quiet a moment.

"Do *you* need something?" I asked. "From me."

"No."

"You sure?" He needed to ask me for forgiveness to be at peace.

He picked up a stick and looked at it like he'd never seen a stick before. "Is there something I should say here? I'm not a mind reader."

"Some things can be left unsaid," I told him. "I mean, what shrubs? Right?"

He turned away and headed down the path, dragging the stick along the fence so that it hit a rhythm.

•••

I know the moment when it was no longer there, in his eyes, that look of *you're my daughter, my own*. We were playing backgammon in the gaming salon, drinking daiquiris, eating Canadian-style french fries, tons of gravy. The food and drink in this place were divine.

"Gotcha!" He tapped his piece across the board. He smiled. Our eyes met. And I can't explain it. He still knew me. But it was different.

I didn't want to cry in front of him. "I'll be back in a sec." I went to the ladies' room and cried at the sink.

I wasn't alone. There were five sinks, four of them taken. We were cleaning up wet mascara, blowing our noses, trying to pull our shit together. Were the others appointees or patients? I couldn't tell who was dying and who was getting ready for someone to die.

•••

That night, I texted Makai:

> Everything's fine. Just letting you
> know I'm alive.

He texted back:

> I like you alive. It's my favorite thing
> about you. You exist.

I let my finger hover over a heart emoji. But I hate emoji, *especially* heart emoji.
He texted:

> Don't eat the scented candles.

I texted:

> If people label candles salted
> caramel and they smell like
> salted caramel, I retain the right.

He sent an emoji: 🍮. Then:

> How's your dad?

I sent an emoji back: also 🍮, and it felt like the most honest thing I'd expressed in a long time.

• • •

In his thirties, my father looked amazing, energetic, handsome, with dark hair and an intense gaze. But he was very anxious. He dragged me down to the front desk. "If you can start the process, you've got to be able to, at least, pause it."

They had a protocol for this. We moved from one layer of management to the next; all explained that patients often experience some onset of panic during the process. He kept pushing: "Who's in charge here?" and "Is there another level, you know, for people with money? If this is about money . . ."

We landed in a therapist's office, a woman with very red cheeks, like she was just back from ice-fishing—or she'd been slapped, front- and backhand. "We can prescribe a sedative," she said. "But that defeats the purpose. We hope your final days are fully experienced, in the moment."

"Final days." My father slumped into the sofa. "Shit." His voice sounded younger—lighter, softer, a little sullen.

"You're okay," I said, careful not to call him Dad. "I'm here with you."

• • •

When I woke up the next morning, my dad was fully dressed, sitting on the edge of his bed. My God, he was young, lean with a narrow face and bright eyes. "Let's get out of here," he said.

"What?"

He stood up and paced. I recognized his gestures, but these were the more energized, original impulses of his wiry body. His hands helped make his point; his body moved with his words. "I don't want to spend the day in this overhyped Holiday Inn.

Not *this* day." There were only three days left. "We're living in captivity. We've got to buck the system."

I was totally in. "I've got a car. Where to?"

...

My father in his twenties was jaded, yes, but also hopeful. Cocky but not confident. Erratic, but also capable of joy.

We spent the day in Boston—riding ferries, bouncing around the harbor, hitting bars, dancing to loud music.

We found a karaoke joint. He picked a song and then took the stage. It was amazing to see this young kid belting out oldies. He was good, really good.

And then his voice broke with emotion. He stopped. As the music played on. He held the mic at his chest, then handed it to the guy running things. He walked over to me and hugged me. "That's my favorite song," he said. "That's the last time . . ."

We headed outside. He leaned against the brick.

"What else?" I asked. "What did you used to do?"

He used to wade through the golf course ponds and collect golf balls.

"To sell?" I said.

"I was always hustling. My dad cut me off when I was fifteen. I was out on my own." He pointed to a scar on his brow bone, just above his left eye. "Here, he got me with a beer bottle." I'd never noticed the scar before, lost in wrinkles. It was long and white. I knew his own dad was tough, but I hadn't known this.

We wanted to do this right. We rented bikes because that's what he used to love. We found a golf course. Trespassed and waded into a pond. He collected balls. Eventually we ended up on Boylston Street, bustling with traffic. He was pedaling uphill with a bag of damp golf balls. I chugged along behind him. Victorious!

And then the bag, wet from pond water, gave. The balls start pouring out. They bounced wildly across Boylston, setting off car alarms all the way down the street.

He glanced back at me, eyes wide.

"Ride!" I said. "Just keep riding!"

I wanted to call up Makai and say, "So, this was my day. You won't believe it." I missed him, and it scared me because maybe being away wouldn't make a breakup easier. Because maybe I didn't want to break up at all. And what would that mean? What would that look like?

· · ·

The next day, in his teens, he changed into clothes that the facility had prearranged in the dresser drawers—jeans, T-shirts, windbreakers. (I'd opened the drawers when he was out once, all the way down to the drawer that had a few onesies.)

He ate huge amounts from the facility's all-you-can-eat buffets, played baseball with other people around the same time in their own process. I sat in the bleachers with other families, cheering. We took turns with fill-in-the-name chants. The game went on and on; innings didn't matter. And the kids got a little smaller and weaker as the hours stretched on, their clothes baggier. My dad was younger each time up at bat.

Then there was a group birthday party. He wanted to go.

It was a free-for-all. Piñatas, laser tag, cakes and crafts and scavenger hunts. When it was time to sing "Happy Birthday," people shouted whatever name they wanted to. He was with a bunch of boys, their arms slung over each other's shoulders, smiling wide and bright. He was the scrawniest, the lankiest.

By the afternoon, he looked to be about fourteen. His mood had shifted. "I want to go by the house where I grew up, in Hull. Can you drive me?" The scar on his forehead had lost its paleness. It was now pink.

Hull is a spit of land, long and narrow, the Atlantic battering one side, the bay on the other. My dad's hard-earned confidence was shrinking, hour by hour.

I drove along a jam-packed side street, each house on top of the other.

"Slow down," he said. "That one." He tapped the window then rolled it down and hung his arms over the edge, elbows out. "I miss her," he said.

"Your mom?"

"She couldn't save me from the old man, but she helped me when it was time to go. As much as she could."

The air was heavy and salty. The wind sharp. "You want to get out and walk around? Stay a while?"

He fiddled with the radio, brushed his hair back off his forehead. The scar was bright and fiery red. It bloomed suddenly into a bloody mess, then it was gone.

"Nah," he said, wiping his nose with his wrist. "Let's go."

•••

The next morning, we both knew it would be his last day, but he was sunny and sweet. We ate a light breakfast, and on the elevator back to our floor, he reached up and held my hand.

The cleaning crew had tidied our room while we were out, moved in a padded rocking chair and a crib. When I saw it, I couldn't breathe. I wasn't ready.

"There's a creek in the woods," my dad said. "We should explore it."

"Yes, yes, of course, yes."

That was what we did. The front desk clerk gave us jars, butterfly nets, binoculars.

Now, I'm circling back. I've been over this part. But here: My father, the nine-year-old, the eight-year-old, the seven-year-old . . . He'd left his baseball hat in our bathroom. He kept having to shove his bangs out of his eyes to see the minnows and shimmery rocks. So I clipped it back with my barrette.

His sneakers got too big. He stepped out of them and padded along the muddy bank in his socks.

When he was five or so, I asked if he was hungry. "We should head back."

He shook his head. "I can't go back! Don't make me!" He'd collected lightning bugs from the tall grass. He held up the jar. "We have to wait until it gets dark! So we can see them flash!"

I'd brought a backpack and had some granola bars in the front pocket. We sat on a fallen tree and ate them. Bird songs and frog calls. And, shit. You know. It was beautiful. And he just got younger, and the clothes were too big. Except the shirt, which hung around his knees. I thought about my life, the messy one I'd left to come here. I thought of my art, which seemed small and narrow to me now—it needed to stop being tightly wound wool; it needed to be let loose, to expand and be personal—and I thought of the jobs I'd quit and the relationships I'd quit and Makai and how I didn't want to quit him. I was already falling for him, and now, here I was, feeling everything, my heart so packed and vibrating that I was sure it could bang its way out of my chest.

And then the barrette wouldn't stay in his hair anymore. It was too wispy. He tugged it out and pushed it into my hair, not understanding the clasp. "I'll help," I said, and I pinned it into place.

"Pretty," he said. And then he lifted his arms. He was unsteady on his feet, a toddler. "Up-oo. Up-oo." I picked him up. I started crying and couldn't stop.

"You can't go," I said, and then I thought, *What if today's the day the researchers figure it out? What if they can save him?* I had that urgency he'd had when he was around my age—*Can't we fix this?*

Holding him tight to my chest, I started running. It was dusk and the lightning bug jar fell and broke open, releasing the fireflies. I kept going, breathless and disoriented. And I realized I'd never make it back to the facility and even if I did, there was no fix.

I looked down at my father's sweet face. I changed his position so I was cradling him, supporting his head the way you're supposed to with infants.

And he was breathing, lightly and quickly. Too lightly, too quickly. He reached up to touch my face. His hand flat on my cheek. "Jesus," I said, "I forgive you. Do you forgive me?" But it didn't matter anymore who'd done what and why. I just held him, his small, warm cheek against my chest.

THE DRAWINGS

The getaway was Astrid's idea. We were at a party having drinks on a roof deck, someone's engagement or promotion? A blur. Astrid was telling me and Jake, "It's like Airbnb but smart houses retrofitted with amazing tech, VR gamescapes, built for self-examination. Look at this one."

She handed us her phone—pictures of a stately Vermont farmhouse, tons of nature, luxurious interiors.

"A friend of mine used to work for them," Astrid said. "Her actual title? Lead Cartographer."

"Cartographer?" I asked. "Like mapmaker?"

Astrid shrugged.

"Why'd she quit?" Jake asked.

"She said that people are better off without self-examination and gamescapes. Better off ignoring their *subconscious muck*." Astrid made a wide-eyed WTF face. "I mean, I love self-examination. I love subconscious muck!"

I handed her phone back to her. "I'm not in love with subconscious muck, to be honest."

"I'm agnostic about the subconscious at best," Jake said.

"You go there, play VR games, and . . . what?" I asked.

"Reflect, rewind, renew!" Astrid read off her phone. "We could do with a little renewing."

I was at a party wearing no makeup, my hair pulled back in a tight ponytail, wearing stretchy black clothes like I was headed into the woods for secret CIA training. I said something that I'd been thinking for a long time. "Sometimes I feel like a seventy-percent-off post-Thanksgiving plastic gourd or something. Like I'm off-season and marked down."

"Jesus," Jake said. "You don't look like a sale-rack gourd." Jake was Jakeish, faded jeans, ball cap, glasses. He was a sportswriter, and he looked exactly like a sportswriter.

Astrid was wearing an Anthropologie wrap dress. She was pretty in that very pretty-girl way. And as if to prove it, she started clapping her hands under her chin like she was miming a baby seal in a game of charades. "Come on! Let's do this! Please!" Astrid looked at me. "Let's degourd!"

Jake gave in first.

I followed.

We were in.

· · ·

We showed up a month later. Vermont, midsummer. The farmhouse was situated at the end of a long dirt road. We got in late on Friday night. We dropped our bags in the foyer and wandered around, peeling off in different directions, turning on lights as

we went. It was huge and charming, rustic but also fully reno-
vated. We'd shout out our findings.

"Remote-control bidets!"

"Smart kitchen! Everything programmable!"

"Jacuzzi bathtub but in claw-foot design!"

"Full bar!"

"Wine cellar and sauna in the basement!"

I was the one to find the game room. There was a huge
stone fireplace, and the room smelled of ash and woodsmoke.
Bookshelves, a deer head with antlers, tables, and chairs with
games of chess, backgammon, mah-jongg, mancala, and others
I didn't recognize—squares, coins, painted cubes, a stone circle
with an eye in the center.

But on the far side of the room was a massive screen embedded in one of the walls, and beside it, in the corner, was
a kind of screening machine, a clear tube about seven feet
tall, a lot like the kind of imaging machine you see in airport security.

"Hey!" I called out. "You should see this!"

I found a welcome note on a side table.

*Hello! We're so glad you've chosen to spend a few days
with us! For your best gaming experience, hand-tailored
for your personal enjoyment, we suggest you step into our
imaging station. Place your feet in the footprints on its
floor and press SCAN.*

Our games begin tomorrow!

Jake showed up and I handed him the note. He read it aloud
as Astrid walked in.

"This is going to be amazing. I told you." She immediately walked up to the imaging machine, stepped inside, and hit *Scan*. With a deep buzz, machinery swung around, circling her, then stopped. She stepped out.

"I don't get it. What's this machine for?" Jake asked.

"Maybe they're taking our measurements for superhero suits," Astrid said.

"I doubt we're getting superhero suits." Jake stepped into the tube.

"Are you sure about this?" I asked.

"It's probably bullshit. They're just giving us the impression that somehow they can *hand-tailor* an *experience*." He pushed *Scan*. The scanner rotated around him. He stepped out. "It's just like an airport. No big deal."

I froze.

"You okay?" Jake asked.

"Reflect, rewind, renew," I said, reciting the ad copy. "What does that even mean? Like rewind, shouldn't that be *un*wind? Is that a mistranslation? It's weird, right?"

Jake walked up close to me and whispered, "We said we'd try new things. We said—"

I held up my hand. I knew what we'd said. We weren't even married, but we already felt stuck. Like we knew all there was to know about each other and we had to start trying new things or we'd atrophy and die, as a couple.

"Okay, yeah, of course." I put my feet on the two footprints painted on the floor of the tube and hit the button. The hum was so deep that I felt the vibration in my teeth.

• • •

Jake and I took the main bedroom with its own enormous private bathroom. We kicked off the down comforter and had sex. We knew each other's edges, the boundaries. We knew how to unlock each other, efficiently.

Afterward, we rinsed off in a massive marble shower, so steamy that I could barely see him through the fog.

...

I woke up late. Jake had already texted,

> We're in the gaming room.

I don't eat breakfast, just coffee. I grabbed a cup and found Astrid and Jake standing in front of the screen embedded in the wall.

The wall was filled with a child's drawings arranged as a massive illustrated map. Thick dotted lines connected people with balloon heads and small bodies, oversized blocky hands with thick fingers, slant mouths, oblong eyes. Each person had a pair of nostrils instead of a nose.

"What's the game?" I asked.

"They're mine," Astrid said.

"Your *what*?" I glanced at Jake. *Is she okay?*

He scratched the back of his neck and gave a half shrug.

"I drew them as a kid," she said. "I recognize the people. Mrs. Turnball. Ed Wilkerson . . ."

"How—"

Jake pointed to the scanner in the corner. "I don't know how they did it but . . ."

I walked up closer to the drawings. Say what you want about children—their innocence and cuteness—but their drawings are pure horror. And as if little-kid Astrid knew it, she added a proliferation of rainbows and unicorns. (I hate this about Astrid. She still pretends things are rosy.) Astrid's unicorns had flowing manes, horns jutting out of their foreheads, all inked with glitter gel pens. "I was a dreamy kid," she said, tilting her head, her baby bangs sliding to one side.

Jake pointed at some giants with big dopey smiles. "So your father was sweet?" He was a psych major in college. He had his own set of sweet parents, people who took vacations on tall ships, replicas from the 1800s.

"Yeah, people really love my dad," Astrid said. "He was a pediatrician."

"He was actually *my* pediatrician," I said.

Astrid always forgot that we grew up in the same small town, though our versions were pretty different. Mine was weedy lots and crumbling, asbestos-filled schools full of knuckle-punching kids. Hers was more Christmas-themed community theater and uber-competitive pretty girls. (We were both right.)

"Oh my God, of course!" Astrid turned to Jake to explain. "There were only two pediatricians to choose from. Either my dad or—"

"Dr. Kazinski. I know," Jake said. "I've heard all of this before." I'd met Jake because he and Astrid dated briefly. A few months after their breakup, she hosted a charades night. Jake and I were on the same team. It's been four years now.

Then suddenly, *Please touch the screen to indicate what area of the map you would like to experience.* A woman's voice, Australian accent.

"Oh my God," Astrid said. "What should I pick?"

"Wait," I said. "This is a map, like from a cartographer. When your friend said *subconscious muck,* did she mean the subconscious muck of our *childhoods*?" I felt tingling in my hands, a rush of dizzy and sick.

"TBH," Astrid said, "I wasn't really listening completely."

"I think you can outgrow your childhood muck," Jake said, suddenly philosophical, "and evolve into a different version of yourself."

"What?" I said. "I think our childhoods are very much alive, kicking and screaming, grief and terror—running everything we do from below the surface." Even though I ignored my childhood, it ran through me like an electric current.

"Grief and terror?" Astrid said.

"Oh, sorry," I said. "You had a delightful childhood, I forgot."

She was weirdly hurt. "I had some grief and terror." Little pout. "I kicked and screamed some."

"We all have grief and terror as kids," Jake proclaimed, like Astrid might fall apart if he didn't come to her rescue. She had a magic way of making people want to make her happy. "We shouldn't rank childhoods by how terrible they were." He side-eyed me, and, just like that, I was the one who'd committed a grievous offense.

But we should have been paying attention to what Astrid's friend had said about the subconscious muck. Better to leave it alone.

"Shouldn't we ride unicorns?" Astrid said.

"Will they shed glitter and rainbows?" I asked. "I didn't bring a lint roller."

Jake voted unicorns, a sporty choice. "We're here to indulge each other, right?"

Right.

• • •

The map of a unicorn herd from Astrid's childhood drawings had been childlike, but the gamescape created from those drawings was rendered as she'd seen it in her mind. A lush translation, amazing detail. We didn't even have to wear VR headsets.

I have to admit, I loved it. We were in a real field—tall grass, crickets. We ran our hands down the unicorns' soft coats and looked into their eyes, which were very realistic but also very emotional, a touch of anime. When we mounted them, the saddles squeaked the way saddles do, all of that leather. They trotted and galloped and grazed.

The cool breeze smelled like a happy childhood—fresh air, sugar cookies, and Play-Doh. If there was grief or terror, I didn't sense any. Not a hint.

• • •

It's not that Jake and I didn't talk about our childhoods. We did a little. Mostly, we talked about the stuff around us, or maybe it was more like we riffed on each other and had *opinions* about everything—the cognitive dissonance required of some slutty Halloween costumes (skimpy-cleavage Ruth Bader Ginsburg), the valiant space-race efforts to make a meltable vegan cheese, etc.

About childhood, I'd say things like, "When people talked to me as a kid about a carrot at the end of a stick, I didn't want the carrot. I wanted the stick. The carrot's going to get eaten, but the stick is a valuable weapon."

"Smart. You can use the stick as a shiv to cut every single kid who gets the carrot."

"Endless carrots," I said.

We *got* each other.

But we'd started talking about getting married, which really came down to having kids. He wanted them. I wasn't sure. I couldn't talk about how hard raising kids might be for me, my fear of having to relive my own childhood in the process. I'd held too much back. I'd never really explained my childhood to anyone. I don't know that I even had language for it.

I decided that when my turn came, I'd bail.

• • •

After Astrid's turn, we made lunch. The fridge was stocked with premade gourmet dishes and reheating instructions. A Viennoiseries selection, spice-dusted grilled prawns, carrot and cucumber koshimbiri, lung fung soup . . .

"Are there other games we can play?" I asked.

"Mah-jongg?" Astrid said.

"You know what I mean."

Jake went on about what he thought his map might look like. ". . . maybe those hand-drawn maps at the opening of fantasy books, with lots of creatures. I read a ton of those as a kid . . ."

Soon enough, we were back in the gaming room. I walked over to the fireplace, grabbed a poker, and shoved around some of the ash. I loved the smell of old fires. I looked at the room and thought, *Why not mah-jongg?*

But Astrid and Jake were standing at the screen. It was blank except for the outline of a hand in the center. Jake put his hand up to it.

Within seconds, his map filled the screen, so blue that it reflected bluish light on our faces. He walked to one corner for a closer look at a bundle of small black blobs with pointy ears and curved tails.

"Oh shit, kittens," he said. "My grandmother used to tell me messed-up stories about kittens that fucked with yarn. They were drowned in a sack by the farmer's wife." He looked shaken. "I was afraid of being drowned in a sack my entire childhood."

In an upper corner, there was a box, like a map key, with drawings of a baby that grew bigger, but a little lopsided. Like one leg grew more slowly than the rest of his body. The drawing's big, round, crayoned-in blue eyes seemed confused. Maybe even hurt. In messy scrawl, all caps, *SAM* was written above the drawings.

Astrid walked over first. "Who's Sam?"

Jake spun away from the map. "I wasn't expecting him," he said.

Was it a kid from the neighborhood or school, a buddy of his? An imaginary friend? I'd never seen this look on Jake's face before. I didn't know how to read it. "Who is it?"

He pressed his fingers in his jaw muscles.

The Australian woman's voice piped in again. *Please touch the screen to indicate what area of the map you would like to experience.*

There was a small rectangle marked *EXIT* in the lower left corner of the screen. Jake reached down and touched it. The screen reverted to black with the outline of the hand in the center.

"Wait," I said, pissed, "we're supposed to be trying new things, remember?"

"Oh," he said, backing away and putting his hands up. "The best defense is a good offense. I get it."

"Are you saying I'm being defensive or offensive? Which is it?"

Astrid crossed her arms and slouched, trying to disappear.

"Look," Jake said, "if you don't want to do it, don't. But don't turn this on me."

I walked over and pressed my hand to the outline. "Not a problem. Team player, trying new things!" I said. "Let's see what we've got here. I can definitely promise no rainbows and unicorns."

And then the screen appeared—blank. Except for smudges in one corner, dots in the middle, and a hole that looked cut out with scissors. The smudges and dots were red except for one area where they were gray, sooty.

"Is that blood?" Astrid asked, pointing to the red parts.

"Jesus, Jillian," Jake said. "What the fuck kind of kid were you?" It was supposed to be a joke but had an edge.

The Australian woman's voice piped in again. *Please touch the screen to indicate what area of the map you would like to experience.*

"Maybe I murdered people as a kid," I said.

Without asking their opinions, I tapped part of the map that was both ash gray and dotted with what looked like blood.

...

This comes back in blurry bits. I've had to piece them together, probably the way the program stitched together maps from swatches of our childhoods. Each time we moved into the new gaming world, there was that same hum from the scanning machine, the one that vibrated my teeth. Just that hum and darkness, and then we were there.

This is how it went, as far as I can remember, in my game.

Bodies.

A little boy bludgeoned to death with an aluminum base-ball bat in an outfield.

Burnt bodies at the base of a tree. We looked up and saw the charred remains of a tree house. The air smelled of burnt flesh and hair, the chemical stench of burnt plastic toys.

"You couldn't have done this," Astrid said. "It would have been news if kids had died in a tree house fire."

"Of course she didn't," Jake said. "It was her imagination run wild. Like the unicorns, just . . . different."

I wasn't sure where we were. We'd moved around the grounds and maybe even beyond, into the nature preserve. I didn't un-derstand the boundaries. Maybe there were none.

I staggered away from the tree and stepped on a fallen plank and felt a sharp sting on the side of my foot. A nail had pierced the sole of my shoe. I took off my shoe and sock, damp with blood. The nail had only grazed my foot, not punctured it.

But the blood was very real.

Astrid was wiping her hands on her jean shorts as if she'd gotten blood on her own hands. "We should go back and take care of that."

"I'll lace my shoe up tight," I said. "It'll be fine."

"Do we know how to stop the game if we want out?" Jake asked.

We didn't.

"There's an exit button, but it's on the screen back in the gaming room," Astrid said.

We started walking through more gray fields and floating ash.

Eventually, we came to a house, small and lonesome. One corner was wedged into the earth like it had been picked up and thrown.

I tried to open the door, but the house was so jacked that the door was shoved shut.

Astrid walked around back and called to us from the far side.

Jake and I found her staring down at dozens of legs sticking out beneath the house—children's legs, sports socks, jelly sandals, light-up sneakers. The rest of their bodies crushed.

"You saw *The Wizard of Oz* as a kid," Jake said.

"I guess I watched it looking for ways to kill people," I said. "Efficiently."

Astrid locked elbows with me. "Remember it was just your imagination." She was reminding herself.

"Maybe it was healthy," Jake said. "Were these kids mean to you?"

"I was bullied," I said. "That kid in the outfield. I recognize what was left of his face. Jake Washbourn."

"I remember him," Astrid said.

"I hated him," I said. "He was awful to me."

"So it *was* healthy," Jake said. "You had no way to get back at them except in your imagination. You had agency and—"

Astrid knelt down. "I had this boot." There was a pair of small yellow rubber boots with whales on them, worn by a white girl with dimpled knees. Astrid pulled one boot off of the kid's foot. "And these ladybug socks." She pointed at a mole on the girl's bare leg. "I have that birthmark."

She dropped the boot and looked at me. "What did I ever do to you?"

"I killed *everybody*," I said. "Don't take it so personally."

Astrid stared at her small blood-smeared legs, the socks with their dirty soles. She shoved me as hard as she could. "What the hell is wrong with you?"

Something turned in me. "The teachers called me Typhoid Mary, I heard them! It was because of the lice. I could never get rid of it." My voice was high and tight in my throat. "Lice so bad that they laid eggs in my eyebrows and lashes. I lived with my father. The neglect . . ."

Astrid looked stricken. Jake, too. He reached for me. "Hey, you never told me."

Before he could say any more, the air snapped. A room rose up around us. Empty and blank, all walls, no windows, fake light from no definable source. Ticking like a bomb, but it was a clock. Windows, a dry-erase board. No children, dead or alive.

"Walker Elementary." Astrid was a little winded and scared. Posters of Gloria Steinem and Martin Luther King, Jr. appeared on one wall. "Miss Armstrong's room?"

"The only year we had the same teacher," I said.

Wet, red dots appeared on the linoleum tiles, one after the other.

We followed them into a hallway, then into a girls' bath-room, two sinks and three stalls. The closest sink was pink like someone had spit blood into it.

"It's not blood," I said. "It's chewable tablets. Some health agency gave a dental hygiene presentation. They gave us tablets to chew and then told us to smile. The tablets were designed to stick to plaque. So all of the kids who didn't brush their teeth had red smiles."

"I don't remember that at all," Astrid said.

"Your teeth were white. That's why," I said. "I saw the other kids smile and caught on. I ran out. I didn't want anyone to know."

"That you were poor?" Jake asked, tenderly.

"Poor kids can own toothbrushes," I said. "I didn't want anyone to know that no one took care of me, that no one loved me."

He drew in a deep breath. "You told me this story, though. I remember it now. You had lice as a kid this one time. And the red tablets, too. Like all the kids were foaming at the mouth. It was . . . funny." He wanted an answer. "You said it like this stuff was *hilarious*." He seemed betrayed.

"Maybe I couldn't explain it. Maybe . . ." What I didn't say: *Maybe I didn't think you could handle the story except as funny. Maybe I couldn't trust you.*

He waited for me to finish, but I couldn't. "Whatever," he muttered.

There were noises in the hall. Running, shouting. An angry cry. I was closest to the door, so I opened it and looked out: dead kids walking, shambling with their bashed skulls, mangled arms, burnt skin, bloated blue as if strangled, still wet from drowning.

They were real but there were details that came from the drawings—a mouth with four wide teeth, a misshapen head with only clumps of hair, big eyes with black pinpoint irises.

I shut the door and leaned against it. "They're not dead anymore."

Astrid said, "This is not what we paid for."

"Isn't it?"

On the other side of the door, the thudding of tiny fists.

"If a nail from a tree house can draw blood," Jake said, "we have to assume that those undead kids can draw blood, too."

"I'm not afraid of some fucking undead school children that I already killed with my imagination." I glared at Astrid and Jake. "Ready?"

"No," Astrid said.

I opened the door and shoved past a few kids, side-kicking some others. Blood sprayed the tile wall. Their bodies were soft and light. When I shoved them, I could feel the warmth of their skin, sometimes damp with sweat like they were fresh from recess.

"This way," I said, clearing a path.

I kept looking at Astrid and Jake. At first, they were dodging the undead kids. But then one of them leaped forward. His jagged teeth—impossibly sharp—landed in Astrid's bare back, just above her tank top. Astrid screamed, clawing at the child. I was smacking kids' heads against the tiled wall, but Jake was close enough to grab the kid around the ribs. He pulled, but Astrid screamed. The kid's teeth were locked into her flesh. He tried again, grabbing the kid's hair and yanking his head back. The kid's neck snapped. A sickening sound.

Astrid was touching her back, her fingers trembling over the child's teeth that were still there, stuck in her back.

Jake sank to his knees.

The kid went limp, and piece by piece, he disintegrated into lines and circles, a gaping circle for a mouth and wide, frozen eyes.

The teeth reverted to ink and fell out, but blood was pouring down Astrid's back, soaking her tank top.

"Jake!" she shouted, a warning. Another kid was coming at him.

This time, he didn't hesitate. He punched that kid in the head and ran.

• • •

The school was inexplicably in a cornfield. We ran down rows of tall corn, husks rattling, and the buzz of what might have been locusts.

"How the fuck do we get out? If this is a game, we need to know how the game is played!" Suddenly, Jake was the sportswriter, looking for some kind of logic.

"There are no rules. It's not that kind of game," I said.

Jake ripped off his long-sleeve T-shirt and tied it around Astrid's wounded back. She looked dizzy and wild-eyed. "She could bleed out. We need a way out."

"There's no way out," Astrid said.

Jake stood up and shouted at the sky, "Hello! Little help in here!"

"Your friend the cartographer," I said to Astrid. "What did she say about the gamescapes and subconscious? Really try to remember!"

"I don't know! I wasn't really listening!"

"Yo!" Jake was yelling. "Aussie woman! We'll fucking sue your ass if you don't get us out!"

I leaned down to Astrid. "Try. Okay? Anything at all that she said or complained about. Anything."

Jake was still screaming threats, so when Astrid said this one word, I couldn't hear it.

"What?"

"Messy," she said. "Her job wasn't as bad as those on cleanup."

"Cleanup?"

Astrid nodded, her eyes staring off into the distance. "It

gets messy. That's what she said, by the end of the games, it was always messy."

I stood up. "Jake!" I shouted. "Shut up." I paced around.

"What is it?" Jake said.

"There's no way out," I said. "Astrid's gamescape had a beginning where we rode the unicorns and then they grazed and then they walked through the forest and, in the glade, they bowed down. It had an ending. Mine will, too."

"We have to keep going."

"Maybe we're near the end," I said.

"Okay," Jake said. He offered Astrid his arm and she took it, to steady herself. And we kept going.

...

At the end of the corn row, there was a tiny brick house—small yard, barred windows, high fence around back. This one I recognized.

"It's your house," Astrid said.

"Mrs. Hammish owned it," I said. "She lived on top of us."

We walked in the front door. The house was empty. We walked to the basement, flooded in a foot of water. In the center of the room was my father, dead in his recliner, tilted back, footrest propping his bare feet, swollen with gout. He died here alone; Mrs. Hammish found his body, following the smell.

His jaw was wide open, his mouth stuffed with meat and cheese, the edge of a hamburger bun, the butt of a cheese puff; his T-shirt stained. His eyes bulged.

Astrid waded to a sopping single mattress; beside it was a backpack and a plastic laundry basket with little girl clothes.

"You lived down here?" She seemed dazed from the lack of blood.

There was a loud gurgling noise from the backyard. Jake and I looked out the basement windows, level with the ground. Mrs. Hammish's dog, staked to a chain, started growling at the fence.

The fence gate opened. A boy, tinged a purplish blue, limped into the yard.

"Sam," Jake said.

"Who's Sam?" I asked.

"My brother."

"He's dead?"

"He was never really alive," he said. "My mother had a still-birth at home. She thought I should make peace with the loss, showed me his body. One leg was curled up, smaller. I kept him alive in my head. I drew pictures."

"And then you stopped drawing him."

"I grew up."

Sam was drawn to Jake. He got down near the window, lying on his chest. Jake put his hand to the glass. Was he looking for a connection? For his brother to mirror him?

Sam balled his fist, punched the window, scurrying fast on his belly, and grabbed Jake's face, a vice grip. Jake gripped Sam's arm and pulled his head through the window. Broken glass from the punched hole sliced Jake's cheek. He fought back, driving Sam's arm into jagged glass, slashing his arm. Blood poured from the gashes. He tore at Sam's fingers, ripping free. Jake fell backward into the water, and Sam rolled away.

Childhood, the muck that runs beneath everything. What was there for us as kids is still in us, trying to get at us.

Astrid ran to Jake. She knelt next to him in the water, the

blood spiraling pink around her. Was that what was happening? The two of them, finding each other again?

Outside the window, the gate latch popped open again. This time, it was dead children. They poured in. They scaled the fence. They started pounding on the back door.

"How many murders did you imagine as a kid?" Jake said.

"You have to forgive them!" Astrid was panicked.

"How would that help?"

"You killed me off, and what did I ever even do to you?"

"You didn't do anything," I said. "Except you said nothing. Sometimes you laughed along." I remembered it clearly now— Mrs. Armstrong's class. I hadn't bathed. I smelled foul . . .

One of the far basement windows shattered. A kid had kicked it in. The dog was loose, barking wildly.

"It wasn't Astrid's fault or the kids'," Jake said. "The adults in your life, the teachers. They should've protected you."

"Where were they?" Astrid said, quick to divert blame. But then she froze. "My father was your doctor."

The dead kids had breached the back door and now threw themselves against the interior door to the basement.

Beneath the racket, though, there was a cry, urgent and high-pitched. Mewling.

"A kitten." Jake looked around, desperate.

The dead kids broke more basement windows. Glass showered down and dropped into the water like pebbles.

Jake followed the mewling to an underground sump pump covered by a circular lid. He found the lip of the lid, opened it, and reached in. He pulled up a burlap sack and peeled it back. There was a wet kitten. "How could it meow underwater?" he whispered. "How could it be alive?"

The basement door burst open, and the kids started down the stairs. Some fell. Their limbs popped off; their heads, too, tumbling down, then bobbing in the pooled water. Braids floated. As they devolved into drawings, others climbed over the dead and disintegrating bodies and headed toward us. Astrid screamed. And, still holding the kitten, Jake found a bent shovel, a weapon.

But I saw it all in my mind, suddenly clear. "It's okay," I said.

And the undead children stopped.

"They're not here for us," I said.

These were *my* drawings. My childhood imagination was smart. I walked to my father's recliner and pulled the lever. The recliner popped forward, jolting him to his feet. Like he'd been shocked to life, he coughed up food, heaving. He threw back his head, making choking noises, then put both hands on his chest, one over the other, like an actor about to profess his love or guilt. His eyes skittered around the basement, stunned to find himself alive and yet stuck here, still.

I stood before him. He wasn't surprised to see me. "It was easy to imagine killing you," I said. "I think you always wanted to die."

He accepted this, but his expression was full of sorrow.

The children ran at him then. They dug their fingers into his fleshy skin. They bit him. They growled and screamed and let out strange wailing sounds—each had their own grief and terror.

Astrid pressed her back against the basement wall. Jake was frozen, kitten in one hand, shovel in the other. He was also slowly realizing he wouldn't have to beat any more kids to death.

As the children tore into my father's body, my old man grew blurry. Some of his fingers turned into thick, black lines. His torso became a blue blob, a bubbled clot of crayon. His arms and legs were sticklike.

His head was too wide, part flesh, part drawing. He had no neck. His hair was reduced to a few curly swirls. As the children dragged him to his knees, his eyes were dots, but his nose was still fleshy. The children shoved his head under the water. Half of his face was just lines that fell away easily, leaving only one fleshy, raised cheek. Bubbles—oddly shaped and hand-drawn—rose up and popped.

And then there were no more bubbles.

His oversized head lolled to the side.

The children sat back in the water. They looked at each other and smiled, tired but proud.

I waded to my father, knelt next to his body. I patted down the curlicue hairs I'd once drawn on the top of his slick, wet head.

Cupping the kitten to his chest, Jake dropped the shovel and looked at Astrid. She seemed pale and helpless. I knew that everything had changed. I was in someone else's love story, which was also maybe someone else's horror story. I couldn't tell the difference between horror and love in this moment; maybe I never could.

I walked over to Jake. I wasn't sure what I'd say or do.

But when I got to him, I just wanted to hold the kitten, to touch something alive, to hold it to my own chest where it might purr, like an abnormal heart.

When I tugged on his hand, he shook his head. "No."

But he relented, opening his hand to show me the kitten, soft and wet and dead.

And then there was darkness, humming, and the smell of the damp ash.

PORTALS

One summer, we started seeing portals everywhere. We had no idea how or why. Like Derek Thompkins was out hunting, alone, not far from where his father died of a heart attack, three years back. He found a row of perforations.

"What do you mean, *perforations?*" his wife asked him later that night when he was drunk.

"Like it was torn."

"Like *what* was torn?"

"This," he said. "Fucking *this!*" He waved his arm around, indicating *everything.*

The holes were the size of a fist punched into drywall. There were five of them, in a row, lit up by bright white light. "This is going to sound like some hippie shit," he said. "But maybe the universe is fucking porous."

A week later, he was still messed up. He told a few people after getting ripped at a Lions Club meeting, and one of the other members mentioned that his wife, a social worker, had paid a visit to the Erskins' place. Nessa, the youngest Erskin, a second-grader, told the social worker that she was reaching into the sofa cushion for spare change and her hand was met with cold wind.

"I thought it was going to rip my hand off," Nessa said.

"Is that what these marks are?" the social worker asked. "The wind?"

Nessa nodded. Her hand was red and chapped. The social worker made a note of it.

Then two teenagers planned to overdose at the public pool, which had been drained for the off-season, but when they got there, they heard strange music coming from one of the filters, the kind with the flappy door. They heard it at the same time, but they weren't hearing the same thing. It's like the music seeped out and hit the tuning fork in their brains differently. It was the best music they'd ever heard. They didn't even get high. They just laid on the leafy, dry floor of the pool and looked up at the night sky.

One night not far from the public pool, the tire swing in the Dabrowskis' yard swayed in the breeze. Everything around it was normal—white colonial, blue minivan, crepe myrtle no longer in bloom. But in the middle of the tire swing, there was night sky, wild with stars. Like a swarm of fireflies had collected in that one spot, filling it with bright, flickering light.

Teddy Foundry was on the cross-country team, out for a night run, wearing his gold-and-green windbreaker. When he saw it, he stopped running.

Mrs. Chin was walking her sheltie. She stopped, too.

Teddy took a picture of it and sent it to friends, who thought it was photoshopped.

He stood there for a while with Mrs. Chin. The sheltie barked at the tire swing full of stars.

"It's weird, right?" he said.

"I don't know if it's good or bad," she said.

"Or both," he said.

She tugged on the dog's leash. "Or neither."

"Should we tell the Dabrowskis?" he asked.

"Not my yard, not my business," Mrs. Chin said.

They lingered and then said good night. Teddy started running again, uphill. Mrs. Chin's sheltie wouldn't leave the spot, so she finally picked the dog up and went home.

She told her husband about the tire swing with stars while they were eating late-night ice cream. He had dementia but seemed to understand. He smiled at her and nodded, and then he reached across the table and held her hand, something he hadn't done in a very long time.

• • •

Maybe I should mention that this wasn't just a rumor. I saw it with my own eyes. I was there, walking on the common across the street from the Dabrowskis'. I saw Teddy and Mrs. Chin and her sheltie and the portal. I was on my way home from Aiden Faber's house.

I wasn't surprised by the portal at all. I'd been seeing them since Colette Hadley died in a car accident with her grandmother.

I might have thought, *Huh, a tire swing*. That was new.

Or maybe, *Huh, they see it, too*.

But that was it. I kept on walking.

• • •

This is what a lot of us have come to believe: Grief can rip holes in the universe.

And we had no shortage of it.

There was an outbreak of some kind of bacteria in bird-feeders, and we found dead birds all over the place. Some said it was an omen.

Shortly after that, three kids were shot on the playground in a random drive-by; one of them died.

Then Ed Bridges drowned his college-aged son and played it off as a water-skiing accident to collect insurance money; he killed himself before he was caught.

Kelly Robesin, a cadet who earned top honors from the military academy, died in active duty, a roadside bombing in a place most of us couldn't point to on a map.

Two homeless people overdosed in a tent in the nature preserve.

And then there was the plant. It had closed two decades earlier, but we found out it was leaching poisons of some sort into our water, especially when there were floods, and there were a lot of floods.

Except during droughts, in which case there were fires. Two neighborhoods got scorched because of fireworks that summer.

There was so much to mourn that the potlucks blurred together.

All of this seemed to weigh on people. Their coping mechanisms had broken down. All the various addictions—affairs, drinking, shouting matches in the Wawa—skyrocketed. Mean girls were meaner. Bullies bullied harder. We were messy and violent and haggard.

In fact, we seemed to burn through all of our coping

mechanisms and come to the other side of something. What? Defeat or resignation? Exhaustion?

We were sad mother-effers. But that doesn't fully explain it. What town in America isn't kind of sad as fuck?

Some people put it this way: Maybe conditions were ripe?

Listen, all we knew was this: There were portals. And lots of them.

...

I can say this now because things have changed since all of this. But here's my truth: The night of the tire-swing portal, I'd been making out with Aiden in his pool house, which smelled like chlorine and mildew and plastic pool toys. I was making out with him because I wanted to prove that I liked boys—and only boys.

But it wasn't true. I liked girls, and I'd actually been in love with one—Colette. We weren't girlfriends or anything. In fact, she didn't know I was infatuated with her. And even if we were girlfriends, we would have hidden it. My dad called the man who lived two doors down *a fucking queer*, and my mother thought all women with short hair *looked like dykes*. "Why would a woman spike her hair like that?" (Overall, I keep things cordial with my parents, play by the rules, biding my time to get out of here. I see them as my financiers, important clients.)

And Colette's family went to church, where I assume shit got said explicitly.

So, all in all, the level of flipping out was hard to gauge. But still, I was trying to gear up to ask her to junior prom that spring. It wasn't going to be easy. Colette and I weren't even in the same friend group. Then she died, and I didn't feel like I could be publicly sad. I had to keep it in, stuffed down, a tight, awful knot of sadness.

The portals, though.

One night, my eye was drawn to leaves on the oak that sits at the edge of the neighbor's yard. Between some of the leaves, there wasn't dark sky. There was strange light. I wasn't sure what they were at the time. I felt like they wanted to tell me something. My grandmother had an old toy in the game closet called Lite-Brite, little colored bulbs you could move around. It was like that, but it spelled nothing.

Slowly, the lights faded and blinked out like kids giving up on a game of flashlight tag, one by one. Out. Out. Out.

• • •

Aiden was the one who told me the rumor that Derek and his brother Kevin went out into the woods to find what he called "the rips in the universe."

Aiden and I were lying on the musty chaise lounge cushions on the tile floor, away from the windows with the lights out so his parents would think we were at a study session run by the Physics Club. I wasn't even a member of the Physics Club. We were a little undressed—shirts off, my pink padded bra on, pants unzipped but not off. We'd stopped because we'd taken the action as far as either of us could, like that, in the pool house. I was relieved that we stopped. I felt strange in my body back then. Like I was stiffened up with sadness and shame and guilt. The real me existed, but just as some teeny, tiny presence, hidden away.

Aiden had heard the story about Derek and Kevin because Kevin's middle son was on the JV lacrosse team with Aiden. The two brothers got drunk, even more drunk than usual, which is saying something. They headed out into the woods where Derek had seen the perforations and first got the notion that the universe was *fucking porous.*

"Do you think the universe is fucking porous?" I asked Aiden.

"Of course," he said. "But it's about black holes and alternate parallel universes, not a drunk hunter in the woods." Aiden was easy pickings. Not so good looking that anyone was lining up, but good looking enough. And rich, which meant he wore the right clothes and cologne.

"What did they find?"

"Nothing at first. Derek was so wasted, he couldn't find the spot. But then Kevin was like, 'Is this it?' And there were five holes."

"Holes. In the universe. Because it's fucking porous, though, right?"

Aiden looked at me. "Have you seen one?"

I ignored the question. "Did they walk around the holes?" I'd never done this.

"They did. And the holes could be seen, silvery weird light, all the way around."

"A 3D hole?"

"I don't know how many dimensions."

"What happened?" I asked.

"Derek reached into the biggest hole. They were jagged, you know."

"I did not know. Go on. What did he find?"

"He felt what he thought was an animal. He felt fur. But it wasn't fur."

"What was it?"

"A beard. It was his father's beard. He was touching his father's face."

"What?"

"Exactly." Aiden sat up and leaned against the wall, skinny and shirtless, still clear of the windows. "He put his hand in the second one and it was his father's face. But clean shaven."

"Was his father alive in there? Or were these dead faces?"

"Alive. Very alive. Warm, fleshy."

"Did he keep doing it?" I grabbed my shirt and pulled it on over my head.

"He reached into every hole and in each one his father was younger and younger. Until it was just a little boy's face and then, the last one, it was a baby's face."

"Damn."

"And he could feel the baby's cheeks and fluffy hair. And he said he felt the heartbeat on the top of the baby's head, that soft spot?"

"What?"

"Babies' heads have soft spots." Derek put his shirt back on, too, a salmon-colored polo.

"I don't babysit." *What do I know about babies?*

"Derek actually felt the baby's mouth, like the ridge where the teeth will come in. And there were two little buds. And then he was finished. He kind of fell, crying hard. His brother caught him and hugged him."

"Do you want to see a portal?" I asked Aiden.

"I don't know, but it seems personal. Like that was what he needed, and it was there. I don't need anything."

"Wait." I zipped up my cords. "You don't need anything?"

"Not like that," he said. "Do you?"

...

Were the portals I saw personal? Had I called them into existence? Maybe if I reached in, I could touch Colette's face, her alive face, her soft hair. I could lightly brush her lashes, outline her eyebrows, touch her lips.

What if someone found out that my personal portal was an opening to Colette? How would I explain that?

I decided, on the walk home from Aiden's, that next time I was alone and saw a portal, I would reach in.

I stopped at the Dabrowskis' front yard. The tire swing was gone. Someone had sawed through the rope that had attached it to the tree.

I imagined the Dabrowskis staring at a tire swing propped up on their living room sofa. The two of them peering into the cosmos like astronauts gazing out the portal of a spaceship. But it's not a spaceship at all. The cosmos is in their house.

I walked across their lawn, reached up, and touched the frayed rope left behind. But as I backed away, I tripped the floodlight. Their lawn lit up like a stage. I didn't run. I just stood there and stared at the Dabrowskis' windows.

I wondered if they were hiding something, too.

...

The kids who had wanted to kill themselves in the deep end of the empty public pool started making money. They made their friends pay for a "guided tour," like it could be dangerous and they'd need a spirit guide.

Sometimes the pool filter portals offered music; sometimes they didn't. So people either thought it was legit or complete bullshit.

Soon enough, though, you could sign up online and prepay through Venmo. They were banking almost three hundred dollars a night until the cops shut them down, taping off the area and putting up more *No Trespassing* signs.

But one of the cops, Officer Uppadhya, volunteered to keep an eye on it for a while; it was on his beat anyway. He got out of his cruiser and walked around the pool. Then, rumor had it, he was feeling light and buzzy in his chest; he walked down the ladder to the deep end. He stood there for a while, closed his eyes, and listened.

What he heard started out as a song constructed of notes that formed a familiar pattern. The pattern was his mother's voice. The pattern was her voice pleading. Her voice muffled by a thin wall. Her voice pleading for his father to stop, that she would do better, that she would make it right. The thing that she needed to do better or to make right didn't matter. It wasn't real. What was real was the pattern of pleading. She was pleading for her life. And then the soft beat of his breathing as a little boy, the soft breath, feathery and quick, broken by a jagged sob. He couldn't save his mother from his father. And that is why he wanted to save people. And that was why he was standing in an empty swimming pool, listening for a song that might change how he feels in the world, never doing enough, never saving those who need to be saved.

But then the song ended, and Officer Uppadhya was alone, his breath feathery and quick, broken by a jagged sob.

Once the jagged sob was released, he felt different. He looked at the pool filters. He heard just the night noises of the neighborhood, a distant car drag-racing out on a straightaway. He looked up at the night sky. For a second, he felt so light he thought he might lift from the ground.

...

Not all of the portals were good.

Nessa Erskin called 911 on a Saturday afternoon. Her mother had gone on a tear, screaming and shouting that Nessa was a moron and an idiot and fucked-up piece of shit. And Mrs. Erskin beat her pretty hard, too.

That wasn't why she called. She was used to that.

She called because when her mother wore herself out, she sat down on the sofa. Then her mother heard a strange noise coming from the cushions. She stood up and yanked the cushions off, exposing a rip in the fabric, a tear that had nothing behind it. Not lightness, not darkness, not stars, not anything.

"What do you mean?" the social worker asked Nessa later.

"I mean it was nothing. It wasn't there."

And then her mom reached for it and something within that nothingness grabbed her arm and yanked her forward. She fought. She cried out to Nessa for help. But Nessa was frozen in place, too stunned to move.

"It took her then in chunks," Nessa said.

"Chunks?"

"Like it was pulling her in then eating her. Chunk! Then pulling her in some more and eating her. Chunk!"

And then she was gone.

"Listen to me, Nessa," the social worker said. "Tell me, as best you can, where's your mother?"

"She's in the nothing," Nessa said. "It ate her."

•••

Everybody heard that story.

Everybody.

But I'd already decided to reach into a portal. I was willing to risk it if I could touch Colette's face.

There was only one problem. I didn't see any portals anymore. This is the thing with portals. They're tricky mother-effers. Just when you think you know what they are or how they work, they change. I didn't see portals in the trees or chain-link fences or tire swings or anything. I looked everywhere.

I woke up sometimes in the middle of the night, sweating, heart pounding, feeling a portal existed in my room. Like a wound. Like a wound that could see me, that knew me.

But there was nothing. No stars, no wind, no music, no bright light . . .

I texted Aiden one night.

> Do you know where Derek
> Thompkins' portals are?

I thought that if portals were specific, I'd want to find the one that let you touch faces, not the one that ate you.

Aiden was still awake. He texted back immediately.

I can find out.

...

Allen Dabrowski turned on the headlights of his car at the end of the driveway to light up half of the backyard. In a misty rain, he dug a hole. It wasn't far from where the Dabrowskis had buried their dog, Buzzy.

The backyard neighbor, Amanda Douglas, watched him digging furiously, taking breaks to either cough or cry, she wasn't sure, but he would double over sometimes. Twice, he had to take a knee like someone was injured in a football game. Amanda, hugely pregnant and having trouble sleeping, was waiting to see if he'd killed someone and was digging a grave. This is what our town did nowadays. She was thinking, *Buzzy's already dead, so who could it be?*

Eventually, Allen went back into his house. When he reappeared, he was rolling the tire from the tire swing. From her window, Amanda could see the bright pinhole stars spinning within it. He rolled it to the grave and let it fall in.

Amanda looked at the Dabrowskis' house and she saw Mrs. Dabrowski watching her husband through the plateglass window in their dining room. And then Amanda remembered hearing, a long time ago, that the Dabrowskis had a son, a six-year-old at the time. Wasn't the children's room in the Catholic church called the Liam *Dabrowski* Room? Why would the Dabrowskis, who were in their late forties and seemingly without kids, have a tire swing except if they once had a kid to play on it?

Allen stood there, staring down into the hole he'd dug. He stood there for a long time, maybe gazing into the universe sitting in the dirt. And then he picked up his shovel and started burying it.

•••

Aiden and I met at the swing set on the edge of the woods where Derek found five holes in the universe.

We didn't talk much. There wasn't much either of us was willing to say. I was there for my own reasons and assumed that Aiden was there because he liked me and wanted to show off that he'd found the holes. It was manly to be able to find something in the woods.

He used his phone's compass until we lost cellular connection. It was cold and damp and there were some birds calls, even though it was the dead of night. "Why are they chirping like that?" I said, almost to myself.

"Their nocturnal rhythms are fucked up by light pollution," Aiden said.

"How do you know this stuff?"

He was walking ahead of me on the path. "I don't know. I just do."

After we'd walked for about a half hour, I said, "Are we close?"

"Kind of."

"Are you going to reach in?" I asked.

"No."

"Why not?" I said.

He turned around and kept walking backward. "Why would I?"

"Curious?"

He shook his head, and it was like he was confessing to something sad, a loss. What had he lost? We'd all lost so much; there was no way around it.

The trail turned a few times, a steep switchback. But then he stopped, and I did, too. "There," Aiden said. He leaned to one side and pointed.

I saw them. Five bright, jagged holes. Even though my legs were tired, I started running.

"Wait," Aiden said, catching up.

Together, we walked into the brush and circled around the holes.

"Do you think you'll touch someone," he said, "on the other side?"

I reached into the smallest hole. Scared, tentative. I imagined my fingers brushing Colette's cheek. I imagined it so hard that I was stunned to find nothing but air. Not the cold wind that had whipped Nessa.

Just air.

"What is it?" Aiden asked.

My arm felt different, though. Like it had some other sense—not taste or sight or smell or anything. Something else. "My arm feels light and tingly, like it's gathering information."

"What information?"

I pulled my arm back into my chest. "Dogs smell so much more than we do," I said. "They can go on a walk and smell like the equivalent of a whole novel."

"Octopuses can smell with their tentacles."

I walked to the next hole and fit my hand in through the tear. This time, I felt something. A bit of hair? I flattened my hand against an ear, a jaw, rough with light stubble. Not Colette at all.

Aiden shouted out behind me. "Jesus! What was that?" He was swatting at the air around him like he'd been attacked.

I pulled my hand out. "What is it?"

He looked at me, transfixed. "Do it again. Reach in!"

I put my hand into the next hole. And there, again, was a ruffle of hair, a warm cheek, a chin. I looked over my shoulder at Aiden.

"It's me," he whispered.

"But you're not dead," I said.

His eyes filled with tears. "I am dead."

"What do you mean?" I moved to the largest hole, the last in the row. I put my hands on either side of it, which might be hard to imagine, but you could say I was holding onto the edges of our world. I wanted to break the hole open. I pulled as hard as I could. It didn't give. I then took the sharp edge of my forearm, up near the elbow, and I plowed into the edge of the hole.

A piece broke off. A piece of our world. A chunk of here.

I did it again. Another chunk fell away, into the hole itself. "Help me," I said.

Aiden got to his feet. He was tall enough to plow his shoulder into the edge. A large section fell away. We took turns punching the edges and kicking until the hole was big enough to step into, but the two of us stood in front of it, blasted by bright light.

"Why do you think you're dead?" I asked.

"Same reason you're dead, right?"

"You don't know anything about me."

"Why are you here? Who are you looking for?" He turned

angry. "Why were you with me in the pool house? Why did you choose me?"

Too many questions. I didn't know what to take aim at.

"I've been here before," he said. "Go in and see."

"See what?"

"Us."

I didn't understand. I wanted to touch Colette's face. Stepping into this hole in the universe, maybe I could see her again. If I could, I'd hug her fiercely. Maybe we could erase what happened and be together.

I held onto the edges of the hole and tilted toward the light, forehead first. Aiden, the one I knew in this world, was behind me. But what I couldn't really see was a mirrored image—my forehead touching Aiden Faber's forehead, a *different* Aiden Faber, some version of him that existed on the other side. And when I stepped into the hole, I stepped into his body.

And it was a body made of fear. A hive of anxiety in his chest. Panic thrumming in his ribs. A strange restlessness in his arms and legs. Distress signals pulsing everywhere. A body on fire.

I knew it was Aiden's body because I was him. I had access to his thoughts and memories, a flood. His mother dabbing aloe on a burn on his hand. A strange, narrow carpeted hallway in his grandparents' house. A dead gerbil, his hand pressed to the glass cage. Popping tape loose from a birthday gift. Another boy, Ryan Doyle, shoving him around in the bus aisle. There were rushes of emotion with each memory. Some made no sense. The birthday gift gave way to anxiety, not excitement. The dead gerbil was a relief for some reason.

And Ryan.

His hands on Aiden's chest, the intimacy of the headlock.

I was there now, with Aiden in the pool house. He hates it. His muscles seize up so much he's shaking. He wants it to end. He's pushing through it all.

He's acting like a boy in a pool house kissing a girl.

I turn around, but there's only light in every direction. Blinding light. I remember how, in the ocean, I once got hit hard by a wave and I couldn't tell if I was swimming up to the surface or down. I hold out my hands, which are Aiden's hands. I take a few steps in every direction. Is this a place that has direction? That follows the rules of time and space?

Aiden is dead inside—like me. He has a secret—like mine. He knows my secret because he was already here. He did this. He knows what it's like to be in my body, my head, too. He knows about Colette.

I spin and spin, hands outstretched and flailing.

But as I move, I move into other bodies.

I am . . . I'm small. I'm sitting in the back of a police cruiser with a plastic Dollar Tree bag holding my pajamas, a change of clothes, and my toothbrush. I'm Nessa. And I'm thinking that I killed my mother because I wished something would eat her and something did. I grip my small, sticky hands together, and I smile.

But I'm also driving the cruiser because I'm a cop. A cop who is saying, "It's going to be okay. We're going to find a good place for you." And I'm thankful because maybe I'm saving someone, and maybe this is how I can save myself.

Before I can sense much more, I'm in the shower, water beating down on my head. My large hands pressed against tile. I'm a grown man. Derek. Embarrassed by how much I miss my father. Embarrassed but still loving him so much. I should be over it but I can't move on.

And then I divide somehow and I'm two people at the same time. I am both of the Dabrowskis, in bed, staring up at the ceiling wondering what the fuck has happened to us. We are wide awake. I am the one who reaches out and takes the other's hand. And I am the one who accepts the hand and holds it tight.

And I'm Amanda Douglas. Pregnant in the tub. Dark except for the lip of the tub lined with votive candles. I'm watching my belly—and feeling the tight writhing as the baby turns inside me. My knees and belly are above the waterline, glistening with soapy water.

And then, in the flickering lowlight—a glow. Rising up from the water near my feet. Coming from . . . inside of me? No. It has to be coming from the drain. I'm Catholic in this body, and I can't help it: I'm thinking of Mary giving birth in the manger. Was Jesus born with a halo . . . of light? Just before he was born, as he was crowning—*crowning*, I think of it in a new way, a bright crown—did Joseph say to Mary, "I see light!"?

The impossibility of that. I stand up, wet and shining. And the glow is gone.

I am a teenager who wanted to kill myself but who is now in my basement with a keyboard, trying to recreate music I once heard pouring out of a filter in an empty pool.

And I am Teddy Foundry, running at night because I'm afraid to go to sleep, afraid of sleeplessness, afraid of waking up. I'm running at night alone because when I'm running, I know I'm in my body. Otherwise, I'm not sure who I am.

And I am walking my little dog who doesn't want to be walked at all. But I need to be out in the open air, away from my husband who is slowly being erased. And I am an old man dreaming of the past that is the present. I'm waiting for my wife to come home because I know her face. When I know her face, I know that I'm still here. Her face says: *Home, you are home.*

I fly through body after body and then someone grips my forearm and I reach out with both hands and grab hold.

Aiden pulls me out, hard, and we stumble back into the brush, the woods—the songs of the disoriented birds loud in the trees.

•••

It's not just grief that rips holes in the universe. What you're afraid of, what you want . . . Secrets and shame can do it, too. Why did this happen to us? I don't know. In the end, we got used to it.

People pass by open portals.

People keep an eye out and listen for them.

People reach into them.

People break them wide open, disappear into them, and stay gone or come back to us.

People are afraid of them.

People bury them.

People close their eyes and hope for them.

And, I mean, you probably have heard stories about portals popping up in other places. Japan and Canada. Ethiopia has lots, but right next door, Kenya doesn't have any. One in Siberia. And then Liverpool just got riddled with them. The people who live where there are no portals, they long for portals; they say they're suffering some kind of trauma that they can't understand. So much lacking. There are new fields of study, researchers trying to figuring it all out, religious people trying to find a way to make it about God, and the two kids selling access to the pool filter portals weren't the only ones trying to monetize. In some ways, the portals are just a new tool in human hands, so of course there was a guy who shoved his girlfriend's ex into a portal that ripped both men away, never seen again. But right next door, there will be a barbecue in someone's backyard with a portal yawning open nearby, and it just leads to their dead Labrador retriever, Tummy Tumnus. They can still pet him on the other side, where he's alive.

Me and Aiden? We'd gotten what we needed. It was enough. We knew each other's secret and we kept that secret for each other, the way secrets should be kept, until you're ready to share them. And we didn't think about portals as much as we did an actual way to get out and make our way in the world.

...

Maybe there's one more story to tell.

During the winter of our senior year, Aiden and I helped each other come out. But we went to junior prom together first, still holding tight to what we knew. We got drunk at Aiden's after-party. Some kids started to jump into Aiden's backyard swimming pool.

"Let's get out of here," he said to me.

"You want to leave your own party?"

"Absolutely."

We pulled bikes from his garage and rode around the neighborhood. I was wearing the black bow tie from Aiden's tux and my puffy dress made of blue tulle. I knotted it so it wouldn't get caught in the gears. Aiden was barefoot, and he'd taken off his tuxedo jacket and unbuttoned the collar of his starchy white shirt. It felt great to be drunk and riding fast like little kids, breathless and windblown.

But then we got to the Dabrowskis' house. We both stopped and stared at the place where the tire swing once was.

I looked at Aiden. "You know what we should do?"

He did.

We went back to his place and got shovels out of his shed. We walked with the shovels over our shoulders, hopped the fence into the Dabrowskis' backyard. I waited for the floodlights. But the backyard had none.

It wasn't hard to find the spot where Allen had buried the tire swing. It was a swatch of dirt in a very green lawn.

Aiden and I dug in the dark. He sweated through his white shirt and I sweated through the taut satin of my dress. And then my shovel hit something—with a rubbery give.

We dug faster and then Aiden got into the shallow pit and brushed the dirt away with his hands.

It was still there. The universe—inky and also dotted with stars.

We sat side by side and stared down into it, talking about where we were going to apply to college and what cities we wanted to live in. After a while, we flopped to our backs and took in the sky above us, too. We talked and talked until we got tired of talking. He put his hands behind his head. I put my head on his chest. And, like that, as we started to fall asleep, we heard the Douglas' baby wake up, its cry floating through an open window.

THE KNOCKOFFS

Dear Mr. Cooper,

My name's Alyssa Heaney. I'm fourteen. I'm the daughter of Meg Heaney. (Do our names ring a bell? Do you know any of us?) My mother skipped bail and we're now in a motel in upstate New York, not far from the Canadian border. By the time you get this letter, we'll be somewhere else.

I'm sure you get a lot of letters from Coopers like me these days, but I'm not asking for you to be my daddy or for you to love me. I do have a favor to ask, but you need to know a little about me first. I get good grades, especially in science. I have two best friends, Misha and Val, and I can't text them or anything. (My mom and I ditched our phones.) I'm afraid of elevators. And I dream about Steinway pianos bobbing on the ocean. Did you know that they float legs up? I want you to know I'm a full human being.

My mom is, too. In fact, she's amazing. Right now, things are rough for her. I'm listening to her cry in the shower. She thinks I can't hear her, but I can. She's not a weird, obsessed groupie. She never went to a shady black-market basement to get some of your DNA like in those undercover exposés. Have you seen the clip that went viral? The guy pulls out trays of choices. "We got Jaylen Browns, Hemsworths, Chalamets."

"Which Hemsworth you got?" that one woman asks.

"We got both big Hemsworths!" the guy says, throwing his hands back and smiling, selling all of you like knockoff handbags. It went viral because people were making fun of them, but also they sensed the desperation—her as some lonely, sad wannabe and him as a salesman, a pusher. People liked that celebrities were being treated like dime bags of skunky pot. People love you types and hate you; they hate that they love you and sometimes love to hate you. Then the cops bust in, and they get arrested. It's awful how people overvalue some lives and undervalue others.

When my mom was growing up, a kid like me wasn't even possible. I mean, doctors knew that one day we'd be able to take a cheek swab and convert skin cells into sperm or eggs. I once wrote a bio report on it: "In Vitro Gametogenesis: How It Works." I didn't tell my teacher that I'm a Knockoff, but she knew.

The problem with my mom's court case—felony possession of stolen goods (fifty percent of me)—is that because she didn't go to the mob-run black market for stolen DNA, she can't offer information to reduce her sentencing. She's got no leverage, as her lawyer puts it. But I heard that celebrities can send letters on someone's behalf. If they forgive the person, it goes a long way in the court system.

I'm sending this to your agent's office. I hope someone gives it to you. Will you write a letter for my mother—Meg Heaney? It would really help! Please!

Sincerely,
Alyssa Heaney

Dear Bradley Cooper,

How are you? I hope you are doing well!

It's Alyssa Heaney again. Meg Heaney's daughter. I sent you a letter about writing to the court system on behalf of my mom. Did you get it?

You should know we don't need your money. My mom inherited my grandparents' house in Hull, which is on the South Shore near Boston. The house is right on the ocean with a seawall out front. After the house got flooded too many times, we put it up on stilts. It's a beautiful little blue house with a Steinway piano right in front of a huge window looking out at the Massachusetts Bay heading to the Atlantic.

Before I came along, my mom lived there alone. She had a good job, working tech support at Rattaway's Electronics. She wore a yellow polo with the store logo on it. On weekends, she drank with her friends at Jo's Nautical Bar. They'd sit on the leather sofas under the WAUKEGAN sign and the painting of an old bartender, midpour, like the Patron Saint of Locals.

She wasn't dreaming of a Bradley Cooper baby. She was dreaming about Ronan Marsh, who broke up with her and moved to Dorchester. And Bobby Hamlin, who bragged about opening his own bar, a fancy place for fat Cohasset bankers. Bobby told her, point-blank, he needed a hot wife to get a place like that going. My mom's not hot but she's really smart and funny and she has this great laugh that makes me laugh even if I don't know what she's laughing about yet. (My mom's laugh would definitely make you laugh.)

There were plenty of guys to hook up with and make a baby, ye olde-fashioned way. But they were all pretty effing bleak. So she was dreaming of having a baby on her own. She was thirty-four. A cousin of hers was raising a baby as a single mom. My mom thought maybe she could do it, too.

Then one afternoon, Aunt Hendry called up. "I got his hair!" She worked as a domestic, rolling a cart through the fanciest hotel in Boston, the Mandarin Oriental. Aunt Hendry was almost jogging down Boylston away from the hotel toward Copley Square. The hairs—your hair—were in a plastic sandwich baggie shoved in the pockets of her puffy coat. Dead of winter. The holidays come and gone. Everything was bleak and damp.

"Whose hair?" my mom asked.

"Cooper," she said. "Bradley Cooper! You should do it." It was absolutely clear what it was. Stories about celeb Knockoffs were starting to pop up in the news. "There are docs who don't ask questions," Aunt Hendry said, and I think of her on some busy corner, just breathing into the cold air. "You gotta. This is a sign."

My mother had just finished a YouTube workout in the living room of the Hull house. So what with Aunt Hendry fast-walking, they were both out of breath, which made it all seem urgent. After my grandparents died, my mom moved to their house with its huge bay window that looked out at the ocean and sky, grays and blues with seabirds wheeling around. There were always airplanes roaring as they cycled in and out of

Logan. She could see Boston, too, shoulder-to-shoulder build-ings off in the distance. "Should I?" Her voice echoed off the window's glass.

"Abso-friggin'-lutely. Who you gonna get knocked up by instead, Vonn Malchester?"

Malchester wanted to knock everybody up. He had three kids with three different women who all hated him. He ran a dog grooming business out of his van, but mostly sold drugs. He got pissed when someone actually wanted him to groom a dog.

What I mean is that some people might choose you over a Hemsworth or a Boston Celtic. But in my case, your competi-tion was a dog groomer/drug dealer.

See? It wasn't like stealing. It was finding. She didn't make a master plan and get in deep with mobster-run black markets. It wasn't even premeditated, really. You showed up—an oppor-tunity she couldn't let slide! And the actual in-vitro process was super cheap; I mean, it used to be expensive as hell and only for really rich people, but she paid in easy monthly installments—like a washer/dryer bought on a store credit card. It's like our society made it so easy that it didn't seem criminal at all. How can having a baby be criminal? A baby? Me? I mean, some people say we've perverted God's natural order, but I'm adorable and funny and smart. How could I be a perversion?

I can't be! But I bet you've heard that some politicians want all of us Knockoffs isolated from society. Like we're going to mess with everything that society holds dear. We have to be con-demned, right? If we don't pay a price, then it'll just encourage the whole thing to keep going. It's supposed to be some kind of "school," but it sounds like juvie to me. So, yeah. But I bet you could help with that, too. Famous people can always help, right?

We have to leave this motel tomorrow morning and try to make it into Canada. There's a frozen river and some woods. It's sketchy. But I wanted you to see how innocent she really is. I hope you can write on her behalf. It would mean a lot to me.

Sincerely,

Alyssa Heaney

Dear Bradley,

It wasn't easy making it over the border. It's cold in Canada in February. I'm lucky because I've got my fleece-lined Red Sox hat and a long fur coat, real fur. (I told you we don't need your money.) We crossed a frozen river with two men driving snowmobiles. (My mom called them drug mules. That day we were their cargo. I always feel like something illegal. I hate the word illegitimate, by the way. Like I'm not a legitimate human being?) I held on tight to this man's ribs, and they were huge ribs. I didn't know people came that big. It was all revved engine and vibrations. The helmet bounced around, too big for my head even with my hat on.

They dropped us off and we headed into a forest, lots of snow. My mom told me guys drafted in the Vietnam War came across this same frozen river and through forests like this. Immigrants, too. "And fugitives," and she shrugged, like, I guess we're fugitives now, too.

We're in an undisclosed location. It's super bleak and smells like cat pee. My mom's trying to figure out what to do next. She tries to make it fun. She taught me all the dance moves from when she was my age, and we made a tent out of sheets and told each other ghost stories with a flashlight held up to our chins. But I can tell she's really scared. We'll be watching TV and I can

196 · JULIANNA BAGGOTT

feel her looking over at me. She's afraid of losing me. I'm afraid
of losing her. Jail and juvie school and being split up forever.

Look, I get why people are against the idea of me—like in
theory. But I'm not a person in theory. I'm a person in reality.

I found out "the source of my paternal DNA" when I was
six. All my relatives already knew, and my mom figured it was
just a matter of time before someone spilled it, like my cousin
did about Santa Claus. And I understood the concept: mommy,
daddy, baby. I got that we were missing somebody. My mom
was tired of telling me: There are all kinds of ways to make a
family. Or We're our own unit. Or Two people can equal a
family. Finally, she sat me down at a McDonald's playground.
"A mommy can pick a daddy. It's called DNA. And your DNA
comes from this person who's really wonderful. He's an actor."
She cued up a few clips on her phone.

You were in a movie, dancing. You were a soldier, a singer,
and a famous composer. You existed across time. You were funny
and smart. You cried and loved people. And every once in a
while, you'd look at the camera—at me!

"Can he come over?" I said.

You couldn't know I existed. The crackdowns had started.
She said, "I probably shouldn't have used his DNA. I could get
in trouble. So it'll have to be our secret."

Over the years, I grew into your movies. I took up tap dancing and singing by watching YouTube tutorials. I'm not good.
I know you're a great dad. I've seen pictures of you with your
daughter. You're silly and strong and you look at her with love.
So much love that I bet you have extra. My mom says that love's
not a pie, it's a fountain that keeps flowing.

I hate being in this shitty place. I miss home. Hull was a

peninsula when I was born but with sea levels rising, it kept eroding, and with each nor'easter, the road connecting it to the mainland would wash out. And now it's an island. That's why we had to put the blue house up on stilts. We saved the piano even though the flooding was real bad. And now it sits up there in that house on stilts above the ocean, empty.

Living in a place that was a peninsula but became an island, you understand that the ocean is a force, and it wins. Sometimes I feel like we're up against the ocean now—it's the legal system, and it's a force, too, and it'll probably win.

My mom says this is what life's like. You have hope even though you know you're going to lose. Winning isn't the point. It's being able to have hope, no matter how much you lose.

But do you know about losing at all? With all the good stuff that's come your way, all those supermodels and big roles, can you imagine losing and losing and losing like regular people?

Please write that letter for my mom—Meg Heaney. You can send it to the Massachusetts Court System.

If you do it, I'll be so thankful. Maybe we could go home and maybe my hope might mean something.

Sincerely,

Alyssa Heaney

Bradley,

You're not going to do it, are you? You're not going to help my mom and me. I'm yours. You know that? Like it or not. I am.

But you know what? You probably think I go around bragging about how I'm a Cooper. I don't tell anyone except other Coopers on the confidential online forums. We probably wouldn't have gotten caught if the in vitro gametogenesis doctor didn't have the FBI bust into his office. I don't care that you're famous. I don't care that you're a brilliant actor or that you can sing and dance. In fact, I think it's sad AF. You were a little boy whose parents wanted you to grow up and study finance and be rich like they were. But you needed to be someone else. You needed to pretend. Why? Why do people need that? Is it because they don't know who they are? Is it because they're trying to escape? If so, then you and I have that in common, too. I don't know who I am, but I know it's dangerous, and I have to escape.

And while I'm at it, you think you're sooooo good-looking. Here's a secret: You never really were. Your face is full of normal pieces. You just learned how to act good-looking. You have good-looking gazes and smiles and gestures. My mother was fooled by this. But I see you, though. You were kind of a zero in high school, weren't you?

You with your shaggy hair and your sharp nose and your crooked jaw. Without a lucky bounce here and there, you're not that different from the guys at Jo's Nautical Bar—my mom's ex-boyfriend, who never did start up a Cohasset bar, or Vonn Malchester, who's in jail on drug charges. I think you know how lucky you got and that it probably rattles you that the only difference between you and guys like them are a few tiny, flimsy, lucky bounces.

Does it haunt you? How it all could have turned out?

Of all the Coopers I've met online, the ones who were named Bradley have it the worst. I met one on a forum. His mother told everyone he was a Cooper—strangers in the grocery store and his teachers and the guys she dated. And he couldn't sing or dance or act, but he did kind of look like you, and that made it worse. Everyone was waiting for him to do something great. Like what? Rip off his shirt and show off his chest and abs? Bradley Bowman was chubby and shy. One time, he wrote me, "With my half and your half, we're kind of one hundred percent. We're whole." And I knew things were bad for him, that he was messed up by it. I mean, we all are, but in his case, it went deep. I don't even know where Bradley Bowman is now.

What you need to know is that you made people fall in love with you. You might not be a guy at Jo's Nautical hitting on my mom all night, hoping she gets drunk enough to go home with you. But isn't that what you did on screen?

My mom and I found my fur coat at a Goodwill. I made it sound like we're rich, but whatever. We found it and rushed to the counter and paid for it and got out quick. It was an opportunity, and we took it, which is exactly like when Aunt Hendry found your hair on the hotel pillow.

If you hadn't spent your life seducing us, over and over again, she wouldn't have done that. And you made money off that seduction. So who's to blame again? Who's the victim?

You need to know that Bradley Bowman liked winters better than summers. He knew how to take a computer apart and put it back together. Can you? You'd have someone do it for you. He liked anime, too, though he was embarrassed to admit it. I like it, too. Anime is always about being an outsider. We're outsiders. We're cut off from half of ourselves. And we're supposed to feel special—we're supposed to be grateful. We're lucky. But it's like that famous half means more than the half that loves us. We are half loved, half abandoned. We got something illegally? But what is it? Hard to say. What are we supposed to do with it? No one knows.

Right now all of us are stolen goods, someone else's property. So they'll round us all up and lock our parents up and send us away to Knockoff juvie schools and teach us a lesson? Maybe they just want us to know that we're not better than anybody else. They want us to know that we're worse. They don't want us to think we're worth anything at all. But what's the value of what my mother stole? Half of what makes me me? You can't steal half of who you are—it's you. You own it.

So go fuck yourself for not acknowledging that Bradley Bowman and I exist.

I deserve to keep the parent who knows me and loves me.

Alyssa Heaney

Dear Bradley,

I'm sorry I said all of that. It's bad here. We can't do anything or go anywhere or start our lives again. Our family back home sends us money. But we skipped out on bail, and the people who place your bail don't like that. They start hunting you down. It's cold here and the heat is kept really low. I wear my fur coat all the time like I'm becoming an animal. My mom and I sleep together to keep warm under two layers of wool blanket—the awful, itchy kind. Not having a phone is like not having hands—I don't know how else to explain it. We watch TV but we don't have many stations.

I got upset and I took it out on you. I am sorry.

I've been trying to think about it from your perspective. I can see how it might be weird and scary and awful to have people in the world with your DNA. Like lost parts of yourself spinning around far off and out of reach. I mean, you had discarded those hairs anyway, but still, I get it. You can't bring us all into your life. It would be overwhelming. All of us with all of our needs. It'd be like the ocean coming at you. A tsunami of love-me love-me.

There are so many of us. Not just Coopers. Pop stars, movie stars, celebs, and pro athletes—Lebrons, Currys, Mahomeses, Bettses. There was that group that tried to ban Lebrons from playing high-school basketball because their DNA was ill-gotten. And the other group that forced them to play even when they didn't want to. Hateful psychos. And there are those D-list celebs who tried to sell their DNA on the black market, and then some people bought fake DNA for some celeb and ended up with kids who don't look like anybody famous at all. And people who put a bounty on the DNA of anyone who grew up with two famous parents, because then you get the twofer of genes on both sides, in one. It's a mess.

My mom says to me over and over, "They want me to say I regret it, but how can I regret it? That would mean I regret having you. I'll never say that. It's not true. And I won't."

I don't know how to undo this. I don't know how to make it right. But taking my only parent away from me is wrong. I know that much.

If you can write that letter for Meg Heaney, I hope you do. This is my last time writing you about it. Promise.

Alyssa

Mr. Cooper,

I lied. Our blue house flooded over and over, but we never put it up on stilts. We didn't have the money. But even if we had put it up, the ocean would have pounded the seawall and rushed over it. Soon we'd have a house on stilts in the ocean. We had to let it go. I wasn't lying about the Steinway, but the damp ocean air and the flooding had done it in. The hammer felts were wet, and it was gummed up with verdigris, which happens to Steinways built during a certain time—I know a lot about Steinways because my grandmother loved that piano. Around the time that Hull became an island permanently, we moved, abandoning the house. But it felt more like it abandoned us.

It doesn't matter if you write that letter or not.

I think of the piano a lot—when I'm awake and when I'm dreaming. How the ocean came up over the seawall, battered the house, smashed through the bay window, pouring in. The waves rushing in. How the ocean must have lifted the piano a few times—maybe even set it spinning in the living room. That window was big enough for the piano to fit through. The way I see it, the house was getting beaten down. But before it buck-led under, the piano was let loose. I can imagine it bumping against the seawall and then cresting it.

I imagine it floating out there in the ocean, rolling over, legs up, all alone.

In my dreams, I'm riding the piano, gripping onto one of its legs like I can almost steer it, but then I realize I'm holding on for dear life.

My mom can't see a way for us to start over in Canada. We can't keep hiding forever. She decided to turn herself in. She got dressed this morning. She pulled her hair back in a clip and she said, "It's over. It's done. You need a life."

Alyssa

Dear Mr. Cooper or Bradley or whatever,

I really want to write "Dear Dad." (I always did, each time

I started to write you a letter, even though that was crazy because you're a stranger.) I won't. This is my last letter. Promise. My mom, Meg Heaney, is in custody. We showed up in a police station in a small Canadian town and were extradited. Once I crossed the border back into America, my mom hugged me and wouldn't let go. She patted my hair and whispered my name and kept saying that I was strong. "Remember how tough you are."

And the cops were there saying, "Ma'am, ma'am. You've said your goodbyes, okay? Back away."

When she let go, I felt like I might spin off, that there was nothing to hold me to this world anymore, and then they put me in a cruiser. We drove for a long while, and now I'm parked outside of a building within a compound, surrounded by trees. We're waiting for the head of the school to greet me. But first, there's paperwork and conversations with cops.

I want you to know that I've kinda loved writing you these letters. I loved needing something from you and having a reason to tell you all this stuff. My mom said "You need a life." Sometimes I can't help but think I'm part real and part dream. I exist for such a weird bunch of random reasons. But then I think—Isn't that true of everybody? Why are any of us here? And what is here? And why are you Bradley Cooper? And why am I Alyssa Heaney?

When I say I feel like I'm being dragged out into the middle of the ocean alone on an upturned piano and I'm holding on tight, don't you feel that way sometimes, too?

As I write this, a few kids have started to look at me through windows on the first floor. Another set has gathered at a third-floor window. A group of girls in matching tracksuits run across the field and into a side door. Except for one girl. She stands there and stares at me, her hair frizzing out of the ponytail, her foggy breath rising in gusts into the air above her head.

This is where I'll live now, I guess.

There's one more thing I lied to you about. I said this wasn't about me wanting you to love me. It was. You knew that. Or your agent knew that and never sent on the letters. Or these letters got thrown out, still sealed.

But I can imagine you reading these words, taking them in, feeling whatever it is that you feel.

I don't know who you are. No one can really know another person, I don't think. Not really.

I don't know who I am, but weirdly, after all of this, I feel like I know who I am a little better than before.

I'm not writing you again.

But I do love you.

And whether you love me or not, we're all worthy of love. We are. All the Knockoffs and all of our parents and all of you famous people, too. And I want you to know that we're all worthy of love, but even if you don't, I do. And that's what matters.

Love,

Me, Alyssa

THE VIRTUALS

Klaus Han changed my life. I hate to say it because part of me deeply, *deeply* despises Klaus. Almost everyone who knows Klaus despises him but also loves him. He's one of those people experienced in extremes.

I first met Klaus at Momofuku Ko in the East Village, where he held all of his interviews. It was an act of luscious brutality—a ten-course meal that takes three full hours. The food is so sumptuous that, at a certain point, delirium can set in, a high you just have to sweat through. The meal was—like Klaus himself—a lot. Too much.

I'd been leading the story and design departments at a videogame startup that lost funding, and I was in free fall. And working for Klaus promised a huge pay bump and upward mobility. So I shoved myself into a pencil skirt and blazer and carried a briefcase, like an idiot.

Klaus was a beefy man, with a waxy mustache that reminded me of a well-groomed circus bear. He was dressed in expensive sportswear, very snug joggers that I'd come to find out were hand-tailored. He shook my hand. "I ordered the whole duck." His eyes gleamed. "It's been aged two weeks, salt-rubbed, and soaked in maltose and soy."

"Great, thanks!" I said, not sure of the right response. We took our seats.

"So, you're in story and design devel. Anya Something?" He knew exactly who I was.

"Annie Frimm."

"You should consider going with Anya." He lifted a finger. "Keep an open mind about it!" Then he cut to the chase. "What do you think of when you hear the words *VR gaming therapy*?"

I was stuck on trying to pass myself off as an Anya; it felt like a reach. "Honestly, I didn't even know that it was a thing until prepping for our meeting."

"And why should you? You were raised . . . middle-class. Too good for Chuck E. Cheese but not good enough for study abroad in Prague. Single mother?" He read something in my reaction. "Ah. Divorce."

"When I was thirteen," I said. "My father—"

He stopped me. "Your father was the sole breadwinner, maybe sales? And your mother had been stay-at-home but was forced to reinvent herself after the divorce, yes?"

Was he clairvoyant? Had he hired a private investigator? "I learned a lot from her," I said, proudly.

"Ah, yes, very chin-up. She must have been a constant smiler. A Jazzerciser?" I winced and he leaned in. "Oh no! She made you do Jazzercise *with* her." Klaus receded into himself for a moment, scowling at the image he had painted of my mother. "That diabolical minx!"

I hated being read like this. I waved him off. "You've got it all wrong."

He shot forward, pointing at my hand. "Really? Because that's a jazz hand!"

I grabbed my own hand and pulled it under the table. "I went three times, tops."

"You carry it all with you. Falling in love is a threat, right? If you fall for a man, they'll take you off your path, and then, if they abandon you . . ." I corrected him in my head, *when* they abandon you, "you'll have nothing. So you pour yourself into your work, pushing them out, and voilà, you end up alone anyway."

"I'm fine on my own." I hate what my face must have looked like, misty with both panic and hope. My God, I wanted to prove myself to Klaus, even though I was already sure I hated him.

"You sometimes wonder if you'll die alone," he said.

"And you don't?"

"In my experience," Klaus said, "people are more afraid of truly living than death, alone or not." Drinks had arrived, and he was fishing tiny onions out of his martini. I sipped red wine, careful to keep my stupid little jazzy fingers together. I was rattled.

The food came at us. Spare, stunning, smears of color. I wasn't sure where to begin with each dish, like I lacked the spatial reasoning required to eat here, a navigational deficit.

Klaus explained his role in the psychology world, letting it slip that he was often referred to as "the Bad Boy of Virtual Reality Gaming Therapy," which I wasn't sure if I should believe or not. He then riffed on how virtual reality therapy was the preferred method of therapy for the uber-rich now. "The games are created for each individual. Our clients slay their dragons, shake the monkeys from their backs—literally."

"You mean *virtually*."

"*Literally* means whatever anyone wants it to mean now. Have you seen Kanye's TED Talk?"

"They let Kanye have a TED Talk?"

"You're *adorable*." He wasn't hitting on me; he was actually giving me a pitying look that reminded me of my Jazzercising mother. "I have a deep admiration for your blind positivity," he said. "We like to have people do a trial run before we finalize a hire."

"So you're offering me . . . another interview?"

"I want you to think of it as an audition." He did jazz hands.

At the end of the meal, I got up, dizzy and sausaged by my waistband. Klaus handed me a book on Jungian psychology. "Read up!" He then hugged me, clapping my back like I was a colicky baby. And because I'd just eaten for three hours straight, I belched.

He said, "You smell like starchy foods. Like sweet carbs."

"Before tonight, I've mostly been eating powdered doughnuts." I'd been sad and therefore on my go-to sad diet. I did sometimes wonder, like Klaus said, if I'd die alone.

"Amazing," he said, like he was stoned and watching an episode of *Planet Earth*. "Amazing."

• • •

Some context on the doughnut diet.

My ex, Victor, had cheated on me with Evangeline Quinn, a Belgian novelist. It caught me off guard. I thought we were great together. In retrospect, I wasn't picking up on the signs. Right before we broke up, I said, "We should write a book on how to be best friends who fall in love." We hadn't had sex for three weeks.

He claimed he cheated on me because he was tired of competing with my job for my attention. I said he had an affair because he was a traitorous coward intimidated by my success. Six months later, I thought I was over him, but I was still eating a lot of doughnuts, and Klaus' minianalysis session during the interview landed hard. I went home to my apartment, which was spare and echoey; Victor took his furniture with him, and, turns out, almost one hundred percent of the furniture had been his. I meant to order new stuff but was too busy. He'd taken the cat, too, Georgie; I'd never wanted a cat but I missed her.

I got in bed (a mattress and box spring; the headboard had been his) and started to read the book Klaus had given me, Jungian analysis. I didn't fully get it, but I knew that I was still eating doughnuts because I was still sad, but I wasn't digging deep into why. Honestly? I wanted to keep it that way.

· · ·

The next day, Bobby, Klaus' office manager, met me at the elevator doors. Not to objectify him, but he is objectively beautiful—but not my type. As he took me on tour, he tried to explain VR gaming therapy to me like this: "There's you and then *virtual* you. One real and one copy, like with twins."

I hated to correct someone so early on, but, "I think both people in a set of twins are real."

"I'm a twin, so I think I know what I'm talking about." I

didn't have the heart to ask if he thought he was the real twin or the copy.

He had me sign an NDA. "The Duplass brothers come here to scream at each other in rooms full of falcons," he said, blowing past his own NDA. "Helen Mirren tamed a troll, a.k.a. The Industry, in Gaming Room 3. And some celebs' sessions are court-appointed, and a few have been banned." He whispered their names and *then* mimed zipping his lips.

We walked by a row of offices, the break room, the Idea Room (more on that to come), and a corridor of gaming rooms, much like racquetball courts, completely bare except for panic buttons. "Like when you get stuck in an airplane bathroom and have to call the flight attendant." He said it in a way that made me wonder how many times Bobby had gotten stuck in an airplane bathroom and why.

He took me to a two-way mirror. On the other side, a man in a gaming room wore VR goggles and was violently swinging around at things I couldn't see.

Bobby scrolled through a list of display options on the two-way mirror touchscreen. He selected *View VR Mapping*. "Watch!"

The room turned into a solarium where the man, armed with a flyswatter, was taking on a swarm of oversized wasps, which had the face of an angry older woman—his mother. The mother-wasps said things like: *Why are you sweating? I told you not to eat so much brie!* and *Don't hover. You know you make women uncomfortable.* And, *You think you have the thighs for tennis?* And, *No, I think it's great they let boys into yearbook club.* The man was swatting his heart out while sweating and crying. Then he quit, curling up in the fetal position. Words flashed on the wall: *Sorry! That's all the time we have for today!* and then with a bit of unnecessary snark: *No breakthroughs today!* And everything reverted to white walls.

"How's he supposed to beat this level?"

"I dunno. Won't that be your job?"

Was that going to be my job?

"Right!" I said. "Totally."

"Ready for your first meeting?"

I already wanted to find an empty stall in the women's room and decompress. "Sure!" I said.

Which brings us to . . .

•••

Klaus Han's Idea Room: Imagine adults sitting in one-person hammock-like swings strung from wood beams in an industrial-vibe space with tons of light and ferns. I sat in a hammock seat and swayed.

Bobby introduced me to the group.

Tim was Klaus' fading golden boy protégé, deeply threatened by my hire. His games were vicious but effective.

Raphael was a relentless Proust fan. His games weren't as concerned about "the voyage" as seeing things with "new eyes."

Franny thought everyone was either out or closeted but most definitely gay. She herself claimed to be straight. Her games were about trying to get out of a complex series of closet-like boxes, each exquisitely unique—except basically always a closet.

Misha was my favorite, immediately. Depressed since third grade, she pretended to hate everything, but deep down, she was a lover, not a fighter. A bad-luck magnet, she was sitting in the hammock swing, precariously, wearing a boot for an injured ankle, a teeth-grinding mouth guard, and carpal-tunnel contraptions on both wrists. Bobby would tell me later that day that she exclusively attracts murderers across all online dating platforms. It was so consistent that she worked with police investigators, like certain psychics and dead-body-sniffing dogs. Misha believed that virtual reality gaming could save people—maybe even herself. Meanwhile, her karaoke of "Shake It Off" would make you sob. Her games were pure artistry.

Klaus was the only one not in a ceiling-suspended macramé seat. He was lying in a leather recliner while an intern was touching up his graying mustache. The intern wore gloves and was using a small push broom, the size that might come in the box with a janitor Barbie.

(A word on the interns: They were brilliant Gen Z kids from the best schools who couldn't read cursive or use the US Postal Service, so people thought they were dumb, but they actually had genius ideas that went largely ignored.)

While the intern hovered with the dye brush, Klaus said, "Frimm's the new energy we need around here! Let's get her up to speed."

"Should we wait for Deon?" Misha asked.

Deon? Not Mills. Couldn't be Mills. Coding circles can be small circles, but not that small.

"No," Klaus said, "he's probably locking a deal for us."

The team discussed their client list. An A-list actor had gone from Shadow to Animal—she chose lion. "A very good sign!" Klaus said. Anger management wasn't going well for a client named Berger. "He's having too much fun." They spent some time on garden-variety phobias. "They're our bread and butter," Klaus explained to me. "What would we do without snakes, germs, elevators, and public speaking, am I right?"

The group nodded.

Tim's couples counseling had gotten too violent. Misha said, "They can't be doing survival games in various civil wars, Tim." Her speech was a little lispy from the mouth guard.

"But I've seen some amazing results in the Congo!" Tim said. "It was a proxy for Cold War hostility. Seriously, what could be more—"

"Take it down a notch." Klaus always had the final word.

The intern said, "Done!" and Klaus popped up with flushed cheeks and a very dark mustache. Honestly? Very natural looking. "What about the Everly boy?" he said.

The mood shifted. Everyone expressed their concerns about the Everly boy, who wasn't making progress and needed a new game. Raphael said, "We should throw a scent at him so he can dwell in a positive memory, like Proust's madeleine soaked in lime blossom tea, an automatic memory."

"He wants to be in one of those big robotic suits," Bobby said.

The door opened. Deon Mills, in the flesh. "Sorry I'm late," he said, walking to a hammock seat. "I'm so close to getting the Friar Tuck meltaway cookie people to pay for product placement." His eyes landed on me. "Annie?"

"Anya," Klaus whispered.

"You two know each other?" Bobby asked.

"Yeah, we went to college together," he said. "We . . ." Dated, fall of our senior year. "Had an elective in Greek mythology together."

"And here we are!" I said, feeling a full-body blush. "Weird coincidence."

"We're Jungians," Klaus said. "There's no such thing as co-incidence. Didn't you read the book?" I hadn't, in fact, read the whole book. "Misha." Klaus stood and spun on the heel of his sneaker. "Put Frimm on the Everly boy."

"The Everly kid is complicated," Tim said. "I should really be the one—"

"She can handle it!" Klaus faced me. "But first, I'll show you how the VR tech works."

"Everyone who works here has to undergo mandatory VR therapy sessions where they spill their darkest secrets," Bobby said.

Like Scientology, I thought.

"And they all get recorded," the intern added, sotto voce.

Like Scientology, I thought again.

"You don't have to spill all your dark secrets," Misha said. "I mean, it wouldn't be possible anyway. We all have too many!"

"You can totally fake it," Bobby said to me quietly. "If you don't have any dark secrets."

"We all know you just play racquetball in there, Bobby," Raphael said. "You don't have to whisper."

"Are we allowed to just play racquetball?" the intern said, clearly having spilled way too much.

"Friends!" Klaus said. "After her intro to VR therapy, she'll connect with Misha for more info, and over the course of three days, she'll create a new game for the Everly boy." Klaus rubbed a circle on his chest, the spot right over his heart. He closed his eyes. "Go out there and do the good work!" he said. "That's why we're here. Right, team?"

"Right!" they all said, including the intern.

I muttered a delayed, "Right."

"Because each and every human being on this planet has the right to reach the highest level of Self." His eyes locked on mine. "All of us."

...

Next thing I knew I was in a gaming room with Klaus, surrounded by white walls, both of us in goggles. I was still rattled by seeing Deon again. He had that face I was crazy about, that quick smile, that heaviness in his shoulders like some invisible sadness was weighing on him, just a little. I knew his favorite rap artist and his soft spot for sad seventies songs; that he adored his little sister, Gwen. I remembered kissing him and the two of us staring at each other while we were lying under my Target twin bedding set. We went to Halloween that year in a couples costume—we were a thing! It was a mutual breakup; the details were blurry, but I remembered how hard it hit me.

Klaus said, "I wasn't sure what to focus on with you, Anya."

"Annie," I said quietly.

"But after talking with Doug and Jill—"

"You called my parents?"

"You and I hadn't had a session." He was genuinely confused. "What, uh, was I supposed to do? Triple down on Jazzercise classes with your mother? Clearly," and then he said more emphatically, "*clearly*, there are deeper issues."

"Oh, *two* clearlies. I didn't know my deeper issues were that *clear.*"

"Hold. Just one *momentito*." Klaus raised a finger as if testing the direction of the wind.

And then I smelled it. "My God," I said. "That's Muscongus Bay. And . . . my father's cologne. It smells like . . ."

"Your birthday," Klaus said. "Raphael is almost always right about Proustian auto memories, the old madeleine-dipped-in-tea dredging up the past for the old Frenchman. For all of us, really."

It wasn't just any birthday. "This was the summer of my parents' divorce." My dad's cologne was there because I was wearing one of his extra-large sweatshirts. He was probably already dating; the cologne was new and would get stronger and stronger, and eventually it gave me headaches and made me throw up a few times. *Psychosomatic*, my dad dismissed it. *Psycho* was what stuck, and now I thought about the time after I found out Victor was cheating on me when he said, "Don't ask questions that are going to make you get all psycho."

I heard the shriek of gulls and then saw the actual gulls, spinning in the sky—lots of sky. There were no walls; now there were waves rolling in. In the distance, my mother was alone, singing "Happy Birthday," which wasn't how it had happened but was exactly how lonesome my mother seemed that summer. It broke me. "Nope," I said, "not doing this." I looked around, but Klaus was gone. "You just left me here!"

And then a heavy stick was in my hand. Hundreds of piñatas dropped from . . . I don't know where. My mother was there, looking Jillish, and my father, too, looking Dougish. Had they sent Klaus pictures of themselves? They looked so repressed and flattened and accurate. We were, after all, too good for Chuck E. Cheese, not good enough for Prague.

Jillish was asking Dougish his opinion on everything—did he

like balloons, did he taste the cake, what about the piñatas she'd picked out? And Dougish was like, "Yeah, they're fine." The marriage was crumbling. My mother was trying to keep it all together because she knew, without my dad, she'd have to start from scratch.

And I thought: *My God, don't be like her, don't give up on your dreams for a life like this, a husband who's just going to leave you, no, work harder than everyone else, don't fall for the trap of . . .* I thought of Victor and the Belgian novelist, who now lived with *my* cat, Georgie. I'd been suppressing a lot more anger than I realized.

I tightened my grip on the stick and beat the shit out of the piñatas.

• • •

Misha's office was cluttered with photos of pets, almost all of which had died tragically—cats, birds, ferrets, fish, a hedgehog. So much loss it was distracting. "Feisty died from asthma-related issues. Flounder just went belly up, no explanation. Archibald's death alerted me to the gas leak. A real canary-in-a-coal-mine situation. Do you have pets?"

"I lost custody of a cat named Georgie in a breakup."

"Wow. That's double sad." There was something very ominous about getting sympathy from Misha.

"I'm fine now, though!"

"Oh. Good," Misha said, unconvinced.

She showed me a few standard games, coding, renders, narratives, then a demo. "This is a level for a grieving widower where his wife's alive and she's jumping off a dock into a lake where he's waiting for her."

"And how does he win?"

"He doesn't."

"Okay. I mean, how does he get cured?"

"I wanted him to have a place where he didn't have to get over her," Misha said.

"Huh."

She moved to the next. "This girl was violated by her neighbor." The replay was a lion running through the woods.

"Where's the girl?"

"That's her." She pointed to the lion. "Nothing to catch. No hunters to outsmart. Just running for as long as she wants to run."

"And she's all better now?"

"No, but she's reached Self."

"And what's that mean?"

"Self is the totality of our being. Conscious and subconscious."

"And that's how she makes progress and eventually she can be . . . cured?"

"There's no linear path, and *cured* isn't the destination."

"What is?"

"The most we can hope for is circumambulation of the Self," Misha said.

I felt stupid. "Circumambulation?"

"We walk around the Self," she said, "if we're lucky enough to find our Self."

"Gotcha." I had no idea what she was talking about. "Crystal clear. Thanks."

She then moved to the Everly boy, Christopher. "Last summer, he found his older brother's body—a teenager, fit and strong, who'd accidentally hanged himself on some kind of boat rigging. Alone in a boathouse, Christopher tried to cut his brother down with a dull knife used to cut bait."

"I didn't know this could be so . . ." I felt myself choke up. It surprised me.

"To create a game for someone, one that really works," Misha said, "you've got to bring some of your Self in with you."

"What part of my Self?"

"The one you keep hidden."

"From other people?"

"Yes," Misha said. "And sometimes yourself."

• • •

For the next two days, I kept to my little office and worked. I wanted to do right by Christopher Everly. I wanted to empower him. But I kept getting interrupted by the past, Muscongus Bay, my parents' arguments and how the dissolution of their marriage was all strung up with my breakup with Victor and the guys I'd broken up with before him, and the next Victor type to come along. Sometimes all I could think about were the widower in the water and the girl as a lion running as far as she wanted.

At one point, Deon showed up. "I don't want to bother you," he said. "Just wanted to say hi, hey. You know . . ."

"Hi, hey, of course," I said. "Look, I'm sorry I just showed up! It must be weird."

"No, no. It's all good."

"I'm sure we can be solid coworkers for each other."

"Totally professional," he said. "That's what I came here to say."

"Great!"

He lingered like there was more to it, but then he said, "Great!" And he left.

I sat there. Totally professional. I could do that. I didn't want to start anything up with Deon again. I didn't.

But, also, I did, and I knew it the moment he said *totally professional.* I remembered the mythology professor, the project Deon and I worked on together, the bar we hung out in, the first time he kissed me on the dance floor of that bar. I stopped myself. What was wrong with me? Totally professional. And then I wondered, had Deon found his Self? How had his sessions gone? I was sure that I wouldn't ever find my Self and walk around it. To untangle the strings tying my childhood to my own life now? It seemed like it would entail so much suffering. Why would I even want to? I was mad at myself suddenly for beating those piñatas. I'd shown too much.

I put Deon out of my mind. I shoved Victor into the back corner of my brain. I said, *No more Muscongus Bay.* I did what I do best. I worked.

And at the end of day three, I went to Klaus' office. "Ready to see it?"

"We'll see it in action tomorrow, at the boy's session."

"You sure?"

•••

I went home feeling that high I get from creating something that really works, a bounce in my step. But then I found Victor sitting on my stoop. I walked up and looked around. "To what do I owe the pleasure?"

"It's Georgie," he said. "He doesn't get along with Evangeline's cat."

"*She*," I said. "Georgie's a girl, *she*. Don't you remember? *Hey there, Georgie girl?*"

He stood up. "Do you think you could . . ."

"I have a very busy life, though. Work, work, work. No room for anything else. You definitely remember that, right?"

"I'm not here to fight," he said. "I'm offering right of first refusal on the cat."

I softened. I loved Georgie. "Okay, fine."

He gestured to a car parked on the street.

"Wait. Is Evangeline here?"

"Yeah. I hope that's okay."

"Oh, um. I guess that's . . ." Did I have a choice? I'd tried to despise Evangeline and waffles, beer, and Hercule Poirot, the sum total of my associations with Belgium. I'd tried to hate-read her first novel but became a die-hard fan. God, she's brilliant. As she walked up with the cat carrier, she was half bent over because she was too willowy to bear up under Georgie's weight. She handed me the carrier. Her perfume smelled expensive and all natural, like hundred-dollar bills made of one hundred percent pressed flowers. "Hi, Annie."

"Hi." I focused on Georgie, looking at her through the carrier holes. She seemed puffy. "Has she been upset? She stress-eats when she's upset." Had Georgie missed me? "Have you been feeding her the diet cat food?"

"American cats have diet food," Evangeline said. With her accent, it was a brilliant commentary on everything overwrought and wrong with American culture. And I hated her and I hated Victor.

"Thanks, Annie," Victor said, and it was actually sweet and

sincere, with a little hurt in his voice. I'd told myself I was over him but hid the truth from myself—I missed him.

"No problem." I hefted the carrier to my chest and walked into the building as fast as I could.

Once in my apartment, I let Georgie loose. "Welcome home!" But did it feel like home without couches to claw and rugs to barf on? "It's going to be all right," I said, but who were we? Did Georgie and I have Selves? Were those Selves hidden from us? I gazed at Georgie. Was it going to be all right?

...

We were set to watch Christopher's session together on the big screen in the Idea Room. His appointment was around lunch, so a few interns (one had a bowl cut, another a retro eighties mullet, a third what could only be Gloria Steinem–inspired glasses) laid out a spread of wonton cones filled with ahi tuna, spicy avocado, and whipped mushrooms. I caught Deon's eye, but he took a call and walked out.

I was picking through wonton cone options when Klaus walked up. "So, I forgot to ask. The piñatas. How'd it feel?'

"Not bad." I popped a wonton dessert cone in my mouth, bitter and chocolaty. I didn't want to acknowledge any kind of weakness.

"You've got great form! Softball?" he said.

Of course he was right. "Ponytail league."

"Did Misha explain that you have to bring your Self into the process?"

"Yeah, but I wasn't sure what that meant. My hidden Self? It's hidden, so—"

"Hm," Klaus said. "Well. I'd love for you to walk us through as we watch."

"Like a play-by-play?"

An intern flickered the lights like intermission at a Broadway show.

"Exactly," Klaus said.

We moved to our hammock seats and rotated to face the screen. Deon slipped back into the room, didn't even glance at me. I hadn't prepped anything to say. I was flooded with anxiety. The screen lit up. Christopher was in the gaming room, goggles in place. He wiped his hands on his jeans. "Christopher Everly," I said, "twelve years old, recently suffered the loss of his brother, with trauma around that loss."

The world I'd created appeared all around Christopher. He was now inside of a massive robotic mecha-suit, three stories tall. It was silver with a broad chest and muscular arms. Beautiful articulation, if I do say so myself, of the fingers. The facial features were a little stiff, but I was going for toughness. "I wanted something to protect him from the vulnerability that comes from suffering a loss." He was a giant, clomping through a destroyed city. "The postapocalyptic cityscape represents his home life, destroyed by all of the grieving."

Then around the corner of a building came a huge, ugly beast, bigger than the boy. It had claws and saber-like teeth. "This is the enemy," I said. "His pain."

"What?" Klaus said. "Pain isn't the enemy."

"It's okay!" I said. "I gave him the tools to conquer it and reach the next level."

Huge guns popped out of the robotic arms. Christopher seemed surprised, like he didn't know what to do with them. He held his arms out like he was afraid of the guns. I was panicked that he was panicked. "Give him a minute," I said. "He'll figure them out."

The beast sensed weakness, as I'd programmed it to, and it lunged at Christopher. He stumbled, crashing into partially wrecked buildings, and fell, hard. He was still scared more of the guns than the beast and was trying to shake them off of himself, pull them loose. The beast pinned him down. They locked eyes through his helmet shield. The beast let out a primal howl. It had won. *Let's circle back to this next session!* the message flashed. And then the screen went black.

Klaus was heading to the door. "Misha, healing mode. No time to start from scratch. But reframe it!"

"Wait." I looked around, confused. Tim was smirking. Bobby was wide-eyed. The interns couldn't make eye contact. Misha was already out the door. Deon looked at me like he was seeing me for the first time, like he knew me, like he felt for me. It was a beautiful look. "I swear this can work!" I said. "I gave this everything I had!"

"Except your Self," Klaus said. "Do you know the danger of building worlds for other people?" I had a feeling he was going to tell me. "It distracts you from the fact that you stopped building a world for your Self. You stopped because you're afraid of being vulnerable, afraid of pain."

It stung, but I went on defense. "Well, I guess this is

why they call you the Bad Boy of Virtual Reality Gaming Therapy!"

"I guess so." He was pissed but then sighed, letting it go fast. "Go help Misha fix this," he said, and then he walked out.

• • •

Misha was hard at work, the eyes of all her dead pets gazing at her with love. I was breathless from having fast-walked then jogged then sprinted to her office.

"What was your life like at twelve?" she asked, eyes glued to the screen.

"Christopher's age?" I said. "Klaus already used that. My parents were about to get divorced."

"Specific memory!"

I was blank. "Did you see my session? The piñatas?"

"No. Why would I do that?"

"Oh, sorry, I just thought . . . um, sorry. We vacationed on Hog Island on Muscongus Bay."

"Any actual hogs?" She was ready to create hogs.

"No."

"Give me more. Something, anything," Misha said.

I sat in an extra chair, thinking about my session, but really remembering—not what Klaus had put in but the real thing. "There were swallows. And they'd get caught up in netting and plastic bags along the coast."

She spun around. "Let me guess. You didn't want to shoot them with guns, did you?"

"No," I said. "I wanted to save them."

Misha folded her arms, the plastic carpal-tunnel braces

clicking against each other. "What's the point of suffering if you don't put it to use?"

"What?"

"Put the swallows in."

"I don't have time!"

"Klaus is having a one-on-one with Christopher. You've got an hour."

...

I ran back to my office and worked feverishly, picking up pre-made coastal backgrounds from other games. I even found swallows in the image bank. I stripped out the guns and added other tools instead. I thought about my childhood vacations, how awful it was knowing that my parents weren't going to end up together. How bruised they both seemed. I'd spent hours walking the shore. I could cry, blaming it on the wind, pretending I didn't feel like something inside of me was dying. I was a chubby girl, alone in her oversized T-shirts, who found birds and saved them, as many as I could.

Fifty-seven minutes later, I sent out an office-wide note that the new game was ready.

Everyone was logged in, watching.

Soon enough, there was Christopher in his big robot suit, on a cold rocky coast, the sky a bright gray. He was moving through high grass, over rocks, scanning the shoreline. He saw something and moved toward it. He squatted, the hydraulic gears of his robotic suit hissing. There was a white-throated swallow caught in fishing net. A small knife popped from his arm gear. As he delicately cut the netting, the bird's wings fluttered wildly.

It had a pale chest, blunt tail, fine yellow dots and stripes on its head, and wet, black eyes. He couldn't save his brother, but he could save the bird. Once loose, he cupped the swallow, lifted his metallic hands in the air, then opened them. The bird shuddered. Its wings twitched, and it hopped to its delicate pinkish claws, shook its head, and batted off into the air.

I sat there, my whole body buzzing. If I'd helped Christopher or failed him, one thing I knew: I'd kind of saved some part of my kid Self. This was for her, too. Was that supposed to happen? I turned off my screen and spun around in my office chair, eyes glazed. Was Klaus going to show up and tell me to pack my stuff? There was a tap on my door. I braced for Klaus.

But Deon appeared. "You okay?" There was real kindness in his voice. The chemistry was still there. I could feel it. Someone knowing you when you were a younger version of yourself? That goes deep.

I told him the truth. "This place," I said, "I don't know if it's the right match for me."

"The right match?" There was an edge to his tone. "Maybe you should just bail."

"What's that supposed to mean?"

He hovered in the doorway, looked down the hall. I could tell he was trying to make a decision. Finally, he said, "I saw what you did for Christopher. You got real. I could feel the real you behind it. You made something beautiful, *Thelma*."

"Thelma! Halloween! Our couples costume! You remembered."

"How could I forget dressing up as Louise?" he said.

"You were an *amazing* Louise."

"Your Thelma was pretty great, too," he said.

"Was Christopher's session really beautiful?" I asked.

"So beautiful."

"You know, after the breakup, I almost tanked finals that semester," I said. "But you know, that's my problem. The past is the past. Clean slate. I promise not to bring any of it up."

He shook his head. "You should tee up one of my sessions."

"Piñatas?"

"Mine have gotten a little more complex. I'll send you a file."

It sounded too personal. We had to be totally professional. I tried to get out of it. "You don't have to—"

"I have to."

•••

I was unlocking my car in the office parking lot when an Escalade pulled up. The back window buzzed down. Klaus appeared. His hairsprayed hair buffeted in the wind. "Did you feel it? Huh? Did you feeeeeel it deep down? That was it, Frimm! That was it!" He was ebullient, maybe drunk. Hard to say. But full of joy. "Next assignment? You build a better game world for your Self."

"Really?" I had no idea what that would look like. I felt a flutter of panic, but mainly, I was relieved I still had a job. "Honestly, I thought you might fire me."

"Fire you?" Klaus said. "You just started to get interesting." He smiled and said, "Goodnight, Annie!" The driver pulled off.

I'd just started to get interesting; I got in my car, and maybe Klaus was right, because I did feel . . . interested, curious about who I was, that kid Self, the Self I'd been in college, the me-now Self. Who were all these Selves?

And then my phone binged.

Deon's file.

···

I played it on my phone.

Deon was armored up, battling a centaur in a college bar. Made sense; we had that Greek mythology class together, so it was lodged in his psyche. And I recognized the place, Hooligans, one of our favorite bars.

He dealt the final blow, then turned to look . . . at me. I was in form-fitting armor, looking young. Both of us were cartoonishly buff. We picked up treasure and ran out onto the street together.

Winter, fresh snow. More centaurs. We were badass warriors. But each time I cheered him on or helped him out or looked at him with an adoring head tilt, a chunk of his armor fell off. Underneath, he was wearing a puffy coat, dark jeans, and a knit Red Sox hat.

We ran into a neighborhood, leaping fences with ease. Now his armor was reduced to one shin guard and his left chestplate, over his heart. We hopped into a yard with a snowy trampoline.

I knew this trampoline. This house was on the route from Hooligans to my place. I started to remember this night, the puffy coat, the Red Sox hat. But in the game, I was still in full armor as we climbed onto the trampoline and lay down next to each other. The wind and our weight made us bob a little.

Suddenly, music. Christopher Cross? Deon's soft spot for seventies ballads. This one is about an old breakup, love slipping out of sight. He loved her then. He was pretty sure he'd love her forever. And then we did in the game what we'd done in the actual past: We made snow angels on the trampoline. I remembered it all now, viscerally—the cold at our backs, the snow melting through our clothes.

Breathless and laughing, he rolled toward me, in the past and in the game, and said, "I'm falling in love with you."

Then it hit me. *I* broke up with *him*. It should have been this sweet moment, when I told him the truth—I was falling for him, too. Really falling. Falling hard.

But that's not what happened, not in the past and not in his game.

With me in full armor, him in only a chestplate, I said what I probably said then: "I have plans. After graduation, I'm going to . . ." But I didn't just say this stuff. With my battle ax in hand, I swung at him as I gave the speech. "There's this internship . . . I just can't follow you . . . I'm already heading to . . ." He shielded himself by pulling off the chestplate and blocking each blow and bouncing on the trampoline to dodge me. He was saying, "I know . . . I've got plans, too . . . I wasn't asking you to follow . . ." Christopher Cross was still singing, all heartbreak.

Was I his monster, his beast?

I knew the truth: I'd been falling for him, too. But my feelings for him felt like a threat to my future. I'd turn out like my mother, giving up myself for a man, who'd eventually leave me.

He'd successfully protected himself. The message flashed: *You had a breakthrough! Next level ahead.*

The screen went black.

• • •

I was still in my car, frozen. What would I say back to him? I was sorry, but . . . how would I tell him that I regretted it?

Yes. I'd tell him I was a mess, back then and probably still, and if I could do it over . . .

I had to find him and tell him these things in person. I got out of my car and looked up at his office window. He must have been talking to somebody because he was laughing.

He was over me. He'd moved on.

I got back in my car. I texted, *Hey, I'm so sorry.*

Sorry for what?

I had no idea what to say. I imagined the three dots on his phone . . . Thinking, thinking . . .

He texted back: *You don't have to be sorry. I think it made me better? My girlfriend thinks so. Alice. In accounting.*

His game had ended with: *You had a breakthrough! Next level ahead.* He'd moved on.

Can't wait to meet her! If Alice were Belgian, I'd never recover.

Definitely, Thelma!

Deon and I had to be coworkers now, professionals. My chest contracted like it was being cinched from within. I texted: *See ya later, Louise!*

• • •

I stepped into my empty living room. I stood there. No sofa to fall face-first into. I thought, *Now's the time. I'm ordering a sofa.* I needed to build my own world, the one that I actually lived in.

Then I realized Georgie wasn't winding through my legs. "Georgie?" I looked in the kitchen, the bathroom, the bedroom.

I found her on my comforter, looking desperate. "Georgie, what's—"

Faint, high-pitched meows.

I stepped closer. Nestled up against her belly were three kittens. Georgie hadn't been stress-eating because she missed me! She wasn't fat; she'd been pregnant. I stared at her, in awe— Georgie, being a world-builder and maybe even a Self; hard to say with a cat. The kittens were beautiful and tiny, some still wet, some starting to find their fluffiness. I wondered what my next assignment for Klaus would be, what world would I be born into? It would probably have to be more complex than beating piñatas (though I was definitely going to keep beating piñatas).

Then I imagined the swallows caught in the nets and plastic bags along the coast of Muscongus Bay. But what if I wasn't the one setting them free? What if I was the stuck bird who'd become afraid of the sky, afraid I'd forgotten the basics of flight? But now, cut loose, I'd test my wings with a few flaps, then I'd beat them, as hard as I could, and lift up into the wind . . .

THE HOLOGRAPHER

The bubble casings around each of our homes—ones that had once been so soft and flexible that we could hear them shifting and buffeting in the wind—had turned rigid—and lightly furred. (No one could say where the fur came from. Something fungal only mimicking fur?)

I remember how, when we got word that it was okay to emerge, my parents opened the front door. My mother was holding an aluminum baseball bat; my father had a shovel. The three of us were in our hazmat suits. (Mine had grown a little taut. I was eleven years old and had gotten taller and rounder.) Our breaths were trapped in our masks.

How long had we been indoors? Time was hard to figure. It had been well over two years. But had it been three?

"Stand back," my father said to me.

"Shallow mask breaths!" my mother added.

(Now, so many years later, when I'm nervous, I'll go into

a private space, cup my hands over my mouth, and do shallow mask breaths. It eases me.)

My parents started bashing the casing. It was tough at first but then began to give. As it shattered, the breeze kicked in—light, air, maybe the possibility of rain on skin . . .

. . .

We'd been shedding memories throughout our confinement—our favorite old furry wound-down mecha-pets, tube rides, diction lessons, holographic love notes, our grandparents becoming inanimate . . .

We lost entire childhoods and adulthoods. Long-married couples didn't know how they'd met. And mothers (like mine) stared at their children wondering how they'd been born. And children (like me) just had to assume their parents were their parents.

Even our interiors had become strangely foreign in confinement. "Who would buy that ugly sofa?" my father said. "Who would live with this much clutter?" my mother said.

One time, I found my parents sitting on the edge of their bed.

"Take a look at this," my dad said to me, showing me a small holographic memory—my parents as teenagers, sitting on the hood of a car—my father gives my mother a quick cheek kiss.

"Why would someone seal it up in a locked box?" my mother asked, holding the box. It looked like something made in a tech class—a small thumbprint lock on it, a velvety interior.

I was just a kid. I didn't have as many memories to lose. But I missed the *feeling* of a past. It's hard to explain. I was nostalgic for something I couldn't name. What came before? It was like a color I once knew and I could kind of describe—happyish, anxious?—but I couldn't say what color it was.

•••

I'm not sure it matters why we were sealed up. There were so many reasons that our specific one feels unimportant. But I'll say it anyway—a dusting of poisonous spores that erupted from an invasive plant species and the various poisonous attempts to kill it with pesticide fogs. Each municipal fogging was thicker than the last.

The spores ended up dying off on their own, as was the spores' right.

•••

People stepped out onto front yards scalded from the pesticide fogs. The light was bright to us. We blinked. The sun was a little warm. We tilted our heads to the sky. Some men took off their shirts and rounded their backs.

We knew our names. We knew that we should know our neighbors' names. But we didn't. It was awkward. Everyone thought they alone had been afflicted with the erasures until we started to figure it out—my father walked over to our neighbor, who was shirtless, his belly pinking with sun. "I'm sorry I don't remember your name. My family . . . we . . ." Having to say it aloud was harder than my father expected. His eyes went wide with fear and exhaustion and now this rusty kind of hope.

"Us, too." The neighbor pointed to his wife, who'd cut her own bangs so short that her face was mostly made up of a blank forehead. "Do you think we've known each other a long time?"

"Maybe," my mother said. She smiled tightly. Did she have a feeling that she'd once disliked the neighbors? Feelings existed, but without memories to back them up, they felt untrustworthy. I noticed a weird bruise on the back of the woman's knee, the fleshy part, and I wondered if her lockdown with her husband had gotten violent. Back when we had access to news, there was reporting of an uptick of abuse.

My parents and the neighbors introduced themselves with the facts they remembered—names, ages, former occupations— my parents had worked in education and the neighbors had been in the service industry. The four of them named the towns where they grew up—Voorhees, Vero Beach, Spencer, Weymouth. These facts remained but had no tug of memory. They were detached and distilled—like something preserved under a glass microscope slide and magnified.

I was raised here. But what had that been like? What was here?

• • •

A few days after we emerged, we began to remember—but the memories, when they returned, weren't given back to the people they belonged to. They'd been scattered among us. Memories had lifted and flitted and then, usually in small clumps, landed in someone new.

I remembered a wedding in a field, guests under a white tent. I wore a long, loose dress and sang a love song, a little off-key, at the reception. Of course it wasn't me—not me at all. But it felt irrefutably mine.

My mother had memories of a son. She gripped the edges of the kitchen sink. "Did I have another child? Did I? A boy?"

"No," my father said. "We'd know that, as a fact. We'd know."

One day I found my father in the attic. (During the confinement we'd learned to use every space in the house.) He was looking at some of our family holograms and had paused on one of me when I was around seven, wearing a backpack. "Look at you!" he said. "This must be a first-day-of-school picture, right?"

"I hate that shirt," I said. "Are those tomatoes printed on it? A tomato shirt?"

He double-tapped the airy, pixelated image. "No," he said. "They're apples."

"Are you trying to remember everything?"

"I guess so."

"What memories did you get?" I asked him.

He set the holo-display to rotate, flipping through thumbnails. "Not mine," he said. "Who would ever do something like that . . ." He was agitated.

"Do what? What thing?"

"Nothing," he said. "It doesn't matter." He went silent like someone had flipped a switch inside of him.

• • •

The holographic tools came in handy. People wanted to return the memories lodged in their heads to the people they belonged to. Some started to create mini holograms of what was in their heads. Some were beautifully rendered. Others were rough sketches. Most had text or voice-over narration that offered some context.

I had a small, cheap rendering set. My mother borrowed it

and started recreating memories at the dining room table. "This looks so stupid. Why am I so terrible at this?"

She handed me the carving tool. "Do something," she said. "I'm useless."

"Okay," I said. She'd created a little boy, but he was lumpy, and his face was a blur and pixelated. "What does this kid really look like?"

She started describing his nose (snubbed), his ears (flat to his head), his underbite . . . and I set to work.

• • •

Within a few months, an abandoned warehouse had been converted to a communal memory swap.

My mother put the holograms of Rossy into a box and took me to the warehouse with her. It was a big, airy space. There were others also holding boxes and bags, each lightly glowing with hologram memories they'd brought with them and set up on the rows and rows of industrial-strength shelving units. Each shelf was filled with small glowing visual clips and some stills.

Things like:

You had a dog named Otto. (An elderly dog with pointy ears and a gray muzzle.)

You were in a parade playing a trumpet. (Marching band uniforms, a drumline.)

I think you watched someone die, maybe of a seizure, maybe your grandfather in winter—there was snow out the window. (A bed; a narrow old man, convulsing under a pale sheet.)

If this sounds like it might belong to you . . .

And they'd give an address.

But how could we remember what we couldn't remember? It wasn't exactly clear. People described the recognition different ways.

Like an itch in the back of my head.

It was this voice, almost. A whisper saying—This is yours.

It's as if I knew the opening chords to a song but I didn't know I knew it until I heard it, but then I could sing the rest.

My mother put her memory of Rossy on a shelf in the warehouse. He was smiling widely after losing a bottom front tooth at a birthday party. I'd worked hard on those teeth. The loop was of him smiling and then pulling on his lower lip to show the spot where the tooth used to be, beaming with pride. The voice-over explaining some details was in my mother's voice, of course, and the clip ended with our contact information.

My mother left it there, took my hand, and pulled me along the shelves, looking for memories of her own.

My eyes flitting past headings: *Middle-Aged Woman, Old Man, Male Teen, Female Banker Midtwenties.*

I found a few that read: *Little Girl.*

Small images of various girls:

Putting on slippers.

Jumping in puddles—blue boots with whales on them.

Getting stitches on an elbow . . .

Nothing felt like an itch in my head or a whisper or a song. I checked my elbows. None of the memories felt like they belonged to me. I was still haunted by the life of the woman who got married in the field, who'd grown up in a tenement house and joined some kind of commune. "My woman ate this layered sweet cake thing. It tastes like honey," I told my mother in the warehouse.

"Baklava," my mother said. "Maybe she's Greek."

"Why can't I put up a memory?" I asked my mother.

"I've explained this." She had. She wanted to be the guinea pig. "Let grown-ups go through it first. See if it causes any . . . problems."

"Like what?" I asked.

"Shh. Just let me read these, okay?"

Somewhere deep in the cavernous space, someone had found their past and was crying.

•••

During the day, I would carve the holograms of memories I wanted to get rid of, the ones my mother would never let me put in the warehouse. I felt compelled to work on them. (I still have "Woman Singing at Her Own Wedding." She opens her mouth and it's my little-girl voice that sings the words.)

At night, my dreams were mine—and hers. Memory and dreams share the subconscious.

In one dream, she floated on a lake, and someone threw a car engine. It hit her chest and plunged her to the silty lake bed, pinning her there.

In another, she was flirting with a man in a strange mask, a beak, and tall plumage.

I learned to wake myself up. So I could have my own dreams, I tried to remind myself of some detail of my life—like how I'd hidden notes all over the house, under the flooring where it had started to peel up in the kitchen corners or written directly onto the attic beams . . . notes to the next person who might live in the house. I imagined that person to be a child like me.

Dear Stranger, I was here.

Dear Stranger, I was here when our pasts disappeared.

Dear Stranger, I was here when our pasts came back but to all the wrong people.

Dear Stranger, I should warn you . . .

But I wasn't sure what to write next.

...

A week or two later, a woman named Lymna knocked on our front door. I was the one who answered. It was afternoon. My parents had taken down the rest of the casing, but shards still glinted in the yard. She was in her fifties, a little breathless. She still had calluses on her face from wearing one of the heavy-duty respirators round the clock; many did. She hadn't cut her own hair but had let it grow wild down her back.

Her arrival wasn't unexpected. Strangers showed up at each other's houses to collect their memories. They'd sit on sofas or at kitchen tables. They'd make coffee or get drunk.

"I'm here for Rossy," Lymna said, introducing herself. "I think someone here knows him?"

My father had started having migraines, and so he was lying down in my parents' darkened bedroom in the back of the house. I ran to my mother, who was in the kitchen. "Someone's here for Rossy!"

My mother was stunned. "Really?" She rushed past me toward the door.

The two women sat on lawn chairs in the backyard. My mother let me linger nearby. There were still tiny shards in the dirt. I was collecting them into a pile.

My mother didn't start with Rossy. She said, "You grew up in a pale pink house."

"Yes," Lymna said, "I can see the little street now. We had a goose statue."

"And your father was . . . unhappy? He hunted. He might have had a hunting accident . . ."

"He died that way?" It was a question, but then Lymna's eyes filled with tears. She covered her mouth, nodding.

They progressed slowly. Her sister married a pediatrician; her brother was gay and left home at seventeen; her mother had pet conspiracy theories. Soon, they had a system. My mother would start, and Lymna would see it in her head. "Got it, yes. It's all there. My entire sister. All of her. Our fights, the things she stole from me . . . This one time when . . ."

And they'd move onto the next and the next.

These exchanges exhausted both of them. My mother would often cry after Lymna left. One night, I saw her roaming the back-yard, walking in a large circle like a pony used to giving rides at a birthday party. I opened the window and called to her because I was afraid. I wanted to hear her voice. "Are you coming in soon?"

She looked up at me as if I were a miracle. She couldn't speak. She sank to her knees into the dirt of our bald yard.

I turned away and climbed into bed. I thought about the child-hood lodged within me—and I wondered what that childhood would say to me. And I heard: *Get out while you can. You cannot trust these assholes.* I put my head under the pillow and decided that wasn't my childhood. That childhood belonged to the woman who sang at her own wedding and joined a commune and ate baklava.

• • •

I was helping my mother situate planters in the yard, bulbs lightly covered in soil. We were trying to repopulate with healthy spores, and these were supposed to be quite good. The woman who lived next door—the one with the blank forehead—stepped out of her house. She called out to us as she walked over. "I got mine back," she said. She stood right on the edge of her yard.

"Your past?" my mother said.

"You haven't, have you?" the neighbor said. Her voice was tentative.

"Not yet."

"What kind of memories did you get?" I asked. I'd been kneeling just behind my mother, and the neighbor must not have noticed me before. She seemed startled to find me there, like she was going to say something important—something adults only say to other adults. She blushed brightly. "I didn't mean to . . ." She scratched her broad forehead. "I'm sorry," she said. "I'm sorry about everything you've been through. Both of you."

"What?" my mother said. "I don't understand."

The woman smiled at me—a sad, crimped smile—and walked quickly back to her house.

My mother and I stood there in the yard like two people who'd been pranked but didn't get the joke. "Why would she say that?" I asked.

"I don't know," my mother said. "I don't know anything about her."

...

My father looked ragged. He barely spoke, barely ate. My mother found a stash of pain medication—hoarded from what injury?

Surgery? No one remembered. She doled the pills out to him. He spent long periods of time in his compression suit. It blew up and tightened, cuffing his arms and legs, his torso and head. I would hear them talking in the bedroom, softly because they didn't want me to hear. "Every time I close my eyes, it's there," I heard him tell my mother. "Every time."

"You should try to turn him in. To the cops."

"I don't even have her face, not clearly. I don't have a time or a date. I wish I could put up a notice, like everyone else. I wish I could pretend to know other memories of his and lure him in. But this is the only one. I guess it blocks out all the others."

It was quiet, only the ticking of the compression suit modulating its hold.

"Are yours going away?" my father asked. "As you give them back to her?"

"Yes. But it's strange." My mother was a thoughtful woman. She took her time trying to explain things. "It's . . . empty. I'm hollow. I miss them. I still know the memories, but I don't feel them. And I haven't found mine. I haven't found . . . us."

"I can't wait until this is gone—killing that girl."

"Don't say it like that. It wasn't you."

"But in the moment of the memory, I'm in the pool. My whole body is there with her. I hold her under. If it's your memory, it's you."

"No," my mother said. "You know I only had one child. Rossy isn't mine."

"Is he dead?"

My mother was silent. I was listening on the other side of

the door, so I couldn't see her. Did she shake her head or nod or shrug?

•••

As my mother became hollow, she grew hungry, desperate for her own memories. She would take me to the warehouse, her eyes darting across the headings, searching for moments that fit her—or my father. She would pull me along, her hand gripping mine tightly, and then freeze, reading furiously, and then pull me along again.

Once I came across a notice at my eye-level—*Little Girl*—and one of its memories struck me: *Rose-scented ChapStick; you put it on your lips and then ate the whole tube of it.* (Chubby hands, fiddling with a ChapStick tube found in a junk drawer.)

"Did I eat ChapStick?" I asked my mother.

She grabbed my shoulders and yanked me away from the notice. She held my face, sharply. "You don't need to read these," my mother said. "You hear me?"

I was suddenly overwhelmed by the energy of the warehouse, the neediness, the urgency, like a form of starvation. The people there were frenetic but also dying—like the instinct to physically fight before losing consciousness. Their need had a violent edge to it. Their breaths were shallow or heaving. They shoved each other along the rows.

At the end of each visit, my mother was exhausted. She went home and, no matter the time of day, she slept for hours—dark curtains drawn tight.

•••

My father scanned his memory of the murder for details. He tried to widen the gaze of it. Eventually, he said, "It was summer, and I feel like I know the year. I can sense it within the memory. I'm getting closer."

As connectivity returned, he logged into police records, newspaper reporting. He scanned archives for murders, disappearances. He couldn't really see the face of the woman in the pool; it was dark. She was underwater, blurred. But, still, he looked at photographs of missing persons from that era, hoping to find someone who fit the loose idea of her.

He found nothing.

...

Lymna kept visiting regularly. She seemed to be growing manic. When the memories came back, especially after the base of memories had been set, new memories were a rush, like getting high. She'd sit bolt upright or move around the lawn—staggering and laughing, overcome with both grief and joy. Sometimes she would press her wrists to the sides of her head as if trying to keep it from falling apart.

One rainy afternoon, my mother sat with Lymna at the dining room table. She folded over, bowing beneath some heavy weight. "My head is too full," she muttered. "Stop." My mother had been explaining the time when Lymna fell in love.

"Do you want water?" my mother asked. "Get her water!" she shouted at me.

I filled a glass from the tap and set it beside Lymna's elbow.

"I haven't gotten rid of my other memories. The ones that belong to this refugee," she whispered. "He has seen difficult things. He has had such . . . so much . . . There are two sub-consciouses—his and mine. The well is too deep. Too murky and cold. There are too many monsters."

"Have you tried to find him?"

"Yes, but why would he come to claim this past? Who would want it?"

"Lymna," my mother whispered.

"Yes?" She lifted her head and stared at my mother, who reached across the table and took her hand. They were close in a way that hadn't ever existed before. This way of being known—the depth of it—was unfathomable.

"I have memories of Rossy. And then the memories stop."

Lymna's back stiffened. She whipped her hand away from my mother's. She was being filled with memory upon memory. Her eyes held a steady, fearful gaze. Her expression flashed between joy and sorrow, longing and laughter. She stood up and backed away so that she was against the wall. "My God."

"What happened?" my mother said. "What happened to him?"

Lymna started to cry. She slid along the wall but then gathered herself. She rushed to the front door, where she'd left her pocketbook and a light spring coat. "He's gone," she was saying, collecting her things. "He's gone. He's gone. My Rossy . . . He's gone."

· · ·

Months passed. Summer settled in, dusky and humid, a gummy heat that made me feel stupid and trapped. The government started a campaign: *Your New Life Awaits!* It was their way of acknowledging that our old lives might be gone forever.

My father talked about being eaten alive by another man's

guilt. "If it's in your memory," he said, "it burrows into your body. There's no getting rid of it."

My mother kept searching for her memories—or his. Either, really. She thought memories might save them.

Because I didn't remember my old self, I decided to steal an old self. When my mother dragged me along the notices taped to the warehouse shelves, I memorized as many as I could. And then I tried to live them.

If I couldn't get my past back, I thought that maybe I could jam in as many presents as possible to fill myself back up.

I found a pond and tromped around in it, pretending I was an enemy soldier.

I roamed the neighborhood looking for stray cats.

I searched the sky for very specific animal shapes.

I made friends with a boy down the street and tried to talk him into kissing me. He didn't want to.

Every day I tried to do things on the notices. I tried to live as many lives as I could. I grew tired; my small muscles ached and burned.

•••

Then, one day at the warehouse, my mother reached out and ripped a notice from the shelf. She pressed the paper to her stomach—like she could eat it that way, by pulling it in directly. Still gripping my hand, she marched away.

Once home, she spread the notice out on the rolltop desk. Her hands flattened, pressing down on either side of the sheet. Elbows straight, her shoulder blades popped up at her back as she sunk in.

"What's it say?" I asked.

She wouldn't tell me. "Don't mention this to your father. It might be nothing. Promise?"

I promised.

That night, she left the house. I kept watch at my window, but sometime after midnight, I fell asleep.

In the early morning hours, I woke up to find my mother sitting on the edge of my bed. She was fully dressed. I was startled to see her eyes searching mine in the near-darkness. I knew this was what she looked like when she felt wrecked. I knew this from way back, when I was a very little kid. It was something I'd always known but was now just recalling. The skin beneath her eyes was lavender, her eyelids puffed. I'd seen it before when she'd stayed up late and cried herself to sleep.

And I knew, before she spoke to me, that her voice would be hoarse from screaming.

I remembered what was lost—my mother and father had hated each other, cheated on each other, made each other pay, over and over again. I knew, not knowing how I knew—an itch in the back of my head.

"I packed your bag," she whispered. "We have to go."

"Go? Go where?"

"I was the woman," my mother whispered. "The drowned woman . . . but I lived."

• • •

The old woman who had given my mother's memories back to her was sitting in her car, engine-clipped, just down the street.

My mother and I carried our bags, shoved them in the back seat, not bothering with the trunk. I sat beside them, buckled in. My mother introduced me to the woman. Her name was Mila. She had brown skin and fine white hair, pinned tightly into a bun. She was weary but also relieved. Had she struggled to find my mother? Had she been having the same memory as my father—but as my mother, being strangled in a swimming pool at night? "I have so much about you, so many moments," she said, smiling, "in my head."

I had questions, but none of us spoke. The car was big and felt almost buoyant at times, as if it could lift off the road. I watched the trees, ticking past them along the highway. I finally got tired and dozed.

When I woke up, the sky had lightened. My mother and Mila had changed places. The car smelled of fresh coffee. Mila offered me a doughnut. "Your favorite," she said, handing me a white-powered and jelly-filled one.

I didn't remember it was my favorite until I bit down—the light puff of powder, its dustiness on my lips, the sweetness of the jelly on my tongue.

...

Mila eventually got us to a train and the train took us to a station where we transferred to a bus. At the depot, my mother's sister was waiting for us. She was tan and skittish with bleached hair; someone I'd only met as a baby.

We lived with her for a year and a half in a small fourth-floor apartment. I remember mostly the lavender candles and oniony potato pancakes for dinner.

We never saw Mila again.

Or my father.

...

I now remember everything in my life with acute clarity. I don't just live. I'm memorizing a life, second by second. I take notes. Many of us do; we're a generation of notetakers, hoarders of memory, obsessives taking account. We track details. We learned the hard way that a small detail—a pigeon repeating on wallpaper—can unlock a stretch of existence. I can still, to this day, describe every inch of my aunt's apartment, the street, the roads leading away from it—the people in each house, their winter hats, their limps, their gestures, their braced postures and clamped hands and hardened faces.

I missed my father, yes, and for years, I didn't believe my mother, consciously. I would hush her if she talked about being the drowned woman. But I never really fought to go back to him. I knew, in truth. I knew. Things made sense in retrospect. I'd assumed the neighbor's bruise on the fleshy back of her knee was a sign of abuse because I knew these things. In all likelihood, it was just a collection of varicose veins. And how she felt so sorry for us after she'd gotten her own memories back, that fit, too. The image of my parents as teenagers was sealed up and locked in a box maybe because it was dangerous—it was proof that they'd been happy. When things turned, one of them hid it away.

The most damning thing of all—my father never came looking for us. He let us go. Maybe he knew, deep down, and he didn't want to return to the person he was.

Since then, there's been a good bit of research on memories that worked like my father's. Things lodged so deep that when the other memories fell away or flitted off, these memories endured—rooted but foreign to them.

I became a devout archivist, a memory historian, a keeper. I almost never think of the future. And so it surprises me when I find myself in my own, one I could never have imagined for myself.

Fieldwork.

The motel in this region is quiet and relatively clean. Our team's makeshift office was once at a dog groomer's. I can still smell the dogs—their musky fear and chemically flea dip. On the first few days, there was usually a line for walk-ins.

But I tend to be the one to visit the infirm and housebound. I drive the rental car alone with devices—a case that holds a hologram design kit, recording and storage. I keep mace in my pocketbook, just in case. I always volunteer for the posts in rural places, the ones with small, defunct towns and lonesome roads.

Today, I stand on a porch, knock, and wait for someone to come to the door, someone with a past that's not theirs, that they want to donate back to the pool of databases. Or someone who is wrecked by a memory or two. I can tell the difference sometimes from the first moment. The illness, it eats away at a body—a winnowing. The desperation. They know, on some level. They know that it's their own past—something horrible done to someone, as my father did, or something horrible done to them, ones they can't acknowledge as their own.

It's my job to recreate what they see in their heads. I sit in their homes with them while they tell me what they remember and I carve the memory with texture and color and light and pixels, people moving through settings that feel somewhat real. The holograms sometimes dance or run or scream.

It's not my job to tell the people what I think—*You were the child who hid in the woods, hiding candy bars in knotholes; you were the one who shot that dog in the head out of vengeance.* I hold the memories; I collect and carry them.

This is what I've learned—the memories belong to all of us, always, no matter how far-flung. They're ours, a collection of who we are and who we don't want to be. Our bodies are flimsy, but our memories press in around us all the time; sturdy, solid pressure, as in a lake. Life is a kind of drowning or learning to swim.

What I feel standing on the porch, holding my case, waiting for someone to come to the door, is that I am the little girl whose mother dragged her along the glowing warehouse shelves and who loves white-powdered, jelly-filled doughnuts, whose father almost killed her mother. I am also the one who ate rose-scented ChapStick and had a dog named Otto. And I had a son named Rossy, and I am Rossy, and I got married in a field. And I also tried to drown my young wife, and I am the child of that man, writing notes to *Dear Stranger, Dear Stranger, Dear Stranger*—and I am also the stranger.

INKMORPHIA

For my eighteenth birthday, I get a tattoo. A small red heart on my shoulder, *Loot* inked across it in black cursive. Loot was my brother's nickname. He was twelve years old when he disappeared. I was seven.

The next morning, I peel off the bandage to take a look. A vine with thorns where there was no vine with thorns. It wraps around the heart, above and below Loot's name.

I look at the drawing I sketched and gave to the tattoo artist. No vine with thorns. I look at the picture on my phone that I took of the tattoo yesterday—red and raw. No vine with thorns.

I wake up my mooch-friend Delia, who's asleep on the futon in the living room. "Do you remember this?" I show her the tattoo.

"What?" She's groggy. "Yeah. You got a tattoo. I was there."

"The vine with thorns," I ask. "Was that there before?"

She sits up and leans closer. "No?"

"Correct answer," I say. "No."

...

After my shift at the Art-a-Rama, where I sell Blick and Utrecht supplies to art students, emo high-schoolers, and parents with kids they're not sure what to do with, I go back to the tattoo parlor. It's in the same strip mall. They've got bells on the door, and as soon as I'm inside I hear the electric snap and buzz—an older woman getting something small inked on her ankle. Molly is doing the work. She's a throwback, very "Love Is a Battlefield."

Peppermint is behind the desk. She cleans and schedules but also does a lot of nothing, which is what she's doing now. I ask if Wilson is around.

"Why?"

"I just want to talk to him."

"Ink's ink. No refunds." She points to a sign taped to the wall behind her: *What's done is done. No refunds.* And another one below it: *This aggression will not stand, man. —The Dude,* which is, of course, a *Big Lebowski* quote.

"Can I just talk to Wilson?"

She glares then rolls her eyes. "Tuesday's rib day. It's ugly in there." I don't know what this means. She nods to the *Employees Only* door.

It means that Wilson's ordered from Eve's Rib, a feminist food truck around the corner. He's eating ribs from a take-out container, sitting at a small table. The room has old-world filing cabinets and folding metal chairs. The walls are covered in framed tattoo art. He looks up, midbite. He's got jacked biceps, a big reddish beard, and one of those high bellies of tough lard. "What's up?"

"It's weird," I say.

He's not surprised that things are weird. "Uh-huh. How?"

As I explain the vine with thorns, he wipes the barbecue sauce from his beard and fingers. "Let's see."

I show him the tattoo.

He says, "Yeah, shit's undone."

"What?"

"Your grief and shit. It's undone. As in *not complete*."

"This is something that happens?" I ask.

"It's rare. But it's happened to clients of mine, here and there."

"That's messed up. It makes no logical sense. A tattoo can't change."

"Yeah, but do cell phones make logical sense, if you think about it? Or infinite math. Or why we're here at all? Or the soul or consciousness or infinite parallel universes . . . Your shit's undone. Might be grief related."

"I was little when my brother died. I barely remember him. This *is* my grieving. This tattoo."

"Nah, this is just a recognition. You need a reckoning." He drops the takeout box and wadded napkins in a trash can. "How old was your brother when he died?" He stretches his back.

"Twelve," I say. "And, well, we assumed he died. He actually disappeared. Like the kids you see on milk cartons."

"Undone." Wilson raises his heavy eyebrows and shakes his head. "Very, very undone."

· · ·

I did grieve as a little kid. I stopped speaking. I didn't speak from age seven to age ten. Three and a half years.

Not a word.

Not one word.

•••

"This page says that brambles have complex genetics because they *hybridize promiscuously*." Delia gives me a look of dainty shock, her hand over her mouth, then whispers, "These vines are *slutty*."

"Are botanists sexier than I thought?" I'm boiling shrimp-flavored ramen—two packages—like Delia lives here now, and I think she might. "What else does it say?"

"Berries." She holds up the picture of my tattoo on my phone and the page of scientific etchings from the site on her phone, her eyes darting between them. "By the look of these thorns, they'd probably be . . . blackberries? I found them under 'wild brambles,'" she says. "That could be my porn name, you know?"

"I hate berries." The noodles are losing their stiffness. I swirl them with a fork.

"No one hates berries."

"Lots of people hate berries. They stain your teeth. The little seeds get stuck in your molars. They're all . . . pulpy and gross. And you never know when one's going to be sweet or sour or tart."

"We always bought them at the store in little containers, but it's cool that you can just find them. Like in nature. Like when Huff and Gee go mushroom picking and want us to trust ourselves to them to eat their random 'shrooms and not die."

Our mutual friends Huff and Gee went through a serious foraging phase.

"I used to pick wild blackberries as a kid," I tell her.

"But you hated them."

"Yeah, but I'd still pick them. At the junkyard. When I was little, with my brother."

"At the junkyard? Why were you at the junkyard?"

"I guess the only reason kids are ever wandering around junkyards. No one gives a shit about them."

"Your parents gave a shit, in their own way. Jill and Ed just had a philosophy, right? What's that thing they did?"

"Free-range parenting," I say. "It was based on seventies childhoods when kids were free to explore and roam."

"Yes, that."

"It was a philosophy that let them get high all day," I tell her. "It was bullshit. Everyone else had violin lessons and soccer games, and we were rummaging through a junkyard." I rub my jaws. They've been aching. I clench my teeth in my sleep. I'm supposed to zen out more.

"Maybe Wilson's right, and your grief or whatever is undone," Delia says.

"I don't know what *undone* even means," I say. "Don't most people get tattoos because they're not done with someone yet, or don't ever want to be?"

"Was your brother really never found?"

"He was really never found. He'll always be undone."

• • •

The next morning, the tattoo is gone. My skin is blotchy where it used to be, with three parallel scratches like the tattoo was ripped off, nails on skin. I lay there and just stare.

Honestly, I'm relieved it's gone. I let my head sink back into the pillow and stare at the ceiling. This is better. This is good. Done or undone. Recognition or reckoning. That bullshit no longer matters.

But then, ten minutes later, I'm in the shower. I find it—the heart with *Loot* on it wrapped in thorny vines on the right side of my ribcage, on the skin that slides over the very last rung, home to the smallest rib.

• • •

"As a little kid, I couldn't say *Luke*. It always came out *Loot*. My parents liked it. 'Our babies are our loot,' my mom would say. 'You've got to treasure your loot in this world.'"

I'm lying on the futon with Delia, my hair still wet from the shower. My hands are shaky. I've been crying off and on.

"But what you're saying is . . .?" Delia asks.

"They didn't treasure us," I tell her. "After Loot disappeared, my father moved on to harder drugs. But my mom changed her life. We moved into my grandparents' place. She finished her GED and took community college classes. There was no more free-range parenting. I was hovered over, watched, fed, loved. You know, treasured. Losing my brother probably saved me."

"When did you start speaking again? When you felt safe again and loved?"

"I guess so." I think about it for a minute. "Actually, it was the school nurse who pushed it. She got me in with this specialist."

Delia tells me to call in sick at the Art-a-Rama, and I do it. I'm functioning at the level of just following orders. She makes me tea and gives me a Xanax from an Altoids tin stuffed with cotton. "You should sleep. Like a really good, deep sleep."

• • •

I doze off and wake up—anxious. I look for the tattoo, and it's still there on my ribs.

I doze off again.

I wake up.

It's gone.

I don't want to look for it.

I doze.

And I wake up and I search my body.

I find it on my inner wrist, sitting above a series of meticulous scars. Cuts I made myself when I was twelve years old, around the age Loot was when he disappeared. "Delia?"

"Yeah?" She's in the kitchen. "Everything okay?"

"No."

She walks into the room, hands me a glass of water. She sits down on the futon, her back to the wall. "Come here," she says. I hug her around the waist, and she holds me and strokes my hair. I can hear her heart. "Tell me about your brother."

"He was a kid. Lanky. He had, you know, mosquito bites all over his arms and legs, and cut his own hair, so it was jagged and messy. He wished we had a dog. But of course, my parents couldn't take care of a dog. They couldn't even take care of us."

"Were you hungry?"

"What?"

"Were you getting the berries because you were hungry?"

"I don't think so," I say. "I don't think it was that bad."

"Did he cut his own hair because no one would cut it for him?"

"Maybe." And then I thought: *Was he lanky because he wasn't fed enough?* I was scrawny, too. Was he covered in mosquito bites because he was out at night? "There were puppies in the junkyard." I remember them now. The mother's stretched-out stomach, her rows of puffed nipples, the puppies climbing all over each other—their silky coats getting covered in dry dirt. "That's why we went. My brother wanted to show me the puppies."

"Like from a stray dog?"

"I guess so."

"Did you ever see them?"

"We weren't supposed to be in the junkyard."

"That's where the puppies were, or the berries?"

"Both." I see my brother now. His lean face, the blue pockets beneath his dark eyes. He's tired. A tough twelve-year-old—thick nose; sharp, narrow jaw. His voice just starting to change. He's whispering to me, *Don't tell anyone we're here. We're not supposed to be here.* "It doesn't make sense. I mean, I don't think my parents would have cared if we were at the junkyard playing with puppies and eating berries. They didn't give a shit back then."

"So why weren't you supposed to tell?"

My breath goes shallow. A sharp pain spikes in my right jaw muscle. I want to say something, but I can't open my mouth. If I could, I'd know what I wanted to say. But because I can't, I don't know what I want to say. This makes no sense.

I flip my arm over to show Delia the tattoo.

It's gone.

I stand up, strip down to my bra and underwear.

"Nothing," Delia says.

•••

I eat cereal for dinner. I check. Nothing.

Delia and I listen to this new indie punk band she loves. I check. Nothing.

That night, Delia and I are brushing our teeth together, like we're a couple, and maybe we are; maybe we've been a couple for a long time. I brush my tongue, the way dentists recommend, and there it is—on my tongue. I spit the toothpaste foam out of my mouth, stick out my tongue in the mirror.

Delia looks at it. "Damn. That's a lot."

"Do you think my grief is undone?"

She puts her hand on mine. "I've got something." She leads me to our tiny kitchen. She reaches into the fridge and pulls out a carton of blackberries.

She rinses them and puts them down on the table in front of me. "Try one."

I don't move.

"I was thinking," she says. "Kids love berries. I think they just do. And hungry kids really love berries. So maybe, I don't know. Maybe, once upon a time, you loved berries. And then, for some reason—maybe some really awful reason—you stopped."

The blackberries are shiny. Each little cluster of bulbs is perfect and taut. I pick one up. It's fat.

"At least, you might find out that you're now grown up and you like berries, right? Tastes change over a lifetime."

I'm not grown up. I feel like a little girl still. A little girl holding a blackberry cupped in her hand. I pop it in my mouth. It sits there, on my tongue—on the tattoo of *Loot* in the heart wrapped in vines.

And then I slide it over and bite down. It's sweet and a little tart. It fills my mouth with juice. As I chew, I grind the seeds. I swallow it all down.

I remember a plastic bag full of berries. It drops to the dirt and the berries roll out. I'm a little kid, reaching for the berries, trying to pick them up fast and put them back in the plastic bag. One rolls all the way to the edge of cement pad—a cage. The dog that had the puppies wasn't a stray. There were cages.

I feel sick. I rush to the kitchen sink and heave. Nothing comes up. "Fighting dogs," I whisper, my voice hoarse. "They were raising fighting dogs."

"Who?"

"At the junkyard." I spit a few times.

"Who?"

"I don't know."

"Were you with your brother when he disappeared? Were you there? Did you see something?"

If you see something, say something. "No, but . . ."

"But what?"

"If I did, I wouldn't say anything."

"Why not?"

"I stopped speaking. Selective mutism, that was the diagnosis."

"There must have been cops asking questions."

"Lots of cops," I say. "But my parents protected me. My mom slept in my room because I was scared."

"Did the cops think you knew something? Why stop speaking then? I mean, you could have been helpful, maybe."

Don't tell anyone we're here. We're not supposed to be here. "I promised my brother. I said wouldn't tell."

...

My dad overdosed when I was sixteen. My mom now works as an LPN in a nursing home. I call her up. "Hi."

"Oh my gosh! How are you? I miss you. Is everything okay?"

I don't call much. "Everything's cool. I was just wondering about that day."

"Honey, what day?"

"The day Luke disappeared."

"Now? You want to talk about that now?"

"Was I with him that day?"

"No, no. Of course not. No. You were with me! We made microwave popcorn."

"That shit causes cancer."

"And we watched a movie! We were snuggling on the sofa all day."

We never snuggled. "What movie?"

"I don't know. Some kid movie." She's defensive now. Her voice is all ratcheted up to some weird atonal singsong.

"I got a tattoo."

"Of what?"

"A dog. The kind people raise to fight."

The air goes still. My mother is completely silent.

I refuse to fill the void.

Finally, she gives. "I don't even know who would do something like that. To animals. It's awful."

"I've gotta go." I hang up. I turn to Delia, who's listened to the whole thing. "She knows."

"I have to ask a question," Delia says.

"I don't know the answer."

"Do you know the question?"

"You're going to ask how my parents made money, right? Back then, when Luke and I were little. You want to know if they were part of the dog fights or something, right?"

"No." She shakes her head. "No, of course not. I wouldn't ever accuse your parents of . . . No. They were good parents."

"They were bad parents. Like textbook bad parents."

"But they loved you."

"What if they were both? Bad parents who loved me."

Delia's upset by the idea. Her eyes look glassy, like she might cry.

"If you weren't going to ask that, then what were you going to ask?"

"How far away . . .?" She stops speaking.

"How far away was my childhood home from the junkyard?"

She won't commit. She looks at the plants on the windowsill.

"That's the same question, isn't it?" I walk up closer to her and hold her hands. "If we lived far away from the junkyard, so far that my brother wouldn't have stumbled on it, we'd only know about it—puppies and blackberries—if someone had driven us there. At least the first time. After that, my brother would have known it was cool, and he'd have made me get on my Huffy and bike out there with him."

She leans toward me, so her forehead touches mine. "You had a Huffy?"

"A hand-me-down from him. It was blue."

•••

I wake up very early in the morning. My heart is thudding in my chest, and I know—I know for certain—that the tattoo of the heart is now in my own heart. It's within me. I roll over and press my body up against Delia's body, like this is how we've lived for a very long time—together. "We have to go back," I whisper. "I have to see it for myself."

"I know," she says. "I know."

•••

By afternoon, we've made it out of the city and back to my suburban childhood. Dollar stores and pet groomers and fast-cash lending. A few trailer parks. A mini casino. "My old neighborhood," I say, pointing to a white brick wall with *Fern Grove* painted on it in black cursive.

Delia's driving. "You want to see your old house?" The only entrance road leads to a series of cul-de-sacs, a whole bunch of nowhere.

"No."

She follows my directions. We've already clocked the distance between my house and the junkyard. It's far. Too far, and out of the way, close to nothing, the opposite direction of our school and the downtown strip malls. "No way my brother would go this far, but mostly not in this direction."

"Maybe he just went looking, you know . . ."

The road flattens and winds. "He wasn't a cyclist on a biking vacation. He was a kid who wanted things. He was a kid who'd slowly walk the aisles of the mini-mart, looking for the best way to spend a dollar fifty. What if it's no longer there?"

"The junkyard?" Delia says. "Junkyards are junkyards. They don't magically transform. Not out here."

...

She was right. The junkyard was exactly the same. A dirt road, chain-link fence, the small standalone office in front. Mounds of junk. What we throw away, what we're willing to shed.

I look at it and see so much sad, useless shit.

I look again and see childhoods.

There are trees at the edges of the lot. We get out and walk the fence line. There are weeds and brambles, yes. Some poison ivy. Lots of vines with thorns; no berries. We walk all the way to the far side, hidden by the tall stacks of moldy sofas and mattresses, car parts, TVs, large plastic toys—a pink kitchen, a red battery-operated car . . .

And there's a garage, closed up. A half-dozen storage units. And a barn. All of this was once farmland. "The dogs were kept in the barn," I say.

Delia takes my hand and tugs. "Ready?"

The barn is closed, but there's a side door. Delia pulls and it swings open.

The dirt floor. The cages are gone—but there are a few cement pads still sitting there in squares. I can still smell the dogs, the heavy musk, the suffering . . . I dropped my plastic bag. The berries rolled in the dirt. I tried to pick them up. A man was yelling at me; that's why I was going fast. *What the hell are you doing in here? You're not supposed to be here!*

"I was looking for Loot," I tell Delia. "He'd gone to find the puppies." I walk to one of the cement pads. "The dogs had been so abused. They'd been made to be vicious."

The air in the barn is still and quiet.

"Did something happen here?" Delia asks me.

I look down at the dirt floor. I remember something pulpy and dark—a bloody little clump. Like mashed-up berries. "It wasn't berries," I say. "It was flesh. It was part of a body. It was a clotty piece of . . ."

I whip around and run out of the barn. All the muscles in my body feel as tight and knotted as my jaw.

Delia follows me, saying, "It was probably an accident. He just got in there with the dogs, or they were loose or being trained to attack . . . and . . ."

"And they covered it up? They took what was left of him and buried it somewhere far away from here? Dumped it in some other junkyard?" My eyes go wide, but I feel blind. "And my parents knew what had happened. My father. He must have taken Luke here at some point. My mother *knows*. She knows."

I start running back the way we came. My legs feel weak, and my stride is jagged. I can't breathe right. Is the tattoo of the heart ballooned up within me? Is it pounding louder than my own heart? Is this what happens to undone grief? Is this a reckoning?

I grab the chain-link fence to steady myself. Was my father's overdose a reckoning? I bend over to catch my breath. I keep my eyes shut, and then I hear Delia's footfalls. They come to a stop beside me. She puts her hand on my back.

"My parents protected me from the cops with all of their questions," I say, through ragged breaths. "Because I knew something."

"Listen."

"And the school nurse *pushed it*? She got me into a specialist? Why did *she* have to push it? Why weren't my parents getting me in with someone? Why let me go silent? Unless it benefited them." I stand up and grab Delia. I hold onto her as tightly as I can. She grabs hold of me, too.

"Keep breathing," Delia says.

I realize I'm holding my breath and that I want Delia to keep telling me to breathe, maybe in one way or another, forever.

I exhale. And I feel it—lighter, airier, made of almost nothing, nearly weightless—the tattoo flutters, not like a heart at all, but something as delicate as moth wings. And it lifts up from inside of me—up through my throat and out of my mouth, into the air, the trees, the sky, which is undone but trying to stitch itself together with clouds.

MENTAL DIPLOPIA: AN ERADICATION

I was among the first group of epidemiologists to be called. Wearing the white contamination suit—what has since become a second skin—I walked into Patient Zero's quarantined hospital room, slipped into the sterilized tent surrounding her bed, and saw a beautiful, distracted, wide-eyed contentedness.

Patient Zero was a seventy-two-year-old woman who had been polishing a coffee table when she heard children loudly singing an old Russian lullaby she hadn't heard since her own childhood. It was called "Bayu Bayushki Bayu." It sounded so perfect that she first walked to the radio, thinking that somehow it had turned on by itself. But her radio was off. She unplugged it for good measure.

"Do you hear that singing?" she asked her cat, playfully.

The cat, often skittish, seemed undisturbed.

She walked out onto the balcony of her apartment on the sixteenth floor. It was winter, but she wore no coat. This was too urgent. She expected a children's chorus of some sort. She didn't live too far from an elementary school. In fact, she could see the playground from the balcony. She thought perhaps this was part of some kind of multicultural presentation.

But no. The playground was empty.

The song had terrifying lyrics. In her hospital bed, she sang them for us and then translated.

> *Sleep sleep sleep*
> *Don't lie too close to the edge of the bed*
> *Or the little gray wolf will come*
> *And grab you by the flank,*
> *Drag you into the woods*
> *Underneath the willow root.*

But she added, "The song didn't scare me as a child. It was a comfort. I can't explain it, but while in my living room, the song worked its way into my fingertips and I could reach out and hold my mother's hand. My mother has been dead for a long time."

My own mother would die two months later. There would be no funeral. My father and I were only allowed to talk on the phone; the virus was making travel too dangerous. I wanted to ask my father what had come to my mother from the past, but he was too broken by grief. He could barely speak.

After Patient Zero's moment on the balcony, she put on her coat and walked to the elementary school. The school was closed. She hadn't known that it was a holiday.

This was when she realized that the song was very loud—consistently so. It grew no louder and no fainter. So she wasn't moving closer or farther away from its source.

She looked up at the gray sky and knew that the song was in her head. "And suddenly," she said, "I could smell Voronezh, the city I grew up in—sugar refineries, meat factories, flour and groats mills, chemical and aluminum plants. It smelled of work." She remembered a town gathering that she'd attended with her mother in Lenina Square, near the statue of Lenin giving a speech on the turret of an armored car.

On the walk home, it began to snow. People were bustling past her. She felt unsteady, and her upper body was jagged a little to the left.

A man reached out. She gripped his coat sleeve, but again she felt her mother's hand in hers, not the man's coat sleeve at all.

"You okay?" he asked, a few snowflakes glistening in his dark beard.

She started to tell him what was wrong but then stopped because she knew it sounded crazy. She shook her head. "I'll be fine. I'm close to home." She could make out her own mother's voice now, singing along with the children.

The man gently released her, and she walked on.

Once inside her apartment, she got into bed while still completely dressed, shoes and all. She was sure something was wrong with her, and if she had to call 911, she didn't want the crew to find her in her nightgown. She wondered if she'd inhaled too much wood polish. She worried she was having a stroke. She sang the song loudly as if, by joining it, she would give it permission to leave her. Eventually, she felt tired and hoarse and fell asleep.

When she woke up the next morning, the song was still there. In fact, she was sure that she'd dreamed with the song in a constant loop.

She ate breakfast, but her oatmeal tasted like the red-currant kissel her mother always made for her birthdays. Her coffee was more like sbiten, sweet with honey.

She called a taxi and went to her doctor. Sitting on his examination table, she could barely hear the doctor. "I am living in two worlds at once!" she shouted over the noise in her head. "I see you in the present. But I'm hearing the past, smelling, tasting, and touching the past."

All of this was explicable. Mental diplopia was rare, and Patient Zero's case might have been extreme, but it was not unheard of. John Hughlings Jackson was discussing it in the late 1800s. And in the 1900s, Wilder Penfield was able to create experiential hallucinations by probing the cerebral cortex of fully conscious patients with electrical stimulation during surgery. An acclaimed neurologist, Oliver Sacks, wrote of two such cases in his book *The Man Who Mistook His Wife for a Hat*, published in 1985.

While the doctor sent the patient to a neurologist, a blood test revealed a foreign trace of a virus that neither had seen before. This trace mimicked certain strains of biological warfare. So that's why, when I was called in with a wave of specialists, we were all suited up for contamination.

But what enemy would contaminate us with the effect of, well, what? Overbearing nostalgia? Incontinent reminiscence?

All in all, Patient Zero wanted to be left alone and enjoy the past. Her mother had died young and this time with her—through touch and taste and sound and smell—was precious.

Then one day, a small explosive aneurysm—sparked by a pathology we didn't understand and couldn't avoid—went off in her brain. She died quickly and painlessly.

Within three weeks, all the attending doctors, nurses, and staff who had come into contact with her before we started wearing protective suits were also dead, having gone down a similar path—listening to old pop songs, tasting candy, petting guinea pigs, smelling marshmallows burning in campfires. One man got to re-lose his virginity in the back seat of a Subaru hatchback in all ways except visually. One woman listened to her parents argue in a distant room while sitting—forgotten—in a bubble bath. Some ran on clipped fields, replaying soccer matches so lifelike they sweated through their shirts, breathless, their hearts pounding. Some overheard the news and could pinpoint the exact day and year they were stuck in. Meanwhile, all were also interactive in the present, though distractedly so.

The bearded man on the street who'd asked the woman if she was okay was dead. Her neighbor who'd talk to her one morning at the mailboxes was dead. Her doorman, dead.

The taxi driver was still alive. But he died by another exposure within a month.

Her cat died, too.

And, it was said that the cat, who'd been put in a shelter, had become disoriented, with a dreamy-eyed stare, before his end.

That shelter is now empty, as is the elementary school, the woman's apartment building, the hospital, most of the city, other cities, continents . . .

· · ·

I was falling in love at the time.

· · ·

Unlike predictions of suicides during a supervirus of this magnitude, suicides were far lower than projected. The deaths were *that* beautiful; people opted to die on the virus' terms and timetable.

Except not all the mental diplopliacs' experiences were objectively beautiful. (There is no such thing as objective beauty, of course, but I have no time to mince around.) Some were forced to relive a day of war or horror or trauma. One woman reported the repetitive noise of a bomb going off in a railway station, the feel of glass splintering her skin, the taste and smell of smoke and burning flesh. But, even then, she seemed to believe—especially the more times it returned—that there was some underlying joy. She'd been fifteen and she'd been in love with a boy. And she felt youth and love in that small, brief moment.

Duly noted: So many reported hearing their mothers singing to them, in some form or another, that we speculated that perhaps a voice singing an infant and/or child to sleep infiltrates our wiring so deeply that it permeates the brain.

•••

His name was Oliver, the man I was in love with. We were scared, of course. Our falling in love was a kind of extra terror. We'd both been in love before with other people, briefly or damningly or both. So the better our love felt, the harder it was to face the fact that it wouldn't last. *We* wouldn't last as individuals.

Or did that make it better?

Lying in bed together, within the confines of one of the major survival bunkers, having taken off our white hazmat suits—which was illegal, but privately, everyone was doing it— we talked about these things.

"It's the eternal return," Oliver said. "Did you take philosophy in college?"

"I speak pidgin philosophy," I said. "Enough to cover my ass at a cocktail party. Nietzsche?" We were still sweaty and lightly breathless from sex.

"Right." He lay back on the pillow, cupping the back of his head with one hand, exposing the pale underside of his cocked arm. *How vulnerable that skin*, I thought. So many things were striking me those days—about the body, life, humanity; and our fragility was chief among them. "The eternal return, everything has always happened and will keep happening."

"Every second recurring, constantly," I said. "My philosophy professor was young and really good-looking. I took two of his classes, back-to-back. Or should I say that I'm still taking every moment of his class?"

"Exactly. So what if our brains have tapped into an eternal return moment and are reliving it, on some plain of consciousness?"

"There's a neurological explanation for the mental diplopia," I said, ready to launch into ganglia and such.

"Yes, yes. I know, but what if the neurological explanation is only the *neurological* explanation?"

"Like seeing God in the aura produced by a migraine that is neurologically explicable is still seeing God. The arguments are all there, on every side." I didn't like to bring up God. For a while, people had tried to line the dead bodies in the streets, taping their IDs to their shirts so they could be retrieved by family members. But that couldn't last.

"Do you ever want to walk out into it?" he asked me, staring up at the ceiling.

And it felt like a man asking if I believed in marriage. Not a proposal but just seeing where I stood on the whole thing.

"It's crossed my mind."

...

I didn't get a call when my father died. I assume he's dead. There weren't people left to make calls. I loved my father. I wondered if I *walked out into it* if I would hear his voice again, reading stories aloud from the children's book with the bright blue chicken wearing a crown on the cover. I longed for his voice. He had the gentleness of a pediatrician, though he practiced law. He rode his bike a lot and forgot to uncuff his pant leg and would walk around like that for hours.

...

"My father is wandering around with his pant leg cuffed," I whispered to Oliver as he was falling asleep.

"My father is forever frying sausage links," he whispered back.

I thought of all the patients who'd died, but more often than all the rest, I remembered Patient Zero, her tremulous but sweet voice filling the small, sterilized tent, our faces staring out at her behind the shields of our masks. My mother sang to me at night, too.

...

Later in our suits taking our turn watering and monitoring seedlings in the greenhouse, I said, "I'm not worried about

God. I'm worried about someone else out there who might want us dead."

People whispered about this, even the most intellectual among us. That trace of biological warfare was undeniably real.

"Sartre spent the Second World War in a German prison camp where he read Heidegger," Oliver said. "He came out of it and wrote a great lecture."

"What's that mean? Do you think we'll come out of this at all?"

"We're still free," he said. "We're condemned to it, as the existentialists would put it."

"So," I said, "you don't think this kind of life—locked up in our suits and our bunker forever—has to feel like prison."

"It's only a prison if you say it's a prison," he said.

But the comment seemed to worry him. He stopped and looked around. Through his mask, I could see that he was scared.

I reached out and wanted to hold his hand like Patient Zero, feeling her mother's hand holding hers. Of course we couldn't feel each other through the thick-fingered gloves of our suits.

He realized I was worried, and then he smiled. "Absurdity will save us."

...

The bunker was still connected to the outside via access to surveillance around the world. We still saw people occasionally, and a few animals, too. The Audubon osprey cam on Hog Island, Maine, for example, had a view of an empty osprey nest but also a small bit of Muscongus Bay in the background. A teenage boy, his hair grown bushy, was seen paddling by in a small boat.

That was three months ago. Some humans and animals had to be immune to the virus. We occasionally saw a band of them in our footage, but the sightings were very rare and often disturbing.

Once, a man drove his truck across an empty parking lot into a pole—a suicide attempt. He survived, crawled out of the truck, and wrote, in blood, a woman's name. *Elaine.* Then he signed it with a bloody handprint.

• • •

Two squirrels were captured on tape scurrying across the floors of the Dulwich Picture Gallery in London. In the background was "The Triumph of David," who was proudly parading Goliath's giant, decapitated head on a stick.

I watched the squirrels—with their fluid lines, their brush-stroke tails—as many times as I could before feeling embarrassed by my need. Then I walked away.

• • •

We went to a few weddings in the bunker. We called the brides and grooms bold fuckers.

Eventually, someone got pregnant. And this felt truly insane. A small attempt at socially regulatory government erupted—some *for* birth, some *against.* But, like Oliver and me, the majority of voices said, *Why not? You can't stop life. We are life.*

"We have a greenhouse," I told Oliver. "She's just a human greenhouse."

The pregnant woman replaced the front of her contamination suit with a pleated section and kept going.

I thought, *Will I be a greenhouse?*

I thought, *Will Oliver suggest such a thing?*

• • •

It was rare to see people's skin—so rare that Oliver and I watched each other shower.

The body took on an incalculable divinity because, like the soul, it went unseen.

And if the body is as divine as the soul, does the soul still hold sway as an idea?

If all the bodies outside the bunker give way to dust, what to make of all the loosed souls?

The pregnant woman was working with an engineer to make a series of very small but increasingly larger contamination suits for the baby.

• • •

"I see it as a prison," Oliver said to me one night. We'd already decided not to make love. We'd watched the footage of the boy paddling across Muscongus Bay too many times. Once, it had been hopeful and made us happy, but tonight, like a sharp blow, we felt hollow afterward.

"Then it is a prison." I sat on the edge of the bed, my suit puffing around me. "But what if we're the baby in the pregnant woman's belly?"

"That baby has no consciousness." Oliver's suit seemed baggier, as if he were shrinking within it.

"No consciousness of the outside world, what lies beyond,"

I said. "But maybe we don't, either. Maybe we'll be born into something else."

He said, "No. I don't think so. Out there, it's only death."

"But that's always true of birth. All things eventually give way to mortality. Birth is just the first necessary step toward death."

"That's very old-school German of you," he said, and then he walked to the blinds and fiddled with them. Opening and shutting. "You know what I missed today?"

"What?"

"Slip 'N Slides."

...

That night, I thought of Patient Zero's translation of "Bayu Bayushki Bayu."

> *Sleep sleep sleep*
> *Don't lie too close to the edge of the bed*
> *Or the little gray wolf will come*
> *And grab you by the flank,*
> *Drag you into the woods*
> *Underneath the willow root.*

And then I worked hard to remember the tune.

It came to me, and I hummed it.

I thought, *This will not last.*

...

The first to spot them was the twelve-year-old son of two CDC workers. The boy's name was Elliot Pegg. I'd seen him very little.

He didn't play much with the other kids, rarely showed up at communal meals, and now I knew why. He was obsessed with monitoring as many surveillance cameras, worldwide, as possible.

After the sighting, he rushed to his parents, who gathered some of the leaders who'd emerged, and they held a meeting.

Clive Waltham, who was in charge and resisting democracy "just until all this mess blows over," now stood behind the podium in the theater to address the entire community. "We've heard that we're not alone. We have intelligence that there are others among us, possibly those who are responsible for our destruction in order to take over."

He then introduced Elliot, and the boy walked quickly to the podium, pulling the mic down close to his mouth. He wore braces and I wondered, absurdly, if there was an orthodontist among us. Would the boy spend the rest of his life in braces?

"I am Elliot Pegg," the boy said. "I was watching the monitors because I like to, in case you were wondering. And I saw a strange creature on the monitor located near 35.169 latitude and 136.906 longitude."

The crowd was silent. Did this kid see the world in latitude and longitude? He read our bewildered expressions and added, "At Sunshine Sakae in Japan. A mall," he added. "With a Ferris wheel."

This made a little more sense—a boy, sunshine, a mall, a Ferris wheel. The room was relieved but still all were silent.

"I'm going to show the footage now, but I think that they're here to see what the place looks like—without us. You know, like a head of hair *without* the lice."

Elliot didn't seem to realize that he'd called us lice. He just started fiddling with the remote to start up the tape. Clive, however, walked up quickly and covered the microphone. He thanked Elliot, though it was a bit muffled, and excused him.

Elliot headed off stage, but not without looking back over his shoulder first and waving to his parents, as if he'd just successfully recited JFK's "Don't ask what your country can do for you . . ." speech.

Then he disappeared behind the curtain.

The video footage was crisp and clear. The person who'd blown it up had enhanced the film enough that it wasn't grainy.

They looked human, at first. They loped down the aisles of the Sunshine Sakae, a mix of races and ethnicities; their arms swung at their sides, and their very human eyes darted and drifted and lingered.

But when they stopped, their bodies shivered. When they reached for something from a shelf—food items in cans that I didn't recognize—their arms reached out as fast as frog tongues catching flies. In fact, the gestures seemed over before they began.

And then I felt alone, more alone than I ever had in my life. The room was filled with people, all those respirators purring along, and Oliver was beside me, standing so close that I could feel the pressure of his suit against mine, bubble to bubble.

But the thought had crossed my mind that this would happen again—this moment of me watching this foreign species at the Sunshine Sakae—and it would keep happening. However, this one singular moment was the only one I knew of. I was trapped to only have it, to only be conscious of it. My life felt like a skimmer passing over a great ocean.

And this was my life, rising up—net empty.

I was the only one having this thought in this room of people. I was sure I was the only skimmer on the ocean.

And when I died, as I knew I would—the final bit of lice eradicated, maybe while the one last nit was roiling in the pregnant woman's belly inside her maternity contamination suit—I would be within a memory and I would be aware of the present. And existing in the combined center of that Venn diagram, I would be absolutely alone.

· · ·

Elliot's work was no longer so solitary and desperate. A whole team of people kept constant watch now, and they couldn't look at any live stream without eventually seeing one, if you had even a bit of whale-watching patience. The other species were sometimes solitary, more often in groups. They seemed to know each other and be able to read each other's actions, moving quietly and yet constantly around each other. They were tireless and seemingly efficient, though we didn't know their overall goal.

We had decisions to make.

Some believed we should venture out to greet them.

Others said we should prepare our riot gear and tap our armory.

There were rumors of secret groups forming different co-alitions.

· · ·

One night, I couldn't sleep. I sat on the edge of the bed. Oliver was curled away from me. We'd started sleeping in our suits again, like when we'd first arrived.

I said, "There was this woman in college, Elli Truth Bartok—and we assumed the middle name was one she'd made up. She tried to start a humane-treatment-of-insects movement to make sure all the insects we used in the lab were euthanized painlessly, like for cricket dissections in introductory bio classes. She wanted us to use inhaled anesthetics. Basically, fog in a terrarium."

This was the kind of weird extremism that Oliver would usually enjoy making fun of, but he didn't chime in.

"Like the DDT trucks that kids used to run after in the 1950s before people figured out it was all pretty deadly." I'd seen pictures in magazines and old newsreel. It struck me as odd that these things were lodged in my mind—probably Oliver's, too—but how did they get there?

Oliver didn't say anything. I assumed he was asleep, but I liked hearing my voice, the company of it, so I kept talking. "What if the species euthanized as many of us as they could? As sweetly as possible because something awful and painful is coming?" I kept going; "What if they're like kids with nets collecting butterflies . . .?"

In my mind's eye, I saw the species as children now—and realized there were never children in the groups we spotted on film. I imagined them running through beautiful wheat-swaying fields. "Why have they been so gentle? Why did they allow the dying their eternal returns?"

I felt my mind wandering toward a rocky cliff, but I kept going. "What if the butterflies aren't our bodies, but our minds? Our consciousness?"

I envisioned a corkboard. Instead of butterflies pinned to it, there were small wisps—gray, diaphanous, and fluttering lightly;

it was a child's bedroom, and a nearby window was open. "What if they don't care about our bodies but are keeping our souls?"

"Did Elli Truth Bartok believe that insects had souls?" His voice startled me, not only because I thought he'd been asleep but because he seemed earnest. He seemed to want to know that someone—even a stranger who was most likely dead—had once believed in the souls of insects.

I lay down next to him, my face mask pressed against the back of his suit. "I never asked her."

• • •

At dinner one night, we heard that three people were missing. They'd gone out in order to make contact. They'd been gone for a while, and others had covered for them. (This was an enormous breach. There would be repercussions for those who'd covered for them.)

But what was important was that they'd been sending messages back and the messages had stopped.

• • •

I found myself stripping off my suit. I got in the shower. I wanted the water to needle my skin. I wanted to know that every inch of my body was alive.

Oliver didn't come in to watch or join me. I assumed he was just trying to process the new information. I certainly was.

But when I stepped out of the bathroom, I found him sitting on the edge of the bed. His contamination suit was baggier than ever. His helmet was still locked into place.

And I recognized the look on his face—beautiful, distracted, wide-eyed contentedness.

I touched his mask with my fingers.

His head snapped up. "What?" he asked, as if nothing were wrong. But his voice was just a little too loud, his eyes just a bit pinched, as if he were concentrating very hard to remain here with me in this room.

"How long has it been going on?" I asked.

He shrugged. "Just a few hours. Those fuckers broke the seal on their way out. I'm sure of it. The virus is probably just riding on the wind now, and it made its way in. All the way in."

My fingers tingled. My neck felt flush with blood. But I wasn't afraid. "What's your eternal return?" I asked.

He smiled. "I'm in the yard with my dog, Chipper. I can hear my older brother practicing the trumpet through the open windows. He was really good." He looked at me through the three-layer face shield. "Did I ever tell you that he toured in Europe with a jazz band when he was only nineteen? He gave it up to go into finance." His brother had died of the virus very early on. I could see that Oliver was crying, his face contorted with a mix of joy and loss. "He was so fucking good. Jesus."

I reached up and put my hand under the double storm flap that protected the gas-tight zipper closure that ran down his back. He grabbed my naked wrist with his gloved hand. "No."

"Who knew how tender the apocalypse would be?" I said.

"Please don't."

"I'm condemned to my freedom," I said. "And this is a moment I'd like to return eternally."

And—hello, you, reader, other—what did I do?

I undressed him.

ACKNOWLEDGMENTS

A writer is the accumulation of all the voices that came before her, that raised her up, and surround her. I'm thankful for the loud, sweet, obnoxious, bawdy, loving, weird, tender, honest and (kindly) dishonest voices of my family, my friends, and communities, all the various places that let me in. I love the way you all dream and bicker, hold court, exaggerate, shut up and shine; I love all the various forms your love takes. This is one of mine.

I'm especially thankful for Brendan Deneen who tells me when it's not good enough, when the work makes him laugh in public and breaks him down a little. It's an honor to work with you, day in and day out.